The Dog Park Club

The Dog Park Club

Cynthia Robinson

Minotaur Books

A Thomas Dunne Book
New York

This is a work of fiction. All of the characters, organizations, and events portrayed in this novel are either products of the author's imagination or are used fictitiously.

A THOMAS DUNNE BOOK FOR MINOTAUR BOOKS.
An imprint of St. Martin's Publishing Group.

www.thomasdunnebooks.com
www.minotaurbooks.com

Library of Congress Cataloging-in-Publication Data

Robinson, Cynthia, 1958–
    The Dog Park Club / Cynthia Robinson.—1st ed.
        p. cm.
    "Thomas Dunne Books."
    ISBN 978-0-312-55973-1
    1. Male singers—Fiction.   2. Dog owners—Fiction.   3. Berkeley
(Calif.)—Fiction.   4. Missing persons—Fiction.   I. Title.
    PS3618.O3235D64   2010
    813'.6—dc22
                                                    2009046146

First Edition: July 2010

10 9 8 7 6 5 4 3 2 1

For Mark, who makes it possible

Part One

1

I saw Amy Carter the day before she disappeared. It was in Berkeley, at the dog park.

Amy was always there. She was a regular. There were eight of us. We, the regulars, dropped by the dog park just about every day. We hung out, sometimes for hours.

Other people showed up sometimes, and then scurried away as quickly as they could, leaving us to our insular, hermetic weirdness. We were the idiot dauphins ruling a shabby kingdom that nobody else wanted.

Amy Carter was different from the rest of us. She was poised and pretty, so pretty you almost forgot she was pregnant. And for a moment I had flattered myself into thinking that she found me handsome. She didn't say so. It was just the way she'd look at me sometimes—with those brown eyes that made me feel like I was drowning in sable.

And, I think it was the way she said my name. She'd say Max Bravo, not just Max. It made me feel important—even more important than usual. Perhaps Amy made everyone feel like that.

2

It started in Berlin. I was there on tour, performing *Rigoletto*.

I had finished the Sunday matinee, tucked away a trencher-man's portion of boiled meats and spatzel, washed it down with several tankards of Riesling, and contentedly buried myself under a bunker of eiderdown. I was sleeping soundly when Claudia Fantini's call rang through.

Like everything else in my hotel, the bedside telephone was old, mechanical. Its clapper stuttered against the bell in drill bursts. It stopped. Started again. Shrill. Insistent. The habitual yelling of a Prussian field marshal.

I reached for the receiver and said, "*Hola*," thinking I was still in Madrid. Claudia was on the line. I braced myself for a bout of transatlantic hysteria.

"Max," she said. She was crying. "Larry wants a divorce."

I'd known Ms. Fantini for years. So I treated the announce-ment like I would a poor review from a provincial critic.

"I don't believe it," I told her.

I fumbled in the blackness for the bedside lamp, then re-membered I was wearing my night blinders. I pushed them onto my forehead. The hotel room was soaked in a sooty, crepuscular darkness. I looked at the clock and cursed out loud.

"Did I wake you up?" she asked.

I tried to calculate what time it was in California. Thursday, around seven in the evening. Claudia was drunk. Gin, I suspected.

"It's four o'clock," I told her. "In the A.M. Are you familiar with the concept of time zones?"

"Max, he came home last night and he said he didn't love me anymore."

"You are in PST, Pacific standard time. But I, being in the Fatherland, happen to be in CEST—which is Central European standard time."

"I couldn't stop him," she said.

"And since the earth is turning on its axis in an easterly . . ."

"He got an apartment."

"Put Larry on the phone."

"I can't."

"Is he at work?"

"No, Max. He's gone. Larry moved out." She choked, sobbing.

I sat up, lit a butted cigarillo, and listened as Claudia stitched together the ragged details of her story. Larry had left without warning and, apparently, without motive.

I told her that my tour finished in a couple of weeks. I'd help her sort it out once I got home. I'd be back in San Francisco before the end of May.

We were going on to Naples next. Then back to Spain, to Catalonia this time—Figueres. Claudia asked me to remind her what the opera was. *Rigoletto,* I told her.

"You're playing him, right?" she asked. "Rigoletto?"

I heard her blow her nose. Her voice steadied.

"Yes, I'm always the clown," I said.

Being a baritone—a hulking bear of a baritone—I generally play the tragic clown or the lumbering villain, while some reedy tenor gets to play the hero.

Opera isn't subtle. If you're rotten on the inside, you're repellant on the outside. That's what I like about it. The clarity.

And so, being the varlet, I'm pretty much always afflicted. My characters are crabbed with spina bifida or lamed with a clubfoot. I've spent most of my career heaving around on stage with a hump on my back and a frill around my neck. I limp and scrape and twitch and scheme and pine for a woman who finds me utterly repulsive, while some salacious duke despoils my desire. And I rail against the injustice of it all with eight pounds of batting strapped to my back. Yes, the hump and I were old friends.

3

I went straight from the San Francisco airport to Claudia's house in the Berkeley Hills. I had to.

She had called me throughout my tour. It was as though she'd constructed a war room in her kitchen and was tracing my movements on an oversized map of Europe. Claudia called me at my hotels. She called my cell phone, incurring outrageous roaming charges.

She even called me backstage in Naples and Figueres, using her supple command of Italian—and her shallow but energetic approximation of Catalan—to convince the stage managers that she was my sister. She told them that she had to speak with me because our mother was suffering from complications following an emergency goiter surgery. Fantastically, people always did her bidding.

And so, I went to her, despite the fact I had just endured a transatlantic flight in steerage because the opera company was too cheap to pay for business class. I got directly on the train at the airport and rode past my stop, the Twenty-fourth Street station, just a few blocks from my own house. I remained on the BART train, in a sullen snit, as it swept under the San Francisco Bay and past all the Oakland stops, pressing farther north into the hinterland—on into Berkeley.

The last of the presentable people got off the train in Oakland. I rode the rest of the way with a carload of Berkeley dwellers. They were wearing the signature look: frizzled hair and drab stretchy mufti and orthopedic footwear. It's a singularly disturbing costume.

I'm uncomfortable amongst people who decided, sometime in the 1960s, to reenact the living conditions of the Middle Ages. That is, people who have denied the modern wonders of dentistry, and hair conditioner, the pedicurist arts, and hot wax depilatory—people who drape themselves in shapeless garments fashioned out of hemp and douse themselves with carafes of patchouli oil. They blithely breastfeed their four-year-olds in public parks. They come to the theater in hiking sandals and wearing fanny packs stocked with dried fruit and nuts that they eat throughout the performance. And they hector you to read pamphlets excoriating condo developers or oppressive civil authorities that deny citizens their basic right to public nudity.

I got off at the North Berkeley station, a stop I'd generally avoid as surely as I would a visit to a Turkish prison, or a Lladro outlet. But this was an extreme circumstance. I was needed. Claudia needed me. And all I had to do was be there.

I stood on Claudia's porch, suitcase in hand. I had to press the doorbell several times. It bonged out a stentorian dirge that sounded like the chimes at a funeral home.

"You've been an incredible pest," I said.

"Oh Gawd, Max," Claudia Fantini wailed and fell forward into my chest.

Larry's wire-haired mutt, Asta, came bolting out from behind her. He jumped up onto his hind legs and yipped and clawed my thighs as though I had arrived to rescue him from a hostage situation.

I tossed my suitcase into the foyer and caught Claudia's arm before she spilled her tumbler of red wine all over my mackintosh—it was 10:00 A.M.—and I grabbed the cigarette out of her fist with my other hand. I packaged her up and dragged her into the kitchen, kicking the front door closed with my heel.

Before the door slammed shut, I noticed a curtain fluttering in a window across the street. The neighbors were watching. They had, undoubtedly, been watching for weeks. Claudia and Larry made good TV: Larry leaving with his suitcase. Claudia screaming on the front porch. Larry coming back for his golf clubs. Claudia tossing an empty bottle of Chianti at his car as he pulled out of the driveway. I'm sure Claudia provided many hours of entertainment. And I was also sure that none of the neighbors offered to help.

Once we got in the house I set Claudia down at the kitchen banquette. The morning sun blasted through the south-facing windows. It hit her face hard. Her skin had turned chalky and dry.

I had expected Claudia to look like hell. But I didn't expect her to look like the madwoman from a gothic novel, the one that the husband keeps locked up in the attic so she can claw at the floorboards wearing nothing but a chemise.

Claudia was in a tatty chenille bathrobe with faded purple wine stains all down the front. Her feet were sliding around in a pair of red satin slippers. The heels, shaped like spools of thread, were worn down at the back so that their satin upholstery had come unglued. The frayed bits of satin curled up to reveal the bare plastic underneath—creamy and shiny and opaque like boiled bones.

I steadied her and lit her a fresh cigarette. I ran upstairs, Asta at my heels. I flung open her bedroom closet and found her velvet caftan hanging on the back of the door. I snatched up the caftan and tossed it over my shoulder. There was a pair of beaded Persian slippers on the floor, with toes that curled up into saucy little napkin rings. They sparkled when I pulled the door open wider and the sunlight flamed into the closet. I picked those up too.

Before I went back downstairs I opened Larry's closet. It was empty. Asta trotted inside it and sniffed around at a couple of clothes hangers left lying on the floor. He looked at me and barked.

"So she wasn't overplaying it," I said to him. "For once."

Asta and I went back down to the kitchen and found Claudia slouched over a coffee cup that she'd just topped off with red wine. A jelly jar full of red wine was standing on the kitchen counter. Then I noticed a third wine pour, this one actually in a wineglass, on the windowsill. The wine was receding, slowly evaporating. It had probably been there for days.

I stood her up and slipped the robe off her. She was naked except for a pair of wispy white panties and a little undershirt, and her skin was pulled tight against her bones and her belly had caved in. I thought my heart would break. And

I entertained a sudden impulse to take her upstairs. But, instead, I pulled the caftan on over her head, and fastened the gold-beaded frog catches down the front, and I slid the Persian slippers onto her feet, noting that I'd take her down to the nail salon as soon as I got her sobered up. I opened the kitchen window and dropped the despairing robe and slippers outside. They fell with a tired thud onto the bricks next to the garbage can.

Her thick black hair—that she normally preened over and cantilevered up into elaborately engineered chignons—was a fright wig. It looked like she had pinioned random pieces of it to her head with a staple gun. A few hanks hung down one side of her face and a couple of errant tresses slithered down her back.

I sat her back down at the kitchen banquette and noticed that the table was set with a half-empty bottle of Claret, a dish containing a handful of chewable vitamin C pills, some vitamin E capsules, and a plastic prescription bottle. The label on the pills was dated recently and it indicated: XANAX— DO NOT TAKE THIS MEDICATION WITH ALCOHOL.

"What the hell is this?" I demanded, snatching what appeared to be a plastic banana comb off the side of her head. I held it in front of her face.

"I don't know. My hair was falling down and that thing— that barrette—was in a drawer," she said, bobbing her head and waving her hand flaccidly in front of her.

"It's a banana comb. And I'm sending it back to where it belongs. The 1980s."

I dropped the banana comb into the wastebasket, marched to the powder room, and started riffling through the cupboards and drawers. Claudia always kept caches of beauty products stashed around the house. She never knew when she'd need to slip away from a cocktail party to regloss her lips or reglue her eyelashes. I loaded up the pockets of my mackintosh with cold cream, some tubes and tins and compacts of color, a brush, and a couple of decent rhinestone hair clips that I found lying in the sink.

I stopped to smooth my eyebrows, noticed I needed a barber. My hair was curling up around the collar. When it was long like that you could see how very black it was. Eight generations in eastern Europe—and the infusion of my own blond mother's starchy Anglo-Saxon genes—hadn't diluted the Rajasthani features. Any wily eugenicist could see it. It was in the darkness under the eyes, and the hint of duskiness about the pallor, and the sheen on the blue-black hair. The signs were there, if you knew what to look for: Rom, Gitan, Gypsy.

"Max," Claudia screeched from the kitchen. I found her trying to light the filter end of her cigarette. I snatched it out of her hand and lit a fresh one for her.

"Aren't you overdoing this a bit?" I asked, meaning everything.

She didn't hear me. Or she acted like she didn't hear me. I slathered the cold cream over her face and then tissued it off. I wiped away the mascara streaks from her cheeks—a tracery of dried tears.

"Can you believe it, Max?" she said through a plume of smoke. She opened and then snapped her lighter shut, apparently now aware that the cigarette was lit.

"How could *he* leave *me*?" she demanded.

"Larry has had some sort of mental break," I muttered—I had several hair clips clamped in my mouth.

"I should kill him."

"Then you'd have to burn the bloody clothes," I said, teasing her hair. "It would be a terrible waste of Prada."

"He didn't even tell me why."

"Maybe he doesn't know why."

"Bullshit!" she yelled. "He knows why."

"Okay, then why?"

"It came out of nowhere," she said. "He was keeping secrets. Sneaking around. Plotting. He rented an apartment for God's sake. That means only one thing."

"What one thing?"

"Larry has been having an affair."

She was right, of course. I'd deduced the same thing. Why else would Larry hide his discontent?

"I should cut out his trachea," Claudia said.

"Oh, stop it, you Calabrian asshole," I said, dabbing concealer under her eyes.

I applied a good base of foundation to even out her color. I leaned back to look at my work. I'd spackled it on rather heavily. She looked painted over, very Kabuki theater. There was no telling what furies were roiling behind that carefully composed mask.

"Okay. So who is this other woman?" I asked.

"Some bitch from work. Some shit-heel sales creep like him. Gray suit. Black sling-backs. Marching through airports, dragging a Tumi computer bag."

"Shouting into her cell phone," I said, "hectoring the thralls back at the office."

I knew the type. Self-important business travelers who pollute the atmosphere in lobbies, and concourses, and cab stands worldwide with their urgent trivialities.

Claudia leaned back against the red leather banquette, smiled in a crooked grimace, and slowly lifted her cigarette into the side of her mouth. Satisfied that she'd made her point.

"We can't be sure it's another woman," I told her. I plucked the cigarette out from between her lips, applied a bloodred lipstick in two strokes, popped the cigarette back in.

"Well, it's not a man," she said.

I winced like I'd been slapped. Not hard, but mean. She must have noticed because she quickly diverted with, "Larry is jealous that I'm so good at making friends, and he's not."

She was slurring. When she wasn't looking I picked up the Xanax and put it in my pocket. I'd hide it in a kitchen cupboard, and call her later to tell her where it was.

I made up her eyes; dark shadow, kohl rims. It was her eyes that made Claudia so dangerous—they were a little louche and a lot languid, heavy lids over molten copper. They were the eyes of a big, hungry cat.

4

As soon as I got Claudia cleaned up she passed out. I had turned my back for just an instant—I was at the kitchen sink rinsing out the assorted wine-stained glasses that I'd collected from all over the house—and I heard a dull clunk. I looked over at the banquette and Claudia's forehead was resting on the table, flanked by her hands—one holding a wine tumbler and the other propping up a burning cigarette.

I frog-marched her to one of the two sofas in the living room. I plumped a couple of throw cushions under her head, careful not to disturb the chignon I'd just pinned up. I draped a velvet throw blanket over her. She began snoring like an elephant seal. I put on my jacket, which Asta took as a cue. He ran to the foyer. I could hear his barks echoing off the mahogany paneling.

"Take him," she said without opening her eyes.

"Take him where exactly?"

"For a walk."

"Where?"

"Walk the fucker."

"His name is Asta. And he knows when you're being a bitch."

"I don't know where. I've never walked him."

"You mean Larry's been gone for three weeks and you haven't walked this dog once?"

She was snoring again and I could see her eyes shifting back and forth under her closed lids. I went into the hallway and Asta directed my attention to his leash hanging from a wall hook.

Once outside, he acted as though he'd just busted out of a federal penitentiary. He pranced down the sidewalk, glancing back over his shoulder toward the house every few steps, just in case the screws were after him.

We got to the end of the street. I wanted to turn right, to make it a quick spin around the block. He could tell what I had in mind and wasn't about to let me off that easy. Asta insisted we cross the street and head down the steep incline toward the Berkeley flatlands. I'm not much of a disciplinarian—not with myself, and not with anybody else. I let the dog drag me along to wherever he wanted to go.

The Berkeley Hills are expansive and hushed, like an expensive columbarium. The houses are big and old, the streets are leafy and quiet and winding. They aspire up to the towering ridge of Grizzly Peak, which marks the eastern edge of the San Francisco Bay Area like the top of a parapet. From its ramparts the wealthy hill dwellers can look out onto the Bay, and San Francisco shining white on its peninsula, and the Pacific Ocean glittering into the sunset.

Asta and I walked under towering redwoods and arching

oaks. The ancient trees loomed over us, casting dapples of shade across the gardens and the sidewalks.

The houses behind the trees lay back on their pricey turfs, languid and unconcerned. We passed through a smorgasbord of architectural fantasies. A Mediterranean villa lounged next to a frothy Rococo pastiche, which flirted with its staid neighbor, an upright Romanesque monastery.

"Asta," a man called out.

It made me jump. I turned.

"You snuck up on me," I said to the tall man. He had a tall dog. Both of them had long, lupine faces.

He smiled, showing me a set of crooked teeth. He was wearing a purple tracksuit. The pants and jacket were covered in little mauve pills. A yellow racing stripe ran down the outside of each pant leg. He didn't wear running shoes. He wore loafers. They were brown with woven uppers that were so brief they showed toe crack—shoe bikinis. His jacket was unzipped and I could read the lettering on his dingy orange T-shirt: ENIGMATICA SYSTEMS, THE CODE WITHIN CODE. I thought he was Yugoslavian.

"Hello, Asta," the man said.

"Oh, you two know each other."

"*Claro*," he said. "I'm Jordi Almirall."

"Max Bravo." I shook his hand. Almirall. He wasn't a Slav after all. He was a Spaniard. To put a finer point on it, he was Catalan.

Almirall bore the signature features of his race. I could see that now. He had the monobrow, the big nose, and the assured, steady presence. Catalans are descended directly from the Roman foot soldiers that slogged across Gaul. Caesar pensioned them off onto small farms in northern Spain, which they worked stolidly. This Catalan who stood before me, this Jordi Almirall, was lean, gangly. He had a clownish air. But his close-cropped hair, sharp eyes, and flaring, big-knuckled hands belied something more beneath the surface. He seemed amply capable. Of what, I didn't know.

I asked him, "Do you work for Enigmatica?"

"This is my dog, Cecilia."

Asta was sparring with the fellow's dog. I noticed the stripe of hair running in reverse along her spine. She was a Rhodesian ridgeback, a rather handsome one—gleaming chestnut coat, legs like a racehorse.

"Bon gos," Jordi Almirall said, mussing his hands over Asta's ears. Asta turned and jumped up onto Jordi, clawing exuberantly at his knees.

"Asta, down," I said. "He'll ruin your . . . slacks."

"Where is Larry?" he asked abruptly.

I stiffened. This was very Catalan too, the directness. But I wasn't about to tell him that Larry had abandoned his wife, and that she was lying in a heap on the sofa. I reached for my cigarette case.

"Cigarette?" I said, thumbing the spring latch.

Jordi Almirall stared at the Dunhills in the case. He swept his hand back and forth over the row of identical cigarettes. Then his hand stopped, hovered over a cigarette on the end. His fingers twiddled, and veered suddenly to a cigarette in the middle. He plucked the cigarette swiftly out of the case. I looked again at the cigarettes. They all looked the same to me. I took the one on the end.

Jordi produced a disposable lighter from the pocket of his jogging pants and lit both our cigarettes. I took a drag and exhaled it in a plume so I could estimate him through a bank of smoke.

"Larry is away," I said.

His eyebrows lifted. I immediately regretted having told him even that much.

"At the moment. He's away just now. Business. I don't know much about it. I'm really more Claudia's friend. Well, I'm both Larry and Claudia's friend. Leaning more in the Claudia camp."

"I think Larry must have a beautiful wife," he said. He narrowed his eyes as if trying to fix a price on her. "We don't ever see her, but Larry is very successful in his business. I work also in the high-tech. I know these enterprise software systems Larry sells. His commissions must be very big."

"Yes. Larry is the great blond bwana. Always bagging elephants—moving the global software installations, multinational players—coming home with the big-ticket contracts."

I didn't know why I was talking like that, mimicking Larry's inane corporate-speak. I despised Larry when he was in that mode, when he spoke in terms of "deliverables" and "takeaways" and "leveraging infrastructure investments."

"Men like Larry get the most beautiful women," Jordi Almirall observed.

"Yes. The world's unfair like that," I said. "That's why the rich tend to be so damn good-looking. They snatch up all the most beautiful women."

"We haven't seen Larry. He is maybe selling software? Overseas?"

"That's correct." I was outright lying now. "Dubai, I think. By way of Buenos Aires."

That threw him. I could see him puzzling over the itinerary, perhaps trying to visualize one of those maps in an airline magazine, imagining the red dotted lines zigzagging the hemispheres.

"We are going to the dog park. You can walk with us."

As soon as Jordi Almirall said the words "dog park" Asta went into a delirium. He jumped all four feet off the ground and twisted in midair. He barked. He clawed at Almirall's pant legs, streaking the soft polyester.

Almirall incanted the words again.

"Dog park. Dog park. Dog park. Do you want to go to dog park, Asta?"

The mantra sent Asta into full-blown Beatlemania. I couldn't manage him, and I wondered whether this Jordi Almirall was perhaps slightly autistic.

"Dog park. Dog park. Dog park."

"You can stop saying dog park now," I told him. "We'll come along."

5

When I got back to Claudia's house four hours later, I was slightly drunk and she was still asleep. I fed Asta and let him poop in the backyard. I didn't clean it up.

I found a yellow legal pad in the desk drawer in the living room. I took it into the kitchen and sat down at the table to write a note:

Dear C.

Took Asta to dog park. Met up with Catalan clown, Jordi Almirall.

Beside Jordi's name I drew a stick figure in loafers. I gave him a big smile exposing a mouthful of jostling teeth.

Also met a hoary-headed old goat named Ed.

Next to Ed's name I drew a stick figure with a potbelly and an oversized head covered in braids.

He has a fright wig—white guy Rasta. Off-putting, I know. But amusing.

I wanted Claudia to be prepared.

Can't draw his hairdo. It is full of green army men. Braids them into his hair. Grenade-throwing guy. Standing rifle-shooting guy. Lying down rifle-shooting guy. Even mine-sweeper guy!

Then I penned a happy face, a question mark, and an exclamation point. Next paragraph:

Met one normal—lovely young woman named Amy. She lives across street from dog park. Has cute pug named Dixie. You would like.
   Amy is pregnant.

I drew Amy as a stick figure with a protruding belly—even though her pregnancy didn't yet show—and it made her look disconcertingly like Ed. I added long flowing hair that flipped up at the ends. I set a little dog at her ankle. It had a smashed-in face and bulging eyes and a tail that swirled up into a tight double curl like a Dairy Queen sundae.

Park is only seven blocks away. They serve beer out of Ed's van. You would like.
   Strongly suggest you attend. Asta would like.
   Am off in the a.m. to Salt Lake C. to sing Don Giovanni—

*just for two weeks. May convert to Mormonism and come back
with several wives (ha!).*

   Luv

   Max

I left the notepad on the kitchen table. I kissed Claudia on
the forehead. Asta followed me to the front door. I told him to
watch over Claudia while I was gone. He cocked his head to
the side then sat down smartly. I pushed in the button lock
on the doorknob and softly pulled the door shut behind me.

6

My next tour was different. Claudia didn't call me. I couldn't stop thinking about her, so I called her house several times. I kept getting her answering machine. I tried her cell phone, and I kept redialing until I got through.

It was a Saturday afternoon. She was at the dog park, slightly drunk, but a happy sort of drunk.

"Here, talk to Amy," she said, and I remembered her—the pregnant woman, the pretty one.

"Hello, Max Bravo," Amy said. I could hear that she was smiling. I remembered how that looked; her plush lips, her dimpled cheeks.

"Everything all right on that end?" I asked her.

"Yes," said Amy. "We're just trashing Larry."

"Fuck him," I heard Claudia squawking in the background.

"Don't let Claudia get too drunk," I said.

"Too late," Amy told me.

7

When Larry and Claudia emigrated to Berkeley three years earlier, I had vigorously opposed the move. Claudia and I had been friends through seventeen years, and between us, three marriages. I was used to having her close by. This Berkeley move put a forty-five-minute subway ride plus an hour walk between us. Driving was out of the question, unless I took a toothbrush—because my visits with Claudia nearly always involved alcohol. Overall, this Berkeley wrinkle was damned inconvenient.

Claudia's and my friendship began in the 1980s. She took care of me when my wife, Connie, left.

We lived in a nine-unit apartment building on Hayes Street. Claudia was directly across the hall from Connie and me. We were all still fairly poor back then, but the consolation for being poor is that it usually happens when you're young and good-looking—which we were.

Connie was a mezzo-soprano, and our agent, Maury, managed to often book us into the same productions. We toured in northern Europe so regularly it became routine. In retrospect,

I suppose that was our undoing—the strain of working and touring and living together. I got too much of what I wanted.

I did love my wife. I can say that now, now that it's over. She was a powerful little mezzo and she looked just as charming in a pair of breeches as in a décolletage gown. I enjoyed being on stage with her—I delighted in those moments when she would march across the planks, belting out an aria, locking eyes with me in that knowing, intimate look. It was arousing. And, even after she started getting fat, I loved how her skin was like gardenia petals, white and soft and scented. And her breath smelled like pastis. And she would pull me into hotel lobby phone booths, and orchestra pits, and bathrooms at cast parties to have quick, furtive sex.

But when we toured together we started bickering over little things—misplaced passports (mine), excessive luggage (hers), cramped hotel rooms. And there was napkin-gate: Whenever we toured Europe, Connie would order me to go out to the nearest store to buy her sanitary napkins for her. She'd insist that I do it because my French, or German, or Spanish was better than hers. And then, I'd always get the wrong kind. "This has a plastic liner." "I didn't want the ones with wings." It would always escalate. "This pad will give me toxic shock." "Are you trying to kill me?" "You never listen."

But, it was more than that. It was more than feminine hygiene products that broke up my marriage—divisive as they, apparently, can be. It was also me; my short attention span that seems to spoil all my treasures. After a while, Connie didn't smell like gardenias anymore. She smelled more like a box of cake donuts. And her flesh wasn't plush and inviting, it was pudgy and pocked with cellulite. And her stage presence wasn't dynamic—she was an inveterate scene-chewer. And her rapier-sharp witticisms weren't amusing. She was just a bitch.

Claudia had never liked Connie. They didn't quarrel, but I could tell by the way that Claudia only spoke to Connie in profile. She could never look directly at my then-wife. Sometimes we'd have Claudia over for dinner and Connie would get drunk and turn into an insufferable braggart. She liked to boast about how desirable she was—which was embarrassing as both Claudia and I could clearly see how, even then, the seams of Connie's jeans were straining and, as she'd reach across the table for another biscuit, the flesh of her upper arms hung down and jiggled. Connie would pry bar elaborate descriptions of her various sexual romps into our dinner conversation. This always put Claudia off her meal and she'd excuse herself and slip back across the hallway.

So when I came home from Amsterdam without Connie, Claudia made no pretense at hiding her glee. She had me over to drink champagne and smoke weed. We ate pizza and truffles and lay on the floor laughing hilariously. I told her how Connie had picked up a groupie in Stuttgart—a hulking blockhead named Stig.

"I don't want to hurt you, Max," I reprised Connie's swan song. "I just want to leave you."

"And then did she waddle out of the room pulling her roller bag full of too-tight pantsuits?" Claudia asked. She handed me a smoking roach on a clip.

"Yes," I said, pausing to take a toke. "And she goose-stepped off to the Baltic, straight into the arms of that inbred Pomeranian."

"Stick?"

"Stig. His name is Stig. Connie thought he was a duke. Stupid cow."

"He's not a duke?"

"No. He's a baronet."

"What's that?"

"That's about as prestigious as being a notary public," I said. "And the bitch thought she was going to be a duchess. Duchess Connie."

"Good grief."

"Guess what the German term for a baroness is?"

"*Hasenpfeffer.*"

"That's rabbit stew," I said. "A baroness in German is *freiherrin.*"

We both collapsed on the carpet in hysterics, repeating *freiherrin* until it ceased to be funny, which, in our condition, took a long time.

"I'm glad," Claudia told me. "I'm glad you got rid of her. She's a *puta.* And she's going to be morbidly obese."

I told Claudia I was glad too.

Claudia and I grew very close in those years, our between-the-marriages years. When I met her, Claudia had just divorced her first husband, a biker who had represented himself as an artist. He was actually a thug and she had found him boorish after a few months.

Claudia was getting her advertising career started. She was working as a junior art director. She painted too. I liked her canvases. They were small studies of small moments—a woman looking at an insect on her pillow, a man trying to write a letter. It takes a certain courage to paint small canvases.

They don't sell the way large pieces do—they aren't as insistent about their importance. You have to recognize what's going on in the painting. You can't just let it run you over.

I bought a few of Claudia's paintings. I liked the way they complemented the Cubist still life oils my mother had painted back in the 1950s and 1960s. Mother was still alive then—still living in the house that I'm in now. She liked Claudia's paintings. She liked Claudia.

Larry came along about five years after Mother died. I don't know if she could have gotten used to him. It took some effort on my part.

I had thought Larry was too square for Claudia. But I suppose after the biker, Larry was just what Claudia needed.

Larry was blond and athletic. He was a sort of a cowboy type from North Dakota or Wyoming or Montana—one of those rectangular states. Larry had attended UCLA on a baseball scholarship. He had majored in business. By the early 1990s when he met Claudia, he had already proven his aptitude for selling corporate software. He was, sale by sale, accreting a minor fortune. His commissions were huge. He had an easy charm and a relaxed manner that made him a brilliant salesman.

Claudia met Larry through work—during a meeting at a client's office. Larry was the head sales guy and he'd been brought in to explain to the agency people how he closed deals. Larry liked the way Claudia looked—all that black hair piled up high, and great clunking chunks of gold jewelry, and olive skin stretched taut across a tall frame and peeking out from under flimsy Pucci prints. Larry liked the way Claudia asked smart questions and cracked wise, the way she made everybody laugh and the way she laughed—brassy and loud. She was so Italian, New York Italian. To Larry, Claudia must have seemed very exotic.

Claudia was smitten too. I knew that night when she told me over dinner about Larry that I had lost her—or, at least, that I had lost a piece of her.

They married a couple of months later. I acted sullen and shitty, but they both humored me. They were patient. Eventually we struck a balance. We found a way for the three of us to get along. I think Larry understood that I came with the Claudia package as surely as if I had been her son from a previous marriage or her idiot brother that she was burdened with for life.

It was around that time that I moved. To Pluto.

Mother died and left me the family home on Pluto Street. I moved in swiftly, before any of mother's starchy white-bread relatives got any smart ideas about the divestiture. The house was a prize. It sat on a steep hillside lookout, in a neighborhood known only as "the planet streets." It was massive, and voluptuous—an aging Queen Anne with crackling, yellowing skin like old marzipan, and it sported an onion dome plump as an Ottoman's turban, and an iron weather vane, a half-moon, spun wildly in the Barbary wind to signify which way the lunacy was blowing.

The place came with entanglements. I had renters in the upstairs flat—a pair of old fags who had lived there for years. Their names were Glen and Mike. I called them Glen and Glenda, which they found amusing.

The first time I started bringing a man around the house, the Glen/Glendas were atwitter. "We always knew you were on our team," one of them said. "I'm not a team player," I told him. And somehow this delighted them even more. "Oh, we'll have to watch you, Max," Glen or Glenda said. "Someone's always watching me," I told him. "I'm a goddamn opera singer." More peals of laughter.

Claudia and Larry bought a house nearby, in Cole Valley. It was a Stickley—tall and skinny and overly ornamented just like the woman who chose it.

Their neighborhood had been fairly crappy—having taken years to recover from the scourge of indigents that arrived during that 1967 disaster that is romantically referred to as the Summer of Love. But by the mid-1980s, Cole Valley was coming back up. Yuppies were buying the gracious Victorians from slumlords, and shooing out the junkies and the speed freaks. Claudia and Larry bought their house from a developer who did all the rehabilitation and then flipped it. He had returned the house to its former glory. It looked like a towering white wedding cake. Typical of Stickley, it was festooned with wooden gimcracks: fish scales, and spindles fanning out from the dormers, and knobs and filials everywhere, and crests mounted gratuitously all over the façade, and any open expanse of wall was overlaid with a tessellated checkerboard of wooden squares.

Claudia's and my house were close. We could walk to each other's doorsteps in twenty minutes, but it was a vertiginous ascent up and over the planet streets. Whenever I showed up at Claudia's door, still panting from the climb, she'd ask me if I just crawled up Uranus.

It was close, but not intimate—not like living across the hall had been. I suspected Larry weighed that in when they bought the house. He didn't want me in their home, in their lives, every single day. Claudia couldn't come traipsing over every time she needed some anchovies or lemon zest. She couldn't just pop in whenever she lost her corkscrew only to find it later in the laundry hamper. And I couldn't knock on their front door and walk right in, telling them about how I'd just learned from a costume mistress that Connie was up to a size 24.

Larry and Claudia's house was divided into three flats, a common practice with those large, ungainly, old houses. They rented out the upper flat to a revolving cast of young women—junior media buyers, and receptionists, and assistant branch managers. The women whose names appeared on the original lease—Kristin, Ashley, and Paige—were long gone and a new flock was always moving in and out. They all looked the same to Claudia: blond highlights, and ankle tattoos, and velour sweatpants that said BeBe across the butt in rhinestones, carrying handbags shaped like cucumbers and talking on iridescent pink cell phones.

The garden apartment behind the garage was just as vexing. There is a certain breed of human that chooses to dwell in basements. They are mole-men with waxen complexions and few visitors and they shop for groceries at odd times of the day. Claudia tended to fixate on the basement dwellers' movements and, occasionally, she'd dig through their garbage in search of clues to some unspeakable crime that she, naturally, could not speak about.

I knew the Cole Valley house was bothersome. But I was still surprised when they moved to Berkeley, claiming they needed to escape their seignorial burdens. I said they could buy a flat in the city. But they had made their decision—without me, which was infinitely irksome. Now the shark-infested waters of the Bay separated me from Claudia.

8

I returned from my two-week engagement in Salt Lake City anxious to see how Claudia was doing alone in that big house. I had guessed that she was better because she hadn't called.

I got in my car and drove out there. I resented making the journey just as much as I had the first time. Maybe more so. But, one consolation, I tossed an overnight bag in the trunk. Claudia and I, we girls, could have a pajama party. I could do that now that Larry was gone.

I had been with Claudia and Larry the day they bought the house. I hated it on sight. It was pretentious and confused; a rambling, Bavarian-Tudor schizophrenic that looked like it took a wrong turn at Avon and ended up in the Black Forest. They bought it on impulse, like you'd buy an alligator handbag, or a fez.

The three of us were driving around the Berkeley Hills one sunny May afternoon, ostensibly just to get a feel for the neighborhoods. Larry urged the Lexus up the steep, narrow streets near the top of Grizzly Peak. The houses were monu-

mental and, I thought, morose. You could smell the musti-
ness wafting off the old money.

Claudia cried out for Larry to stop the car. She saw an
open house sign.

"This place looks crazy," I said from the backseat. But
Larry and Claudia were already out of the car.

"Let's just look," Claudia insisted.

The Tudor aspect of the house faced the street, hunkered in
the shadow of an old redwood. It was low and heavy, crushed
into the earth beneath a thick, brown roof that curved over
its wattle and timber walls like the cap of a mushroom. Big
black hinges—jagged and pointy like short swords for close
fighting—held the heavy plank door in its arched frame. Dor-
mer windows pinched up through the roof thatch, soft yellow
light glowing out of their mullioned panes of watery glass.

A hulking gray stone castle loomed up behind the Tudor
cottage. At first I thought it was the neighbor's house. Then I
read the sales sheet and realized that the castle in the background was actually part of the Tudor house—it was an
addition grafted on in the 1920s. Claudia and I paced around
the outside of the edifice.

"It's Disneyland," Claudia said.

"It's Neuschwanstein," I told her. "Did you know that Mad
Ludwig named his castle after the Wagner character, Lohen-
grin?"

A row of arthritic camellia trees grew along the wall. They
were flowering pink and white, but that didn't soften the marshal architecture. The place still looked more like an armory
than a residence.

"Look, darling," I told Claudia, pointing up at the archer's slits. "You can hurl your empty wine bottles down at passersby."

"And it's even got a crenellated roofline." She clapped her hands with delight.

"For pouring cauldrons of boiling sewage onto the heads of troubled yokels."

"Who would live in such a thing?" Claudia said.

The window in front of us popped open. Larry stuck his head out. He was grinning like an idiot with a piece of shiny foil.

"Hey, get in here," he told us.

We breached the threshold and a Realtor marched toward us, her sling-back shoes clicking on the polished fir floors. She stretched her arm out, the hand opened stiffly. I couldn't tell whether she meant to shake hands or give us a karate chop. She was a starchy blonde in a puce pantsuit and a preternaturally orange suntan. She said her name was Stephanie Saint Claire. We were welcome to look around.

The front of the house was a hobbit dwelling. It had wide plank floors and whitewashed plaster walls and low ceilings boxed with chocolate beams.

We passed through to the addition and the whole space opened up into a grand living room. The ceilings soared fifteen feet high, and all that air above your head made you feel as though you were being drawn into the stratosphere against your will. Our voices echoed off the hard white walls. The oak floors were polished high, gleaming like an ice rink after the Zamboni machine gives it a good going-over.

Stephanie Saint Claire flung open a pair of soaring glass

doors and bullied us out onto the redwood deck. I asked her if the deck was safe. She swept her arm across the vista and instructed us to note the "commanding view."

It didn't feel commanding though. Not to me. I got the sense that the house was slouched up there, bewildered and wary, wondering how it had gotten stranded on that rock.

Claudia pointed out how you could see the full spans of both the Bay Bridge and the Golden Gate Bridge. That impressed her. She'd be able to tell people, "We have both bridges," like she owned them. I could already tell she liked looking down across the steep decline at the inferior houses assembled like courtiers on bent knees. Their roofs were bowed heads. All around them, the tops of tall trees wavered in the breeze. The red and brown rooftops floated between billows of leaves. The whole landscape seemed to be adrift.

Larry called to us to join him and Stephanie Saint Claire in the kitchen. They were sitting at the red leather banquette in the breakfast nook, in the cozy Tudor section of the house. Contracts and forms were set into neat piles all over the table.

Larry asked Claudia if she liked the house. Some sort of secret married-person signal must have passed between them. Larry turned to Stephanie Saint Claire and told her they'd like to make an offer. I looked at Claudia. She thrust her hands into the pockets of her coat. But I could see that her fingers were fidgeting.

I looked at Saint Claire's card. Her picture was on it. Her smile was manic, and her teeth were as white as mausoleum marble. Her eyes were slightly crossed. She looked like a cobra about to strike.

Larry started negotiating. I had never seen him in action. It was unnerving. He remained cordial, but his pleasantries became hard around the edges.

He forced Stephanie Saint Claire to split the commission with him, saying he was acting as his own agent. He hammered down the price. He made her stretch the warranty out to cover a full year. And, just to confirm who was in charge, he made the sellers pay for his moving expenses.

Stephanie Saint Claire's fee was dwindling with each concession. But still, she was smiling. She liked it. She liked playing rough with Larry—it was better than money.

Larry had wanted that house so much. Once he got it, he didn't last three years in it. He walked away from his house, his dog, and his wife. Larry left his whole life lying out there like so much curbside recycling. Maybe he knew Max Bravo would come along to clean up his mess.

Claudia greeted me at her front door looking strong and tanned. She stood up straight and her eyes were clear and she smiled easily. Asta scrambled to greet me, his claws clattering across the hardwood.

The house was clean. There were no pills in sight.

"Not playing with your dolls anymore, darling?" I asked her.

"They were making me retarded," she said. "The Ambien gave me panic attacks. The Xanax punched holes in my brain. And the Paxil made me shit my pants. Literally."

She walked away, still talking. I found a half-full bottle of Chianti neatly corked and tucked away beside the bread box on the kitchen counter. I poured myself a short tumbler.

"Don't take your coat off," Claudia called from upstairs. "We're going to the dog park."

Ed, the hoary-headed Vietnam vet, was in the park with his big yellow hound, Colonel. Ed greeted us as "amigos" and offered us a beer. Claudia, to my surprise, counteroffered. She reached into the pockets of her oversized Parisian sack coat and pulled out three beer cans.

Ed told us about how he was having transmission problems with his van, which was also his domicile. He said that he knew a guy in Richmond who could replace the transmission in exchange for a brick of weed that another guy was going to drive down from Humboldt County as soon as his Harley got a new starter. Claudia commiserated with him. I found it tedious.

As they spoke, I watched two unkempt women lumbering down the sidewalk. They were typical Berkeley citizens: people who looked like they slept under bridges but probably owned million-dollar homes.

The women shambled along, shoulders hunched, feet scraping. They wore mustaches and their hair hung in frizzled, salt-and-pepper shanks. Their faded ankle-length skirts looked like they'd been laundered on washboards for several generations. And their pendulous dugs lolled across expansive bellies, scrimmaging like litters of puppies under their T-shirts. I imagined them at age twenty-two, loping up that same sidewalk, slightly pigeon-toed, with their unrestrained breasts bouncing saucily under their peasant blouses, great clouds of cannabis wafting in their wake. You can get away with that sort of thing when you're twenty-two. But not when you're sixty. You can't carry an AARP card and still go around dressed like one of the Manson girls.

"And so Dan and Indio are riding in from Chico . . . ," Ed was telling Claudia.

"We should be going," I interrupted.

"And I told those guys, what goes around comes around," Ed said.

"It's getting late," I insisted.

"Hey, there's Amy," Claudia said.

I looked across the street. Amy was on her front porch with Dixie. She smiled brightly and waved as she walked across her pretty front yard. Her little dog pranced at her heels like a sprite.

"Amy has the most beautiful garden," Ed observed.

Amy's front yard was full of blooms. Her tidy rosebushes espaliered around an oval of shiny green grass. They were bursting with red and peach and yellow and pink blossoms. Amy kept them well trimmed so they bloomed continuously.

"Hey, guys," Amy called as she entered the double gates of the dog park.

"Hi there, Max Bravo," she said, nestling next to me on top of the picnic table. She had changed a little. Amy looked pregnant by then. She rubbed her hand over the back of my shoulders.

I tried to remember what had passed between us when we met that one other time. What had made Amy feel she could be so familiar with me now? Nothing. We had just chatted about general things; the dogs, rising real estate values, a horrific tale in that morning's newspaper about a woman's corpse washing up on the Berkeley shore. I had heard that the dead woman was pregnant. But I didn't want to mention that part, not with Amy.

It had been a casual meeting. And this was only the second time I'd met her, unless you counted the telephone conversation. But the warmth—the heat—that was coming off of Amy was real. I felt it. She made me feel like we were close. Like we had been close for a long time. I recognized then that Amy had a talent. She could make somebody—anybody—feel bigger, more worthy. It was addictive. It was a feeling that you wanted to keep. She was a woman who you wanted to keep, all to yourself.

Claudia knelt down to pet Dixie and said, "High-five, Dixie, high-five."

The little pug jumped up onto her back legs so she could press her front paws into Claudia's palms.

"Are you still working?" Ed asked Amy.

"I'm working right up to my due date," she told him. "I don't want to go stir-crazy."

"Isn't your job stressful though?" Claudia asked. Amy's job had something to do with loans. Her office was in downtown San Francisco, in the financial district.

"It's only stressful if you let it be." Amy smiled. "I was actually having some trouble with the darn computer system. But Jordi helped me straighten it out."

Amy smiled and gently ran her hand across her belly. She'd gotten bigger, yes. But her belly was round and neat and her arms and legs were still slim. Her fingers were long and her nails were filed square and varnished a buff color. She wore one ring—a baguette-cut yellow diamond faceted into a platinum setting. She didn't wear much makeup. But her eyebrows were professionally shaped and her long dark brown hair was cut precisely so it bounced and curved round her face.

"You look great, Claudia," Amy said, just as I was thinking that Claudia looked garish in the sunlight; black eyeliner applied with a paint roller and a black birthmark glued to her cheek.

"Thanks, sweetie," Claudia said. "You want to know the latest?"

"Larry's getting a sex change?" Amy asked. She grinned and wriggled closer to me, squeezing my elbow.

"Larry is stalking me," Claudia announced triumphantly. She tapped her cigarette sharply. The ash fell to the ground and scattered.

"Oh, that doesn't seem—" I tried to interject.

"He's rented a car," Claudia said to Amy, ignoring me. "It's a gray Ford Taurus. It's a dedicated stalker vehicle. He knows I'll recognize his Saab."

"Now that is going a bit too—"

Claudia held her hand up to my face.

"You saw him?" Amy asked. "You saw him in the stalker vehicle?"

Claudia told us that she'd been at Trader Joe's earlier that week. She was loading her groceries into the car when she felt someone watching her. She pushed the cart back to the cart corral, then she walked up and down the row of parked cars, jingling her keys. The cars were empty. She turned and walked back to her own car. She heard a car start up behind her. When she turned again, a gray Ford Taurus pulled out of the row of parked cars. It drove away from her, straight to the exit. She saw the back of the driver's head. It was a blond man. The Taurus had been empty when she walked by it just a few seconds earlier.

"Larry must have been lying down on the front seat. Hiding," Amy said.

Claudia reached out to Amy. The two women clasped hands. They laughed. Their laughter sounded like wavering light, like fingertips circling the rims of crystal goblets.

I was hurt. Claudia hadn't told me about Larry. She'd been saving the story for Amy.

"Would Larry do something like that?" Ed asked me. "Seems pretty intense."

I looked at him and crossed my eyes. He shook his head. We both knew to keep our mouths shut.

9

"They are my friends, Max," Claudia told me.

It was later that same evening. She and I were seated in her dining room. She ladled a murky seafood bisque into my soup plate and said, "Can't I make friends?"

"You have friends," I said. "You don't need to pick up vagrants at some park."

She marched over to the desk and opened the drawer. She walked back to the table holding up a yellow legal pad.

"Perhaps this will refresh your memory," she said, brandishing the note that I had drunkenly and ill-advisedly written to her a couple of weeks earlier.

"It says right here," Claudia said, then reading from the memo, "Park is only seven blocks away. They serve beer out of Ed's van. You would like. Strongly suggest you attend. Asta would like."

"That document is inadmissible," I said. "Why is this bisque so pink? It looks like it's been irradiated."

She ripped the sheet of paper off the pad and set it next to my plate. I picked it up and crumpled it into a ball and threw it at her. It bounced off her forehead just as she was reaching for her wineglass.

"I scanned it into my computer too," she said.

"You're insane," I told her. I lifted my napkin to my mouth and spit out a rubbery mussel that a hyena couldn't have masticated.

"I knew you'd get shitty. You're so jealous. I knew I'd have to preserve the evidence."

"Of what? Some crime?"

"You're the one who told me to go to the dog park in the first place. It's on the record."

"Claudia," I said after taking a moment to calm down. "When I told you to go to the dog park I just wanted you to get out of the house. I didn't think you'd join a cult."

"Are you done with your soup?"

She whisked away my soup plate and brought out the entrée: a pork roast that she had scalded into a desiccated lump of carbon. She presented it wreathed in brussels sprouts that were blackened into buckshot pellets.

The food was as bad as I'd expected. But the wine was good. I had expected that too. We started with a toasty champagne during the soup course. Now I poured the wine for the entrée—a full round of pinot noir that nicely offset the charcoal in the pork.

"These dog people?" I asked. "These are your *friends*?"

"Why do you say it like that?"

"Say what?"

"*Friends,* Max. The word is *friends.* Why can't I have friends?"

"Claudia, it's just that, to me, friends are people with whom you share common interests. The only thing you have in common with these people is the fact that you all own dogs."

"I know," she allowed. "It does seem a bit thin."

By then I was struggling with a briquette of charred pork. I couldn't saw through it and so I staked it down with my fork and tried to rend it to pieces with my knife. Somehow, burnt up like that, the meat reminded me, very graphically, of the animal that it once was. My thoughts ranged wildly to sordid abattoir scenes. I could picture the frightened pigs marching single file up a ramp and into a concrete room, mincing into the jaws of death on their delicate little hooves.

I moved the meat slab to the side of my plate and took up the pile of brussels sprouts. I popped them into my mouth, one at a time, and ate them like cracklings.

"Claudia," I said. "You are different from those people. They are not your species, dear. So what's the point? Why bother with them?"

"I need friends right now, Max."

"But these people aren't friends, Claudia. They are just . . . just clutter."

Strategically, I should have encouraged the dog park connections. These people were, after all, picking up a lot of the Claudia babysitting duty that I—that Max Bravo, as one man, as one human being—could not possibly handle on my own. They were useful.

But they were also what are referred to in movie trailers as "a ragtag bunch." On-screen, they'd be an ensemble cast of hard cases who are released from a military brig to carry out some complicated, certainly suicidal, mission behind enemy lines. Or, I could see them as the crew aboard a rusting old bucket of a space freighter—kooky but capable individuals who each had his own signature eccentricity like singing Little Richard tunes or reading comic books or reciting snatches of James Joyce.

"So is the dog park where carnival workers go to retire?" I asked Claudia.

"They're not that bad, Max."

"Really? Let's review."

We went down the list. There was Jordi Almirall, the software engineer from Barcelona, forty-five years old, single. Understandably single. Almirall had amassed his entire wardrobe for free by collecting the giveaways at high-tech trade shows. The man's T-shirt collection broadcast more slogans than the Gang of Four. He had been cordial enough when we met, but I disliked him. As the instigator who first dragged me, and then by association Claudia, into the dog park, I thought of him as a sort of human gateway drug. I hadn't liked his assumptions about Claudia. He had no business thinking about whether she was good-looking or not. I decided Jordi Almirall was presumptuous and intrusive. And he was sartorially offensive—dressed like a head injury victim on the caregiver's day off, which, in Berkeley, meant that he blended.

"Gator is presentable," Claudia said. She cleared away the burnt pork offerings and set out a couple of salad plates.

"Gator? What is that?"

"Open the claret please, Max," she said. "Gator is a man."

"And why is he called, what is it, Gator?"

"I don't know. But he's ruggedly handsome."

"He is probably like your first husband," I said. "Ruggedly penniless."

Gator didn't have a job. He showed up every day at the dog park with a pair of affenpinschers—sinister-looking little black terriers with the faces of monkeys. They weren't his dogs. He said they belonged to a couple of old women whom no one had ever met.

I was sure that Gator was some sort of drug dealer. And that was the last thing I needed—for Claudia to find another drug pusher, besides her medical doctor.

"Stay away from him," I said.

"Maybe you'd like Gator for yourself, Max."

"I have Wolfgang at the moment."

"It's always just at the moment for you," she said.

Claudia hadn't met my latest paramour yet. I'd just acquired him on my last German tour. But she'd heard enough to speak about him—about Wolfgang the subject, not Wolfgang the person—with some authority.

"I like Ed, don't you?" she said.

"He's nothing but a decrepit, wizened old hippie," I said, and then I put a finer point on it. "He's a bum."

"He's a sweet old man."

"He lives in that Chevy van," I countered. "That's exactly the sort of van that's popular among the serial killer set. Handy for stowing victims."

"He's a gentle, harmless old man."

"Bullshit. People who live like that—people who live under the radar—are hiding from something. He's probably wanted by the FBI."

"His dog is very sweet."

I reflected on Ed's dog. Colonel was a big yellow brute with dull weeping eyes and a set of jaws that could puncture a tractor tire.

"And furthermore," I said, "when we left the park tonight Ed told me to 'keep on truckin'.'"

Claudia cleared away the salad and brought out the dessert. It was, happily, something she hadn't baked herself. She'd bought it from the Tunisian bakery in Oakland. She drove an hour there and back to buy me a box of Cornets de Luna—dense, crumbly pastries made out of sifted flour and powdered almonds and shaped into crescent moons and dusted with powdered sugar.

"Amy is lovely," I said. I bit the tip off a smiling moon.

"You say it as though you're attracted to her," Claudia said. And she lit a cigarette, ignoring the dessert on her plate.

"She's attractive. Around here that's remarkable. Like being a Martian, or a Republican."

"She's pregnant," Claudia informed me brusquely.

"I noticed," I informed her right back.

"And married."

"What's he like?"

"Steve? He's a big cretin. An oaf. Good-looking—if you like the jock types. Square. Golf shirts. Lantern jaw. Bosses her around."

"Sounds a bit like Larry. Without the bossing, of course."

"He's nothing like Larry," Claudia said. She smashed out her cigarette.

"How does he boss Amy around?"

"You'll see," she said, lighting another. "Everybody hates him. He's a big prick."

"I like a big prick now and then."

"That's your other problem, Max. You like a bit of everything now and then."

10

I frowned and cast a lizardly gaze about the park. It was getting well into autumn, and the air was cold as ice tongs. The sky had turned the color of lead. It hung heavy over the top of the leafless landscape.

Claudia had come to expect me to squire Asta to the park every day. The dog walking had quickly progressed from a favor, to an imposition, to a form of indentured servitude.

I felt caged inside the park fence, on display. I was the mad pacing bear, living in a zoo diorama for the amusement of the local bumpkins.

For a while I had distracted myself with Gator. He was as interesting as Claudia had promised he'd be. He was good-looking—in a rustic, "I reckon so" kind of a way. And, at first, I was intrigued by his epigrammatic conversation. But I soon found that Gator was as deep as trail dust. When a fellow isn't pronouncing sentences comprised entirely of "You bet" or "Evidently" from a saddle, they lose their commanding resonance.

"There's a rather interesting book about the old West," I

said to Gator. We were alone in the park, sitting on top of the picnic table. "I didn't read it, just skimmed the review," I said. "Social anthropology. The theory is that out on the frontier, a great many of the cowboys were actually gay."

Gator didn't look up from the cigarette he was rolling.

"This is the part where, in normal discourse, you ask me to elaborate."

He didn't. That's what happens to one's social skills when most of your conversations are with your horse or, in Gator's case, with a pair of affenpinschers.

"Bisexual, to be precise," I continued, undeterred. "The cowboys were gay out on the trail, and hetero in town—down at the saloon with Miss Kitty and the girls."

He struck a match on his jeans by running it under his thigh. He took a drag, and blew the flame out. Then he turned and gazed upon me with a mild indifference.

"What are you, Max? Gay? Straight? Or what?"

"Or what," I told him.

He flicked the spent match across the lawn and rested his elbows on his knees. He watched Asta running along the fence with a tennis ball in his mouth, the affenpinschers on his heels.

"I hate that," I said. "Categorizing people. It lacks subtlety. Demanding that people declare an orientation. I will not be boxed in! You know Gore Vidal had a long love affair with Ayn Rand."

"Anaïs Nin," he said.

"Pardon?"

"Gore Vidal was with Anaïs Nin. Not Ayn Rand," said Gator. "Big difference."

Ed pulled up in his van. That put me in a state of alert. Ed was a confirmed ear-banger. If he trapped you, he'd chew your ear until there was nothing left but a strip of bacon hanging from the side of your head.

The trick was to stay away from the perimeter. The park had a very Balkan borderline—it was an irregular hexagon with seven corners. If Ed managed to trap you in any one of those corners, he could blast you with one of his dissertations on how the United States had secretly carpet bombed Laos or what a bastard Bob Dylan was for having gone electric.

Of course, Ed wasn't the only regular that required special handling. They all had an autistic disregard for personal space.

I had learned to sit on top of the picnic table, at the end, so as not to get sandwiched in between two people. I'd take the added precaution of placing a beer can on the table beside me. If I neglected these measures I'd end up with someone's fleece-encased thighs rubbing up against mine. They would sit right on top of you—these dog people. Maybe that's what comes from years of locking arms at sit-ins and sleeping with fourteen other people in a yurt.

Amy came out of her house just as Ed was getting out of his van. That was a relief. She'd dilute him and Gator—when they were together the entire discourse was comprised of monosyllables and stonerisms.

"Max Bravo," she said. "Have you heard the latest?"

I picked up my beer can and Amy slid onto the table beside me. She reached up and tucked a strand of my hair behind my ear.

"Larry is stalking Claudia," I said.

"That was last week."

"Update me."

"Claudia and Larry are talking again," Amy said.

"What? A détente! Without consulting me?"

"Keep your voice down," Amy said. "Claudia just got here."

She tilted her head toward the far end of the park. Claudia was there with Ed and Gator.

I waved at Claudia, airily, smiling. She waved back. I muttered to Amy, "If Claudia reconciles with Larry, after all this, I'm going to have her committed."

Amy pressed in close to me and conveyed her story in a low, conspiratorial tone. For the first month that Larry was gone, Claudia didn't hear from him. Not a word. I knew all about that.

Then Amy told me something I didn't know. Larry had started telephoning Claudia. It was sudden. And, perversely, Larry chatted away as though nothing had happened.

He wanted to talk about the car. The Lexus was due for its 50,000-mile tune-up. She told him to fuck off. She hung up. He called back. Larry urged Claudia to take the car in to the dealer. Again, she told him to fuck off. He persisted. Finally, she relented. They arranged for Larry to come and get the car while Claudia was at work. He returned the Lexus to the driveway the next day; tuned up and cleaned inside and out. The gas tank was full. The brake fluid and the windshield wiper fluid and the oil were all topped up. The dashboard shone with Armor All and a new pine-tree air freshener hung from the rearview mirror.

"Strange," Amy said. "Isn't it?"

"Yes. I never take my car in for those dealer tune-ups."

"I mean it's funny the way Larry used the car as an excuse to keep up contact with Claudia," Amy said.

"Is that what was happening?" I asked. I honestly hadn't read it that way. I just thought Larry was worried about keeping up the terms of the warranty.

"You are such a typical guy," Amy said, laughing.

No one had ever called me that before. Amy placed her hand on my leg. It was so delicate, and her fingers fluttered. They were long and slender. I wanted to reach down and put my hand on hers and hold it there. I lit a cigarette instead.

"Larry wanted to talk to Claudia," Amy said. "But he didn't know how. He had to make up an elaborate excuse—with the car."

She smiled. The dogs were barking in the background. Amy's teeth were softly rounded at the edges. Pearls.

She was saying, "It's so sweet, isn't it, Max?"

"Sweet? I was thinking deceitful."

"But, Max, sometimes we have to be creative to get what we want."

"The jails are full of creative guys."

"Oh, Max Bravo! Is it a crime if nobody gets hurt?" she said. She flashed that winning smile again. "Larry couldn't be direct with Claudia. She's still so very angry. Claudia is deeply hurt."

I looked over at Claudia. She was standing with Ed and Gator, swinging her beer can like a burgermeister at the local hofbrauhaus. Claudia was doing all the talking. The two men were laughing. She described figure eights in the air with her long black cigarette holder, still talking. She paused to let

Gator light her cigarette. She pressed on with her story. They laughed louder. Now she was braying.

"She doesn't look very hurt," I said.

"She's just being brave."

Claudia was walking in short steps on tiptoes. She bent her arms in close, hands hanging down. I knew what she was doing. She was imitating one of her clients, a female monster that Claudia had named "Roo."

Roo was famous for getting out of her chair at agency presentations and strutting around the boardroom in four-inch heels, her lazy, distended guts hanging over her waistband. Claudia had accurately identified her as looking like a kangaroo with a joey in its pouch. Claudia was performing the Roo walk, and it was good. Ed was laughing so hard he was gasping for breath. Gator laughed and stamped his boot in the dirt. Claudia took a few more rounds as Roo, this time with the cigarette holder clamped in her teeth. She waggled it up and down.

"Yes," I said. "There she is now, smiling through the tears."

Suddenly, a chorus of birdsong filled the air.

"That's me," Amy said, and she pulled her telephone out of her pocket. "Okay, yes," she said into the phone. I could hear a man on the other end. I couldn't tell what he was saying, but I could hear his tone.

"Steve is getting hungry," she said to me, smiling thinly as she closed her phone.

"Then he should eat something."

"He wants me to get dinner started. He doesn't like to snack between meals."

I looked over at Amy's house. Her husband was standing

in the living room. He had his cell phone in his fist and he was watching her through the front window.

"Come on, Dixie," Amy called to her little pug. Dixie came running with a wide smile broken across her flat, creviced face.

I watched Amy leave, Dixie trotting along beside her, like a cocktail wiener on legs. Amy opened the front door for Dixie and followed the dog into the house. She shut the door quickly behind her.

I saw Steve fling the curtains shut. They quivered. Then they hung still and stiff.

11

Opera singers have a lot of free time. It's one of the great luxuries of the profession. And, like all luxuries, it can be an enervating opiate.

I was playing Major-General Stanley in *The Pirates of Penzance*. I already knew the part—I'd played it three times. We were in rehearsals, four nights a week and Saturday mornings. That leaves a lot of daylight.

The empty days unfurled before me. And I deliquesced into the emptiness. I stopped charting and parsing time. I let time rundle out before me like an immense roll of butcher paper, dislodged from its brackets. Unraveling.

Claudia's situation was the mirror opposite of mine. She was madly busy at work. It was early November and the workload in ad agencies always picks up at that time of year. The clients are trying to empty out their marketing budgets so they can ask for even more money the next year. Claudia's agency was overwhelmed with hard deadlines and she was working twelve hours a day. I volunteered to help by extending my dog-sitting hours. Claudia didn't thank me. She just accepted my offer, and then treated it as an imposition.

"Why are you here so early?" Claudia demanded one Thursday morning.

I had showed up at her doorstep, unannounced. She was leaving for work, dressed in some sort of Mandarin costume—a jade green Chinese jacket, cropped black pants, and pointed slippers embroidered with fire-belching dragons. She was just stepping out the door.

She didn't wait to hear my answer. She clipped across the walk, slippers slapping, to the Lexus in the driveway. She kicked the dragon shoes off into her hand—she always drove barefoot—and disappeared into the car. I let myself into the house as she sped away.

As usual, I riffled through the pile of mail on the table in the foyer. Nothing from Larry. Not today at least. I sighed. I did love to find notes from him amid the junk mail and the bills. A Larry letter cropped up every few days. It was always something banal. Handwritten in a careful script meant to look dashed off. Something about the dog needing his shots or the property taxes coming due. He was forever offering to attend to these pedestrian little errands.

I had started monitoring Claudia's mail more closely since Amy had told me that relations between the two of them were thawing. Larry had caused so much anguish, and I had worked so hard to peel Claudia off the walls, that I didn't want him to come sailing back into his old life. He didn't deserve it.

I could have just walked away. But if I'd done that, I

wouldn't have been Max Bravo. And so I cleaved onto Claudia's melodrama—her troubles, her fabrications and machinations and byzantine plot twists, both real and imagined. I reveled in it. I embellished it. I even invented a musical score to accompany Claudia's greatest dramatic moments: hysterical violins colliding in a modernist discord of stridulating screeches and pizzicato plucks.

But just how crazy was Claudia? After all, she had sustained a terrible shock. Apparently, Larry was crazier than she was. He's the one who did the crazy thing. He's the one who ran off like a mental patient bolting for the fence.

Larry—good old dependable Larry with his MBA, and his blond good looks, and his healthy, uncomplicated sex drive. He had always been so dependable for running the finances and having the rain gutters cleaned every spring. And you never had to worry about Larry's income. He was the perennial favorite at work—an A team guy who never got laid off even as the efficiency experts were obliterating entire departments full of expendable worker bees all around him. An entire company could go out of business and, somehow, Larry would still be there, handing out business cards and drawing a salary.

That was the Larry who Claudia and I knew—and took for granted. And, we were just a tad bored with him. I could say that now that he was gone.

But now, Larry had changed. Somehow his aberrant act, this abandonment, had made Larry something new. It made him interesting.

We realized—and this was titillating—that there must be

a seamy underside to Larry, a cloaked world of secrets, which Claudia and I had never even thought to suspect was there.

"What do you want?" I said to Asta. He was standing by the door, staring at me.

Then I remembered why I'd come over. I got Asta's leash and his halter-top thingie and got him outfitted.

As was our usual routine, Asta and I set off down the street. I started singing, very quietly, almost whispering, Major-General Stanley's song.

"I am the very model of a modern Major-General, I've information vegetable, animal, and mineral."

Asta's ears flattened back onto his skillet-shaped skull. He didn't like distractions when he was trying to get to the dog park. But, I thought, to hell with him. It wasn't as though these walks were for his sake.

We promenaded along our usual route, the seven blocks that descend—geographically and economically—from Claudia's hilltop chateau to the proletarian dog patch on the Berkeley flatlands. It was like passing into another country.

The houses shrank as the terrain leveled out. And they began to line up in duplicates and triplicates of the same cracker box Craftsman bungalow. Same squat, single-story elevation. Same generous porch flanked by two hefty pillars. Same two bedrooms, one bath, built-in dining-room cupboard featuring stained glass doors, same fireplace in the living room, same oak floors throughout.

The bungalows weren't strictly identical, not like they had been when they were all built in the early 1920s. They shared the same DNA, but each house had mutated into a wholly unique curiosity. Now the neighborhood no longer looked like a multiple birth family—it looked like a gathering of inbred cousins.

These houses were suffused with the personalities of all the generations of people who'd lived, and cooked, and slept inside them. The plaster and paint and wood were alive, as surely as if it were skin and blood and bone.

The wee little hovels were painted every color in the Crayola box. Some were defaced with aluminum case windows or asbestos siding. Others were draped with Tibetan prayer flags and weeping wisterias shedding handfuls of purple teardrops. The gardens were spritzed with spinning pinwheels flashing silver amid beds of trumpeting white calla lilies. Glossy green hydrangea bushes lofted their iron blue pom-poms. And primordial palm ferns patiently waited to witness the end of mankind, just as they had watched the dinosaurs come and go.

"I'm very well acquainted, too, with matters mathematical," I sang, a little louder. "I understand equations, both the simple and quadratical."

We strolled by a house that had been wrenched off its foundation and raised up fifteen feet in the air. It was perched on a forest of pillars. They were building a new first floor, doubling the house's size and, presumably, its value. The flatlands were full of these houses on stilts, houses growing taller and bigger.

People were buying up these shacks for 420 times their original price, then sinking small fortunes into completely changing them. The little proletarian village—originally populated by shipyard workers and secretaries—had become a real estate bonanza. People were betting everything they had on these houses.

"I know our mythic history, King Arthur's and Sir Cara-doc's; I answer hard acrostics, I've a pretty taste for paradox," I sang on.

The dog park came into view, and I picked up the patter, singing louder. I stopped at the gate, threw open my arms, and gave the Major-General's song a rousing finish, "I am the very model of a modern Major-General!"

Jordi, Ed, and Gator—milling around the picnic table— applauded and cheered with gusto.

"What ho, lads," I called out as I clanked through the double gates with Asta. I unhooked his leash and he bounded across the dirt to join the other hounds.

No matter what time I got to the dog park, at least one of the regulars was always there. At first, it had put me off. If I saw someone inside the fence, I'd walk past the gate, acting as though I hadn't intended to stop there. But they'd call out to me. They'd beckon me to join them inside the chain link. They didn't have to bother anymore. I went inside all too willingly.

"Say," I said as I took my place on the picnic table. "Have any of you fellows heard from Larry?"

"What are you trying to shovel up, Max?" Gator said, re-folding his newspaper.

"I suspect Larry is trying to patch things up with Clau-dia."

"No," Jordi said quickly. "This is not possible."

Gator handed Ed his newspaper and said, "Did you guys see that thing today about some guy, killed his pregnant wife and took off. They looked all over hell for her and then they found her body, in the backyard. Half cooked. In the barbecue pit."

"Well, that was in Mississippi," I said, as if that explained it.

"The world is so big," Jordi said. "And one body is so small. So perishable. Is that the word? *Perishable?*"

"Depends on how you look at things," Gator said.

"To hide a body where it can never be found sounds very easy to me," Jordi said.

"Check out Steve," Ed said, without looking up from the newspaper story about the barbecued woman.

Steve had opened his garage door. And there, sitting on a trailer, was a twelve-foot fishing boat. He rolled the rig out onto the driveway, set the brake, and started washing the boat.

Jordi pulled a wad of toilet paper out of his pocket. He yanked at it, methodically straightening out sections of tissue, which he then used to blow his nose into.

"Must you?" I said to Jordi.

"*Qué?*"

"When did Steve get that boat?" Ed asked.

Jordi slid off the table, stuffed his hands into the pockets of his jogging pants, and walked to the fence. He leaned on it and called across the street.

"Steve. Steve. Steve. Steve."

Steve didn't look up. He was now in the boat, bent over, rearranging the life jackets and the seat cushions.

"Steve. Steve. Steve," Jordi kept calling.

"He can't hear you, dude," Gator said.

Jordi swung back around to us. His lips curled up, his nose crinkled, and his eyes squinted. He looked like this often.

Confused. His yellow T-shirt bore the words THE CLARITY OF QUINTESSENCE LOGIC.

Jordi stepped out of the dog park. The gate clanked behind him.

"What the hell is that goofball doing?" Ed said.

Jordi walked up Steve's driveway, making large hailing motions with one arm. He kept the other hand in his pocket. Steve stood up tall in his boat, polishing a spiked grappling hook.

We couldn't make out what they were saying, but the pantomime was legible. Jordi made long interrogative speeches, all smiles and scrapes. Steve fired back staccato answers. After a few moments, Jordi waved good-bye—a big wave like he was on a desert island trying to signal a low-flying plane. He came bouncing back across the street.

Steve put away his grappling hook and his rags and wash bucket. He pushed his new boat back into the garage, closed the door.

"What did that horse's ass have to say for himself?" Ed asked.

"He says he likes fishing, so he bought a boat," Jordi said.

"That's kinda, I don't know what," Ed said. "Sudden, I guess. Out of the blue."

"Should he have consulted us first?" I said.

"I think it's kinda out of the blue," Ed said.

12

"You are nothing but a dancing bear for the *gadji*," I heard an old woman say as I walked through my front door later that afternoon. The voice was coming from the living room. And, although I couldn't see her, I knew exactly whom it belonged to. I could hear the aspirated, cigarette-raked tone, the broken Balkan accent pebbled with Romany cadences.

I stepped into the living room and there she was—my grandmother. She wore a long red skirt printed with tight bunches of petite roses, a faded yellow blouse, and a pair of Soviet-issue lace-up army boots. A metal amulet—the size and shape of shooting skeet—hung on a string of beads around her neck.

She raised her face to me: a crooked snippet of a mouth set into a puckered, brown walnut of a face. A pair of long forelock braids, the hair stubbornly black, hung along her temples and past her shoulders. Her eyes—so dark they looked permanently dilated—clapped onto me, unblinking, from under a periwinkle scarf.

"We agreed you wouldn't come back," I told her. "Never. Do you remember that conversation?"

"I don't know what you are talking about," she claimed.

Maybe she didn't. Gypsies, the more primitive Gypsies of my grandmother's ilk, have no sense of time. They don't wear watches. They don't keep records. Most don't even read. My grandmother couldn't tell you what year she was born. I reckoned her birth date to be between 1912 and 1920. Varying family accounts put it at somewhere just before or just after World War I. "Before" and "after" can be abstract concepts to Gypsies. So can death.

Baba's birth date may have been a mystery, but her death date wasn't. I was in college, and had come home for the funeral. It was 1978. I suspected that I hadn't heard the last from her when we buried Baba. I was right.

She folded her hands in the lap of her skirt. She gazed out the bay window as if something interesting was happening on the street.

"You need my help now. That is the only reason I am here," she said.

"I can't imagine what for," I said.

I chose to stand by the fireplace, my elbow resting on the mantel. I wouldn't sit down. To sit would have insinuated we were having a conversation.

"You cannot see because you are as blind as that *gadjo* mother of yours," she said.

"Oh." I looked at my watch. "That took exactly three and a half minutes."

"What minutes? Taking what?"

"Three and a half minutes. That's a measurement of time. It's exactly how long it took from the moment I stepped through the front door until you brought up Mother."

"Her *mahrime* pollutes your life," the old woman said.

I let that one slide. There's no arguing *mahrime*, the pollution that comes in many guises, carried by many vehicles. Gypsies follow elaborate rituals and strictures to avoid *mahrime*. And then my father went out of his way to marry it. My mother was *gadjo*, a non-Gypsy, and my father's very involvement with her was *mahrime*. It was my grandmother's great tragedy. But within that tragedy, there was hope. There was me. She always came back to me, the tenacious old woman— ever hopeful to reclaim me, to cleanse me.

"I'm not here to talk about your father's unfortunate marriage."

"Father's unfortunate marriage had a name," I told her. "Grace. Mother's name was Grace."

"A terrible evil will soon be committed," she said.

She bent her elbow and raised one crooked finger. Then she inscribed slow circles in the air with her gnarled digit.

I made a mental note of the gesture. Baba was a treasure trove of aberrant mannerisms. I plundered them regularly and kept them in my repertoire. I'd pull them out and reenact them on stage whenever I was portraying a particularly eccentric character.

"You are woven into the evil like a thread in a bolt of cloth," she continued. "You will be made part of it."

Baba looked small, and terribly rustic, tucked up against the armrest of my Eames recliner. The iconic modern chair seemed to swallow her up, skirts and beads and all. I had gotten the chair from Claudia. She was throwing it away be-cause she was frustrated with it—the swivel base was broken and it would sometimes tip over backward if you leaned too far into it. You never really knew how far back was too far back. I half hoped the old woman would relax back and the chair would topple her to the floor. But, of course, she would have to have weight for that to happen. She would have to be corporeal.

"Oh, for God's sake! Can't you save this stuff for the hicks? Honestly, I may be half *gadje*, but I'm Gypsy enough to know that all your cardomancy and palmistry and tea leaves and all the rest of it is just for the tourists."

"I don't talk to you now as a sideshow fortune-teller. You know that I can see."

"All right. What is this evil thing?"

"Murder," she said. She shut her mouth and her head shook left and right, the Balkan gesture for yes.

13

The phone rang and I heaved myself out of the bathtub.

"Max Bravo," the voice said.

"This is she."

I was feeling giddy. And I suppose I thought it was that asshole trying to sell me a time-share in Maui again.

"Johnny Miranda," he said.

"Oh," I drawled. "Mr. Miranda. And what can I do for you?"

"I've got a package for you to pick up. Down here at the Sans Souci."

"Really," I said, my party atmosphere having abruptly dissipated. "And does that package happen to be five foot eight? Nose like a Medici?"

"I think the nose part is stretching it," he said.

"It always looks bigger when she's a pain in the ass. Why don't you just put her in a cab?"

"It's beyond that," he said, and he hung up.

The Sans Souci was empty. One glance around the dark shotgun barrel of a tavern confirmed that. Johnny Miranda was standing behind the bar reading the newspaper, *The New York Times*. He was standing perfectly erect, as he always did.

The Sans Souci affected the 1890s Barbary Coast theme that was in vogue in the 1970s. The former owners—surely under the influence of cocaine and Quaaludes—had tricked it out in gold wallpaper with red flocking, and stained-glass pendant lamps that glowed burnt umber and harvest gold, and green and gold paisleys that ran in a faded riot across the mashed and sodden carpet. It was a nautical pastiche. The thick-roped nets hanging from the ceiling, and the ship's wheel on the wall, and the framed etchings of old whaling ships were meant to make the patrons feel hearty and salty. Johnny Miranda wasn't salty though. He was smooth and neat. Johnny Miranda was always brushed and pressed with sharp creases.

Claudia's leopard print coat was draped over a bar stool. Her handbag was sitting on the bar.

"Where is she?" I asked him.

Johnny Miranda nodded toward the doorway that led down the steep dark stairs into the basement. She was in the powder room. Miranda didn't put his newspaper down. He held a stubby golf pencil in his left hand. He was doing the crossword.

"Why's she here by herself? Where's Jeff?" I said.

"The partner?" he asked, and he raised one eyebrow and I was struck all over again by how deep the heat smoldered in his eyes.

"Yes," I said. "Jeff."

"His girlfriend called three times. I told him to clear out. I told him I didn't want to have to vacuum up the cat hair."

"Yes," I said, vaguely recalling the last time Jeff's girlfriend came to fetch him from drinks with Claudia Fantini. "Both those kitties have sharp claws, don't they?"

"That's not why I called you," Johnny Miranda said.

"What's she doing?"

"Drunk dialing."

"Not Larry," I cried.

"No," Miranda said. "Some guy named Jordi. Ever heard of him?"

Yes, I told him. I'd heard of Jordi. I thanked Johnny Miranda for calling me. I said I'd take care of it.

"Max!" Claudia called out.

Her voice was full of fanfare. If somebody didn't know her—somebody who didn't know she could carry more liquor than a Greek oil tanker—they would have thought she was just being exuberant.

"Max!" she repeated herself. "I've been working on my runway walk. Watch."

She set her face in a glower and started across the room, flicking her boots in front of her at the ankle like she was trying to knock dog shit off her toes. She slid onto her bar stool.

"Max, sit down." I was sitting. "Johnny, darling, get Max a drink, will you, love?"

"Max is driving," Johnny said. He put his newspaper down—now that she was there—and he picked up one of the bar nozzles and sprayed a glass of soda water, no ice, into a tumbler. He set out a fresh coaster in front of her and put the tumbler on it.

"*Que diablos haces?*" she demanded.

"I'm surprised you didn't just sign for that package yourself," I told Johnny Miranda. "Seems like it could be delivered right to your door."

"I wouldn't want the rightful owner to show up and say I had no business claiming it," he said.

"So what brings you to our festive Sans Souci, Max?" Claudia asked merrily.

She was drinking the soda water, just like Johnny knew she would. She would have drunk de-icing fluid if Johnny were pouring.

"I was in the neighborhood," I answered, looking straight ahead at Johnny. "And guess what neighborhood I'm on my way to next."

Of course I had to spend the night at Claudia's, lying in the guest bed, my head up against the chiffon-thin wall, listening to her snoring through that outsized Guinea beak of hers. In the morning I got up early. I made her breakfast— more soda water with an Alka-Seltzer sidecar, black coffee, a piece of dry wheat toast, and a shot glass of cranberry juice. I set it all up on a tray. I thought about bringing her a rose in a bud vase. Then I decided I shouldn't spoil her.

"Oh, take that shit away," she said.

I yanked her up by her armpits, plumped her pillows, and propped her up. I set the tray in front of her. Then I sat on the bed and drank her coffee while she sipped her fizzy water and picked pieces of crust off her toast.

"Why did you get so hammered at the Sans Souci?" I asked her.

"I don't know, Max. Maybe because it's a bar?"

"Well, if I wasn't there to intervene you'd be waking up in a Murphy bed," I said. "Next to your greasy bartender."

She set the tray aside and got out of bed. She was wearing a sheer nightgown. The morning sun punched through the window behind her, and I could see the sharp outline of her angular frame. Her eyes were as hard as stones. Her hangover had vanished. And it occurred to me that, if she really wanted to, she could kick my ass.

"Don't orbit too close to me," Claudia said. "You're liable to singe those downy little wings of yours."

She flung open her closet door, pulled out a pair of slacks and a sweater. She tossed them on the bed and headed for the shower.

"I'm going to the dog park," she said.

"Why?"

I heard the shower turn on.

"That's even worse, you know," I called out, still sitting on her bed. "Johnny Miranda I can understand. But surely you can't be serious about that Catalan idiot in the polyester tracksuit."

I heard the shower shut off.

"He's not like us, dear," I called out. "Sleeping with Jordi would be like crossing the species barrier."

"Get me a towel, would you, Max?"

I called Wolfy that evening. I always called Berlin whenever a new development in the Claudia Chronicles surfaced. I told him that Claudia wanted to make Larry jealous. Any man would serve. Johnny Miranda. Even Jordi. Larry was too hetero to notice that Miranda was socially inappropriate, and that Jordi was patently unattractive. And Claudia knew that.

Wolfy disagreed. He suggested that Claudia actually saw something in Jordi that I didn't, something about his personality. Then he laid out a tedious theory about a person's inner character being more important than his outward appearance. Naturally, I wasn't buying it.

But we both found the topic delicious. In fact, most of our conversations revolved around Claudia by then. We were as hooked on her as we had been on Egyptian soap operas when we were together in Berlin.

Wolfy and I were drama addicts. And hanging around with Claudia was like smoking crack. But we knew it. And isn't that the first step to recovery? Admitting you have a problem? Or is that the first step to an overdose?

14

On a bright Sunday afternoon a cadaver walked into the dog park. It was a woman, a dried-out husk of a woman who had been beautiful once. She was walking an enormous, brindle-coated brute of a dog. She guided him by a length of yellow nylon rope that she'd knotted to a heavy chain around his neck.

The dog was a pit bull. But he was like a pit bull from the Ice Age—enormous. Some deranged drug dealer had likely taken up crossbreeding pit bulls with mastiffs and rottweilers. I was imagining a race of lunkheaded killer dogs multiplying in some junkyard in Vallejo or El Sobrante—one of those shithole towns in the North Bay.

The dog had a massive head. He walked with it held low in front of a solid mound of shoulders and chest. He looked like a cement mixer on four legs.

The woman walked her dog along the outside of the fence. She had an Oakland Raiders cap pulled down low. But we could still see that her cheeks were sunken in like someone had gone after them with a melon baller.

She wore a shiny leather jacket with a rabbit-fur collar. Her jeans hung off her fleshless legs like empty denim bags. Her sneakers were dirty and blown out at the seams.

She lifted the U-latch to the outside gate, stepped into the vestibule. She became flummoxed when she found herself confronted with yet another gate.

"Safety gate," Jordi called out to her. "Close the outside, then come in."

"This gate's fucked up!" she yelled back.

"First close the outside gate," he said. "Then come in. Is for safety. Is safety gate. So the dogs don't escape."

"I don't want to escape, dude," she said. "I'm trying to come inside."

"Should I go help her?" Jordi asked us.

"No," Ed said.

In what must have been the tweaker equivalent of a eureka moment, she closed the outside gate and saw that she then had enough room to swing open the inside gate.

Her dog's head loomed through the open gateway. He swung it slowly around like it was a searchlight running along the perimeter.

"Good Christ," I said. "That's the biggest Gila monster I've ever seen."

"Once when I was down in New Mexico, me and a buddy were making a run from up around Truth or Consequences, and we pulled over outside Gallup to take a leak," Gator said. It was the longest string of words I'd ever heard him put together.

"On yer bikes?" Ed asked.

"Yeah," Gator said. "And we're just standing there taking

a leak on the side of the interstate and this Gila monster, big as a dog, comes up out of the gulley and clamps onto Jake's boot."

"Unprovoked?" I asked.

"Sure," Gator said. He started to laugh. "And that booger would not let go. We tried shaking the hell out of it. Stompin' it. Hammered on it awhile with a wrench. Finally, ended up I kept a set of fence cutters under my seat and we took his head off with them. And that son of a bitch still wouldn't let go of that boot—after he was dead."

This was just the sort of dust-blown, black-leather-vest-wearing, Harley with extended forks, tools-and-killin' humor that Ed and Gator loved to share between themselves. They both laughed heartily, reveling in their grit.

"Well, I suppose I'm just a sissy," I said. "Because I've never actually sawed a Gila monster's head off of my friend's boot."

"It was more of a snipping motion than sawing," Gator said.

The tweaker woman approached us. She kept a few feet back, careful not to penetrate the social membrane. But she was close enough that we could see the outline of her skull under her dried, pocked skin.

"No leash park. Right?" Skeletor said.

I heard a click. Claudia was lighting a cigarette.

"No leash," she repeated. "I can take him off his leash, right?"

"Yes." Claudia was the first to speak. "As long as he's okay with other dogs."

"He won't fuck with your dogs," she said. "If they don't fuck with him."

She cackled in a loose volley, then bent down and untied the pit bull. He swung away from her, reared up on his back legs, and pounded down hard on the dirt with his two front paws. He traversed the park with his nose in the dirt. His balls, big as iron shot puts, clanked against the tightly bunched muscles on his legs.

"Smoking okay?" the Skeletor woman asked.

We nodded. Gator took a drag on his cigarette, squinting at her through the smoke.

"You never know what's cool anymore," the Skeletor woman said.

"How so?" I had to ask.

"Heck a lot a rules. They got a law against everything now."

And I thought, yes, including class five narcotics. Claudia made some chitchat with her, extracting the usual data points. The woman's name was Candy. Candy Bates. Her dog was Troy. Someone named Tate had asked her to take the dog while he was away—in the Vacaville Penitentiary.

"Will you get your dog fixed?" Jordi said.

"He ain't broken," Skeletor said. And her smile looked like two slabs of uncooked liver pressed together.

Gator said, "Makes him more aggressive, doesn't it?"

"Yes," she said, and she tapped the ash off her long, skinny, menthol cigarette.

I looked over again at the pit bull. It slowly, methodically, stalked around the tuft of madrone bushes at the far end of the park. Then it disappeared behind them.

The gate opened and Amy came into the park with her

little pug. Dixie trotted ahead, cheerily approaching us. A smile creased her flat face. Her eyes shone like two bright brown buttons.

There was the sound of pounding across the hard dirt. Then screaming. Women screaming—Amy and Claudia. And Dixie was screaming—but the little dog's screams were more of a high-pitched keening. Troy came out from behind the madrones. He slid to a stop in front of Dixie. A cloud of dust went up. Troy's jaws clamped onto Dixie's shoulders. He stood, upright and inert, as though he'd surprised himself. Dixie hung limp in his jaws. The dust swirled in the air around the two dogs, and slowly fell to earth.

Gator and Ed and Jordi were up off the picnic table. They surrounded the big dog.

"Leave it, Troy!" Candy Bates screamed.

But Troy wasn't leaving it. He didn't look at her. He just lifted his eyebrows, pinching them together. He shuddered his head in a quick shake. Dixie's little legs flailed in the air like she had no bones. He paused, looked at the three men. Then he shook the little dog again.

Ed kicked the pit bull in his flank. When it pivoted to face him, Gator kicked it on the other side. There was a lot of yelling. Then everything seemed to slow down.

Jordi ran across the street to Amy's house. He came back with a long iron pry bar.

"Don't you hurt my fucking dog," Candy Bates said.

She started toward Jordi. I stepped in front of her. "Back off," I told her.

She twitched, started to say something, then walked back

to the picnic table and sat down. She swiftly tossed one bony thigh over the other and spastically swung her crossed leg up and down.

The pit bull was lying on its side with Ed and Gator thrown over its body like a couple of rodeo cowboys on a steer. Jordi stood over its head. He had shoved the chisel end of the pry bar through the edge of Troy's mouth, rammed it into the dirt, and flipped the dog onto the ground. And still, pinned, piled on, and bleeding, Troy wouldn't open his jaws to release Dixie.

Jordi ratcheted the pry bar back and forth, then he gave it one hard thrust. I heard a crack and Troy's jaw fell open. Dixie tumbled limp onto the dirt. She tried to stand, but collapsed. I scooped her up and rushed her over to Amy. She and Claudia wrapped Dixie in Claudia's coat. Claudia told me she was going to drive Amy and Dixie to the veterinary emergency room. It was close, she said. She assured Amy that the little creature was more stunned than hurt.

More people filled the park. Uniforms. Claudia had dialed 911. A pair of animal control officers took Troy. Candy Bates, apparently, had outstanding warrants.

The police put Candy in the back of a squad car, her hands cuffed behind her. The window was open just a few inches. As the car pulled away, she sprung forward on the seat and tilted her head sideways so she could poke her face out the window.

"I want drug tests on all these fuckers!" she screamed. "They're all fucked up!"

The squad car rolled down the street, Candy screaming out

the window. It reached the stop sign at the end of the block. Its taillights flicked red, and I could clearly hear her.

"I know who you fuckers are!" she was yelling, her voice now rasping. "What goes around comes around, assholes."

"I knew she'd say that," Gator said.

"I'm coming back, assholes!" Candy was yelling. "Don't you fucking sleep. I'm not sleeping. I'm not fucking sleeping."

15

It was the middle of November. Amy was nine months pregnant. She was due to deliver the baby on Thanksgiving weekend. She had explained to us that although the doctor gave her a due date, his calculations could be off by as much as a month. This uncertainty provoked Ed.

"Amy shouldn't be at work," Ed said.

"She told me she feels good," I said.

"What if her water breaks?" Ed said. "That quack doctor doesn't know when the baby's coming. Why is there so much mystery around the damn due date?"

"A thirty-day window does seem a bit broad," I allowed.

I'm not an expert on childbirth. I find it mildly terrifying actually. But I, too, had thought that the ambiguity around the due date was odd.

"Amy's fine," Gator said. "She's not out in a goddamn rice paddy. She's on the twenty-second floor of Embarcadero Two. If she goes into labor, they'll get her to a hospital."

"Have you been to her office?" I asked.

"She's better off at work," he said sharply.

I had visited Amy at her office—only recently, and just the once. I was downtown having lunch with Claudia. We had dropped in on Amy and invited her to join us.

It was a little dislocating, seeing Amy in that environment. We were so used to seeing her outside, in the sunshine, surrounded by dogs. None of us ever pictured our cohorts in their lives beyond the dog park.

We got off the elevator and stepped into the reception area. It was so quiet I felt like my ears were plugged, like we were underwater. The receptionist talked in a whisper and led us to Amy's office. It was very masculine, but in a cartoonish way. The decorators were going for an English gentlemen's club effect. Foxhunting prints cantered across the oak paneling. Forest green carpeting sucked all the sound out of the air.

You couldn't see the loan sharks circling. But you could sense them threshing, just beneath the clubby décor and inside the brokers' Brooks Brothers suits.

Amy was in a private office, sitting behind a massive rosewood desk that looked like it had been deposited in the middle of the room by a glacier. She seemed flustered to see us.

Maybe twenty years earlier, Amy really would have been the helpful loan officer she pretended to be. But the industry had changed; it had turned feral and had grown tusks. I could see by the product brochures fanned out artfully on Amy's credenza. The loans she sold were specious arrangements— reverse mortgages, subprime mortgages, balloon mortgages. Loans like that could ruin you if you weren't careful. It didn't square with Amy's kindly demeanor, but maybe that's why she was so good at it.

Amy quickly composed herself. She acted like our visit was a pleasant surprise. But her smile was static, and she quickly ushered us out, saying she had an appointment. Claudia and I were unsettled by the incident. We didn't tell the others we'd been to Amy's office. It felt like a dirty secret.

"I wonder how the other wage slaves are doing," I said. I didn't want to think about Amy, not in the context of Evergreen Mortgage.

"All work is just an elaborate form of crowd control," Ed observed.

"I wouldn't sit for one day in an office," Gator said.

"The man," Ed said. "Keeping you down."

"Larry I can see in an office," Jordi said. "But not Claudia. The routine crushes your soul."

I was certain that, at that very moment, Claudia was playing ringmaster in the office she shared with her copywriter, Jeff—also known as "the long-suffering Jeff." They'd been together for eight years, and in three agencies. Jeff knew how to get along with Claudia. He didn't make a lot of noise. He left that to her. Claudia was the one who always told the traffic manager to push back the deadlines. She was the one who demanded their raises. She was the one who decorated their offices: red walls, Astroturf carpeting, speakers blasting out Swedish death metal.

"I could never be cooped up in an office," Ed said. "I couldn't take the boredom."

"Yes, Ed," I remarked. "The workaday world can't rival the adventure of sleeping in your van every night and sitting in this park every day."

Ed stood up and went to his van. He came back with a

beef joint the size of a war club. He threw it toward Colonel. The beast took it up in his mouth and raised it like a military standard. He loped around the park with the bone, Asta and Cecilia and the two affenpinschers trailing behind him.

"You come here every day too, Max," Jordi said to me.

"I'm between engagements."

Ed came back to the picnic table and sat down.

"My wife had four kids," Ed said. "And for every one of them, the doctor called the date within a week. Amy should know when that baby's coming."

"Can we stop talking about it now?" Gator asked.

"Why are you so touchy?" Ed asked him.

Gator's tone had stopped me too. There was something in his voice. An anxiety.

"We must have a party," Jordi said. "A baby bath."

"Shower," I told him. "It's called a baby shower."

16

Everyone wanted to go to the baby shower. But no one wanted to host it. We debated the party plan for nearly a week.

Ed suggested we host the shower at Claudia's house. I said no way. Claudia would have been furious at the inconvenience. But I couldn't say that.

I argued that it should be held at Amy's house. It was a surprise party, I said. And surprise parties always worked the same way: You invade the subject's home. You vandalize it with streamers and balloons and other vile pastel-colored crap. Then you hide a mob of people behind the potted plants. When the intended victim arrives home—tired and cranky after a day's work—you jump out and terrorize her. I'd never actually been to a surprise party, but I'd seen them depicted on television.

I had them convinced until Jordi distracted us with logic. He pointed out that my scheme would require coordinating with Steve. That killed it, but only temporarily. Gator hit upon the idea of asking Kim and Marcy to host the party.

"The lesbians," Gator described them. "The ones with the golden retriever. Bill."

"It should be at a chick's house," Ed agreed.

"Why?" I asked, genuinely bewildered.

I'd seen Kim and Marcy around the park, but didn't think of them as part of the core group. Marcy was a gruff bruiser who always wore a red fleece jacket and a gray, wire-bristle mullet. She looked like a hockey coach.

Kim was younger, around thirty, and she was cute, of Korean descent, and obviously heterosexual. The rumor was that Marcy had lured Kim away from her husband and young son.

For some reason, no one ever asked Kim if she was gay, or straight, or what. They certainly never asked Marcy; her situation was obvious.

And that chafed me. People were forever insisting on labeling me, on forcing me to choose a camp. But they allowed women—in this case, Kim—to skip back and forth between the borders of gay and straight as if they had some sort of diplomatic immunity.

"Marcy and Kim's house would be the best," Gator said. "Chicks always keep their places nicer."

"Kim and Marcy are sort of chicks," Jordi noted.

We didn't know Kim and Marcy that well, but that didn't stop us. We elected them in absentia because they were cordial and pleasant and socially neutral. Gator told us they kept an orderly household and, I suppose because none of us four did, that impressed us. Marcy was a full professor of political science at UC Berkeley. Gator said he'd sat in on a few of her lectures on anarcho-syndicalism, Keynesian economics, and the Trotsky-Stalin rift. He said she was quite good. Kim was a plumber. She drove a big red truck with built-in, locked toolboxes. Her tagline was: "Flooded to the brim? Quick, call Kim!"

When they weren't working, the two women enjoyed the usual lesbian recreations. They installed retaining walls in their garden and hosted tailgate parties and took Kim's young son on camping trips.

"Why is Marcy always in that fleece jacket?" I asked.

"It's from REI," Jordi said.

"I can see where she bought it. It has a tacky logo on it. The point is, it's execrable. Particularly the fabric. It's all pilled and covered in lint. And it's some sort of synthetic, like recycled 7-Up bottles."

"Fleece, dude," Ed told me. "It's called fleece."

"Fleece is the action fabric of the nineties," Jordi added.

"Kim's really cute," Gator said.

We all concurred. Kim was cute. And then Gator did something curious. He became animated. He talked about how Kim—a compact gamine with a saucy walk and bandy legs— looked so good in clothes. He gabbled on about her playful flights of sartorial fancy: her short skirts and thigh-high striped socks and her positively Asian penchant for successfully clashing patterns—paisleys and plaids and polka dots. He even liked how she clipped up her hair into little tufts with bright plastic barrettes.

"Gee, Gator," I said. "I didn't know you were such the fashionista."

He pulled out his tobacco and papers and slowly rolled a cigarette.

"I studied fashion design for a while," he said.

He licked the edge of the cigarette paper, folded it down with one neat swipe, and stuck the cigarette in his mouth. I clicked my lighter.

"Perhaps I underestimated you, Gator."

"Don't read anything into it, Max."

17

When Marcy opened the door, a pack of dogs came crashing out onto the porch. I could hear Ed braying in the background. Marcy beckoned Claudia and I in and herded us quickly through to the backyard, where everyone was busy setting up the party.

"Amigos!" Ed called. I couldn't see him. He was standing in the shadows of the trees at the back of the yard.

"Comrades!" Claudia called back.

They had set up a buffet table on the deck. Claudia dropped her contribution onto the table and removed the Tupperware lid to reveal a runny parfait of Dream Whip polluted with yellow, green, and purple mini-marshmallows.

"Oh, that should round out our food groups," I said. "Fruits. Vegetables. Meats. And—thanks, Claudia!—petroleum products."

Claudia twirled to face the group. She flung her arms up and let her cape fall from her shoulders and puddle onto the deck planks behind her—a ripple of ebony. The sun glinted off the bands of silver bangles stretching from her wrists to her

elbows along the skintight black sleeves of her turtleneck—
Evita Perón addressing a multitude from the palace balcony.
The outline of her arms showed through the tight-knit
sweater—her muscles were wiry and hard and manic and
they looked like they could bend tensile steel. She strode forward in cigarette slacks, on a pair of stacked mules, black silk
dahlias atop her black lacquered toenails. Kim and Jordi and
Gator crowded round her to receive her benediction of air
kisses.

"Max." It was Ed again. "Come and help me hang this
piñata."

Ed and I found a short stepladder. We opened it, and
planted it on an uneven piece of grass. Ed climbed it to the
top step.

I held him by his belt as he worked—the little ladder jerking sharply back and forth, knocking the ashes off the cigarettes that we both clenched in the sides of our mouths. Asta
came over and lay down on the grass at my feet. He watched
us dolefully, his chin on his paws, his eyebrows fretting on
the narrow ledge of his forehead.

Ed tied the piñata to the branch of an ancient, gnarled
apple tree laden with hard, sour apples the size of a child's
fist. The piñata was meant to be a dog. It was wrapped in
fringed paper to suggest a fluffy coat. But the paper was
pink, and I thought it looked like a pig.

I had told Ed not to get onto the top step of the ladder. So
did the instructions on the side of it. The instructions indicated in English, Spanish, and pictogram what would happen.

Ed shifted his weight suddenly as he started down off the
ladder. His belt—which I hadn't noticed was not buckled—

slipped through the loops and came off in my hands. He fell. He landed on his back and lay there, in the grass, looking up at the sky.

"That hurts like a son of a bitch," he said.

"Oh God, Ed," I told him, still holding his belt.

"Landed right on my shrapnel," he said.

"Hey." Marcy looked up from the burgers she was tending on the barbecue. "You guys okay?"

"I gotta go to my van," Ed said. I pulled him to his feet. Colonel had run over to him and clamped his big mouth around Ed's hand.

"Want me to go with you?" I asked him.

"No. I just need to take something for this."

Having helped Ed with the piñata, I decided to wander over to the gifts table, where Gator was working. Marcy was the kind of bossy dyke who gave everybody a job. I knew I had to keep looking busy or she'd have me shoveling dog shit.

"I started arranging the gifts by color," Gator explained to me. "But then we got so many blues and pinks, it couldn't get a balance."

"You're so gay," I observed.

"This looks good here," he said, placing the champagne that I had wrapped in Christmas paper. "This bright red makes a color accent, and the shape of the booze offsets the square packages."

"Right," I said. "And the 'booze' is an $185 bottle of Moët et Chandon."

"We've got party favors," Gator told me. He and I started pulling them out of a bag. We had pointed clown hats. I put one on and could feel the elastic strap slicing into the puffy flesh under my chin. Even without a mirror, I knew it was unflattering. I took it off. We found whoopee cushions, then hid them in plain view all around the yard—on deck chairs, on chaise recliners, along the deck bench. We unpacked the noisemakers and blew them at each other until we got bored, which took way too long for two grown men. And we pulled a long roll of name tags out of the bottom of the bag.

"Don't we already know each other?" I asked.

Gator took a tag and wrote on it "Hi, my name is Max Von Baritone." He peeled the tag off the backing and smoothed it onto my chest, over my heart. I saw my reflection in his sunglasses. I looked small.

Gator's lips curled up in the suggestion of a smile. Little crescents formed at the edges of his mouth.

I pulled the name tag off my chest and crumpled it up. I took Gator's pen from his hand and wrote on a fresh tag "Hi, my name is Waldo Lydecker!"

"Nothing is more baffling than the truth," I told Gator. And I looked again at myself reflected in his glasses. I felt as though I were falling.

The moment was blown apart by the blare of a furling trumpet. A chorus of snorting laughter followed. I looked over and saw Claudia—cigarette holder in one hand and beer bottle in the other—clomping across the deck. She went from the bench, to the chaise, to the chairs, dropping her bony ass onto one whoopee cushion after another.

"And check this out," Gator said. He wrote the name Bill Gates on his tag and stuck it to his shirt. "You see why I go by Gator. This is my real name, dude."

"So you're one of the richest men in the world," I said.

"Waldo Lydecker," Gator said. "Is that your real name?"

"I don't know anymore," I said. "It doesn't matter."

"You can't tell who anybody is, Max," Gator said. "Especially the crazies."

"Crazies?"

"Psychos. Your serial killers. I knew a guy—went to high school with him—and he was just arrested for killing his wife. Then they found out that his girlfriend from senior year—the one that everybody thought had killed herself—turns out he killed her too. He shot her. And all these years we thought it was suicide."

"What was he like in high school?"

"Normal."

I started to feel a little faint, a little out of control. I didn't like that I kept staring at Gator's raw knuckles, and his slim hips, and those little crescents arching around his lips. And I didn't like this talk about killing.

"He could have killed lots of women," Gator said. "Women we don't even know about. Could be dozens."

Gator took a swig of beer. I was unsettled, torn between feeling attracted to him and repelled by his conversation. I told him I needed to find Claudia. Typically, she was stationed at the bar.

Claudia was standing between the ice chest and the beverage table, presumably so she could pull beers out of the ice with her simian toes while she continuously uncorked wine bottles with her clasping fingers. Jordi was standing close to her. He was holding a paper plate. It sagged heavily under a heap of her marshmallow salad, which he was eating with enthusiasm.

I had expected Jordi to show up dressed up for a Romanian disco—gold chains, black ankle boots, maybe a nice pair of burgundy Sansabelts. But he surprised me. He was dapper in a tan Guayabera shirt and cream-colored slacks and a pair of suede desert boots. He had a daffodil yellow flat cap on his head and a pair of perfectly round, perfectly black sunglasses on his face. He looked like a Cuban man—a Cuban man in the carefree, well-fed, pre-Castro days. I had to admit that Jordi was notionally handsome. He was also in my way.

I needed to talk to Claudia. Alone. I was bothered by my exchange with Gator. He hadn't overtly come on to me. Or had he?

I sidled up to Claudia and addressed her in what any idiot could see was meant to be a quiet, confidential aside.

"They put roofies in the punch," I said.

She grinned broadly.

"Date-rape drugs," I whispered urgently.

She laughed raucously.

"I mean it. Stay cool."

"Yeah," she issued a loud drunken pronouncement, "I think they put Viagra in the hot dogs. Bastards."

Everyone stopped talking. They turned to look at me.

"Fine. Don't believe me," I said and stalked off to the bathroom to throw some cold water on my face.

"Hey, Max!" Kim called out. "What do I do if my erection lasts longer than four hours?"

Now they were all laughing.

I looked back and saw Jordi stroke Claudia's neck. He bent down and kissed her on her eyebrow and that, somehow, struck me as more presumptuous, more intimate, than if he'd actually kissed her on the lips.

I was in the bathroom. I'd just toweled off my face when my cell phone rang. I opened it and saw a name I hadn't seen appear on the little screen in months.

"Larry," I said.

"Max," he said.

"Long time no hear," I told him. I made a point of not asking how he was. I'm sure he didn't notice.

"Max, are you in Kim and Marcy's house?"

"Yes. Why? Are you staked out across the street in an unmarked car?"

"Pretty much," he said.

"Why so creepy, Lar?" I said.

"I'm stalking you guys," Larry said. Then he chuckled. "Hey, Max, so can you come out front without anybody seeing you?"

Larry was parked in an oyster gray Ford Taurus. He had squeezed it in front of an old Volvo station wagon, and behind a big truck, across the street and halfway up the block.

I opened the passenger door and slid onto the front seat. It was an older model, maybe 1992, and the front seat was configured like a sofa so there was nothing between Larry and me—no cup holders, no handy compartments, nothing.

"Did you ever watch *The F.B.I.* on TV when you were a kid, Max?" he asked.

"Sure."

"They always drove Fords." He took a sip of coffee from a Styrofoam cup.

"I know," I said. "So are you with the FBI?"

"No. I'm just tailing Claudia."

"What do you want, Larry? You're confusing everybody. I mean, you run off—but you won't just go. You're lingering. You're malingering. What do you want?"

I almost added the words "from us." But I stopped myself.

"I don't know what I want, Max. I don't know how to articulate it. I think I was just exhausted. Claudia is—she can be—so exhausting. You know?"

I did know. But I didn't say so. I pulled a pack of cigarettes out of my jacket and lit one. I kept my arm outside the window so the smoke wouldn't fill the car.

"Is this a rental?" I asked.

"No. It's just an old beater I picked up."

"You went out and bought a stalker vehicle. That's a lot of premeditation, Larry."

"Max, it's the only way I can keep an eye on Claudia. I'm worried about her. She won't talk to me."

"Oh, you care about her well-being. That's good. That's rich. Coming from you."

"Max, I can't explain it," Larry said. "I'm not going to try."

He turned and looked at me and hit the high beams on those startling blue eyes of his, those eyes that could close a two-million-dollar software deal in a single meeting.

"Are you trying to sell me, Larry?"

"I'm trying to do the right thing."

He reached over and grabbed a wrapped gift off the backseat. He gave it to me. It was for Amy.

I told him so long. I watched him pull away from the curb and drive off before I went back into the house with his gift.

Amy arrived right on time. She had believed the story

about Marcy being caught up in a traffic jam. And she didn't even question the part about Kim having to dash out to staunch an overflowing toilet. Amy had rushed right over.

'She pulled herself out of the front seat of her VW Bug and came up the walk, her belly big in front of her. She'd gotten so big that we'd stopped talking in terms of "the baby." We had felt his first fluttering kicks, like a goldfish in your hand. And, later, we'd seen his heel arching across Amy's belly. Now we called him by his name. Henry.

Dixie jumped out of the car after Amy. She was wearing a plastic cone around her neck that made her look like a little circus clown. It kept her from biting the stitches that ran, in seams of puckered flesh, up her right haunch and onto her back. Amy had painted yellow flower petals all over the plastic cone. Dixie's face was the center of a smiling daisy. When we jumped out and surprised them, Amy covered her mouth with both hands and screamed. Dixie ran in mad circles around the yard.

Her husband, Steve, missed the cake. And then he missed the opening of the gifts. He finally came, straight from the golf course, he said. He was wearing a pink Polo T-shirt and a pair of khakis and what I imagined were expensive sneakers.

I had only ever seen Steve in passing. This was my first chance to study him up close, and I found him fascinating. His brown eyes were clear and empty and his mouth was bow-shaped and oddly feminine. He had perfect teeth, American teeth—they connoted an upbringing that included regular trips to the orthodontist, and vaccinations, and plenty of beef and milk at every meal. Steve moved his big frame with the shaggy, muscled movements of an ex-football player—never good enough to make pro, but good enough to play college ball, good enough to always get what he wanted. Cheerleaders. Jobs. Promotions. Amy.

"We never see you at the dog park." It was Gator talking to Steve. He was interrogating him, in a light and breezy way.

Steve said, "Dixie is really Amy's dog."

"We all love Dixie," Gator said. He pulled a beer out of the ice and cranked the top off it. "And we all love Amy."

Steve made an announcement: Amy was getting tired. He started packing up the baby gifts. He did it by himself. Amy just looked at him, looked at his back as he bent over the table shoving gifts, some of them still unopened, into big shopping bags. She turned and walked back into the house.

Steve ran out of shopping bags. Now he was dumping the baby's gifts into a green Hefty garbage bag. I couldn't watch anymore. I decided to look through Kim's music collection. I passed the kitchen. Amy and Gator were standing by the sink, facing each other. Their faces were close. Their mouths were practically touching. Amy's arm was raised. Gator held it, mid-air, by her wrist. Amy said something. I couldn't hear what. Gator said something back. I think he said, "I don't care."

I hurried into the living room before I was caught spying on them. I got there and stood confused in the middle of the room. Then I noticed the shelf of CDs and remembered. I started flipping through them, looking for anything loud.

I put on an AC/DC album and cranked it up for "You Shook Me All Night Long." When I returned to the backyard, everyone had reconvened there. Steve was holding the bags stuffed with gifts. Amy was talking to Claudia and Kim.

"Let's go, Amy," Steve said, and he shook the bags.

"Okay, hold on," she said. She turned and started talking to the women again.

"You can't go now, man," Ed said. "We haven't even broken the piñata."

Steve shook his head and grimaced. He told Amy to come on again.

"Yes," said Jordi. "The piñata. Is necessary."

Everyone joined in. The piñata, they said, could not be denied.

"Okay," Steve said. He tossed the bags onto the ground. "Where's the bat? Give me the bat."

"We were going to use this stick," Marcy said, holding up an old piece of a broomstick.

Steve snatched it from her and strode over to the piñata. He made a bid at humor. He tapped the stick against his shoe, like he was knocking dirt from his cleats. He lifted the stick and pointed it toward the horizon, indicating he intended to knock this one out of the park.

"Dude," Ed said. "Wait, dude. You gotta put on the blindfold."

"Wrong, *dude*," Steve said. "I don't *gotta* do anything."

Steve coiled and swung the stick. He hit the piñata so hard it burst, tearing all its appendages off with one blow. The torso twirled on its string, suspended from the tree branch— legless, headless—in the quiet that followed.

The rest of us stayed until after midnight. My last memory of the baby shower involved the Ohio Players, the song "Fire," and a raw but stirring simulation of a Chippendales performance by Jordi, Ed, Gator, and, possibly, myself.

18

Baba Luminitsa was a pest. But I realized that I had no control over how long she'd stay so I assumed a Gandhian posture of passive resistance. I went about my business as if I were alone in the house even though she would hide my reading glasses, and she'd rummage through my collection of scarves and wear two or more at a time and not put them back where she had found them, and she'd dither around in the tea leaves at the bottom of my cups and make offhand comments like, "It says you'll be impotent by age fifty-seven."

I had too much to do to bother with her. Wolfgang was coming for the holidays. He was flying in the day after the 25th, so we'd celebrate it when he arrived. I had to get the house ready.

I decided to do a Mexican Day of the Dead theme for Christmas. I bought a silver aluminum tree and strung it with white lights. I went to the Mission and purchased a large box of fist-sized, white sugar skulls—their crystalline faces tattooed with pink and green and purple filigrees. I hung the skulls all over the silver tree branches. I stood on a chair to place a wooden Calaveras, a skeleton, at the treetop. The Calaveras was a man, a mariachi, and he had a brightly colored blanket thrown over one shoulder and he wore an upturned white sombrero. He was playing a little cardboard guitar with three strings. I opened his hinged jaws so it looked like he was singing. Finally, I carpeted the floor all around the base of the tree with piles of marigolds, the flowers of death, fashioned out of crinkly orange crepe paper.

I plugged in the lights and stood back to admire the glowing tree in the deepening twilight. My grandmother appeared at my side.

"It is beautiful," she said.

She offered me a cigarette. She tapped the pack against her index finger, coaxing out a cigarette. I noticed that she still kept the photograph of my grandfather tucked under the cellophane wrapper. Every time she tossed out an empty pack and opened a new one, she would carefully transfer his photo to the fresh pack.

My grandfather stood there, in black-and-white, with his violin in one hand and his bow in the other, both hanging down at his sides as if he were about to drop them to the ground. He was wearing his shallow-brimmed felt hat and a jacket that was shiny from being vigorously, and often, hand-scrubbed against a wooden washboard. His baggy pants had gone out at the hem. His wrists stuck out too far from his sleeves and he could only fasten the top button of his jacket, leaving the other two undone. The jacket splayed out to the sides revealing his shirt. It was dark—probably scarlet or indigo—and it was covered in light-colored, delicate little flowers.

He died in one of the camps. He was methodically destroyed—starved into bones, flamed into ash, scattered into dirt, given up into the wind.

19

Steve banged open his front door and came across the street. Most of us were there—Claudia, Jordi, Ed, Gator, myself. We had him outnumbered. But he still scared us.

Steve demanded we tell him where Amy was.

"Dude, if you don't know where your old lady is, why would we?" Ed blurted.

Steve turned to look at Ed, to single him out. He didn't just turn his head. He turned his whole torso, slowly.

"I mean," Ed said, "we haven't seen her."

"What's happened?" Claudia said. She was the first to regain her composure.

"I've been up all night," Steve said, and his voice cracked.

Claudia motioned for him to sit down. She twisted open a beer and handed it to him. He took it without looking at it. He rested his forehead on the neck of the bottle. His chin was quivering.

"Amy didn't come home last night," Steve said.

Claudia put her hand on his shoulder. I resented the gesture, I felt vaguely as though Claudia was a traitor.

"What do you mean she didn't come home?" Claudia asked Steve.

"I got home and she wasn't there."

"There must have been a note," Gator said. "She went to her mother's maybe."

"No, I called her mother," Steve said. "And her sister. I walked around the neighborhood. And I came back and got in my car and drove around looking for her."

"What about her clothes?" Gator said. "Did you look? Did she take a suitcase?"

"What the hell are you implying?" Steve yelled.

"Is Dixie gone too?" Ed asked.

"No," Steve said. "She showed up later. She was just sitting on the sidewalk, in front of the gate."

Ed stared over at Gator. He wouldn't look away until Gator returned the eye contact. I thought I detected Gator shake his head.

Steve said he had gone fishing in the early evening, out on the bay. When he got home, Amy was gone. She had started dinner—Steve found a steak marinating on the kitchen counter. And the dog's leash was still hanging on the hook. But he knew that there was a spare leash somewhere around the house. He assumed Amy had just stepped out to walk Dixie. He waited. By 10:00 P.M. Amy still wasn't back. Steve walked around the neighborhood looking for her. Then he called the police. But they said he couldn't file a missing persons report on an adult until twenty-four hours had elapsed.

"Just tell me where she is," Steve said. "Before I call the cops again."

"We said we don't know," Jordi said. "Now you call us liars."

I was surprised at Jordi's tone, his sudden vehemence. So was Steve. But he quickly matched it.

"Liars?" Steve said to Jordi. "I'm calling you more than that, you snaggle-toothed fuck."

"You are the fuck," Jordi said. Steve stood up, and Jordi stepped forward, right into his face.

"*Pendejo*," Jordi said, as he poked Steve in the chest with two fingers.

Steve grabbed Jordi by the front of his jacket. He twisted the stretchy polyester in his fist.

"Where's my wife, shithead?"

Steve tugged at Jordi's jacket and the zipper came apart in the middle. Jordi looked down at it, at the teeth torn off their tracks.

"You wreck my zipper."

Steve tugged again. There was a ripping sound and the zipper gapped wider. Jordi tried pulling back, but Steve stepped behind him. He yanked at the jacket, pulling it off Jordi's shoulders, then his arms. He let it go and the jacket hung down around Jordi's waist with the sleeves turned inside out.

"You destroy my jacket. Is part of a set. Now I must buy a whole new suit, new track pants too."

"You fucking dork," Steve said.

Jordi swung at Steve's head, but Steve feinted to the right, so Jordi only clipped his ear. Ed barreled in between them, threw his arms around Jordi and walked him back away from Steve.

Gator got in front of Steve, but he didn't need to restrain him. It was obvious that Steve was done.

Ed had to keep holding Jordi. He shouted at Steve, "*Chupame la polla, maricón!*"

"What time is it?" Steve asked Gator.

"Five o'clock," Gator said.

"It's time. I'm going to the police station," Steve said. He added, looking away, "They told me they'd need her dental records."

Part Two

20

Amy's disappearance was all over the news. The local stations interviewed Steve standing on his front porch. They interviewed us in the dog park. Then the national news networks swarmed the park, and they interviewed all of us all over again.

The twenty-four-hour news networks designed key art specially for their Amy Carter segments, which they aired every hour. They liked to use the same photo of Amy—pregnant and smiling with her dog. They'd also gotten hold of some home video showing Amy cooking spaghetti sauce at a family gathering in Stockton. She was laughing and waving a wooden spoon around. She was wearing a man's checkered apron, probably her father's. They liked to show that too.

I was jealous that, despite my eloquence, they aired Claudia's interviews more than mine—by a ratio of about eight to one. I suppose the TV tabloid people liked the way Claudia came across. She was telegenic. And she spoke with intense vacuity.

She'd dolled herself up to look like a femme fatale in a

1980s nighttime soap opera. She wore a shocking red scarf—which, not coincidentally, matched the key cards they'd designed for the Amy Carter news sections. She'd painted her lips a dark and mournful aubergine and she covered her eyes with big sunglasses—dark, murkily reflective squares that looked like unplugged television sets.

Claudia spoke in sound bites. And the news crew treated her vapid pronouncements as though they were profound: Amy didn't have an enemy in this world. It is so surreal. It could have happened to any of us.

Claudia became a favorite lead character in the Amy Carter show. She was helping to keep Amy in the public's mind, to keep people looking for her. I knew that. But I was jealous of the attention Claudia was getting for herself.

"How are your ratings today?" I'd goad her.

She ignored me, even when I accused her of being a habitual whore of an advertising hack. "You're not selling cars here," I said. "A woman, our friend, is missing. Probably dead."

There was a genius to Claudia's on-camera persona, her splintery statements—more whispered than spoken. They augured into the heart of the collective fear: disappearing into the maw of an uncaring and anonymous world. It was something that happened to other people. Teen runaways went missing. Truck stop hookers vanished from the shoulder of the interstate. Adult schizophrenic wards of exhausted, tattered families wandered off and died, muttering and alone amid rushing crowds on city streets.

Legions of people disappear every day. They become ghosts, looking wan and bewildered in pixilated photos taped onto lampposts. Karly Bekins—Last Seen January 2.

Have you seen Lakeesha, age fourteen? Ed Chin—Missing Adult at Risk. They were marginal people, laggards culled from the herd. They got, maybe, one minute on the local news, one inch of type on page nine. And in the end a decomposed body washes up from the bay. Or a construction crew at a new suburb on the outskirts of town churns the dirt and a packet of bones tumbles into the teeth of the grader. And the rainfall washes the photos on the flyers white.

But Amy was Anglo, and pretty, and pregnant. She was a professional, a wife, she and her husband owned their home. Bad things didn't happen to people like her. So when they did—when the world turned the other way around and the seams of reality split open to admit the monsters sleeping under the bed—it made good television. Amy's story scared the shit out of people.

Inside the dog park, we invented our own reality. Marcy came up with the theory that Amy had left on her own. She proposed that Amy ran away from Steve.

Surely, she reasoned, Amy was secretly staying with her sister in Stockton. We swirled the story around tirelessly, mixing facts with conjecture, until we spun Marcy's speculation into reportage. We all crowed at the thought of Amy's bravery, her pluck, in walking out on Steve when she was nine months pregnant.

But our theory was soon punctured. The sister, Sharon, drove in from Stockton with her parents three days after Christmas. We all watched as Sharon edged her Camry into the driveway across the street.

Steve watched them too. He stood in the front window, not stirring from behind the glass, as his wife's family pulled themselves out of the Camry and came to his door. The mother, earthbound and stout, swayed side to side as she walked—an old woman staggering across the deck of a storm-tossed ship. The father supported her by the elbow, his head bowed. Steve closed the curtains. He waited until they rang the bell before he opened the door.

"It's the fuzz again," Ed said later that afternoon.

He waved at the two Berkeley detectives as they pulled up in their black Buick. We had all spoken with them several times already. One was McGuire—tall, laconic, and skinny as a rope. The other was Estevez—short, chatty, a man who always cleaned every bean off his plate.

They spoke to us as a group and individually. McGuire moved slowly and deliberately like a lemur. He looked at you with dispassionate gray eyes when you answered his questions. He wrote your answers down in his notebook in full sentences. Then he would ask another question that didn't follow from the last one. His interviews jumped around in a random sequence that tested whether you were lying. At least it felt that way. And he wanted it to.

"Has Mrs. Carter seemed nervous or upset lately?" he asked me.

"I don't know," I said, worrying the tassels of my saffron-colored scarf.

"Did Mrs. Carter ever mention that she wanted to leave her husband?"

"No," I said. "But if she had a secret, she wouldn't have told me."

I laughed—it was more of a bark really than a laugh.

"Why?" McGuire said.

"Amy knows I can't keep a secret. I'd have to tell Claudia, and then she'd have a few martinis and . . ."

I looked down and saw my hands were actually twirling the ends of my scarf. McGuire's eyes flicked to my twirling. He looked me in the face again, and waited.

"Have you tried her girlfriends?" I asked. "Old college mates, perhaps?"

I willed my hands to stop. They wouldn't. I shoved them into my pockets, but as soon as I restrained my hands, the twitch moved to my face. My eyebrows flickered up and down while my lips alternated between puckering and compressing into what was meant to be a smile.

"I'll need your address, Mr. Bravo," McGuire said.

Estevez was the opposite. He called your name from ten feet away as he approached. He walked briskly—in fact, all his gestures were quick. He took notes in shorthand. Where McGuire clearly interrogated you, Estevez engaged you, as if you were having a normal, but animated, conversation. He would nod his head as you spoke. He kept it very breezy, until you said something that interested him, then he'd pursue it like a terrier following a rat down a drainpipe.

"Steve doesn't really socialize with us," I told him.

"How so?" Estevez interrupted, lifting his pen from his notebook.

"He's not sociable, I suppose."

"Is he hostile? Or shy? Maybe something in between."

"What do you want me to say?" I asked, feeling pinned down. "That Steve is a quiet man?"

"If he is, yes."

"Isn't that what people always say when they find out the guy next door is a serial killer? He was so quiet?"

"Was he quiet?"

I started to answer and came unraveled somewhere between yes, no, sometimes, and I don't know. Estevez gripped his pen in his fist and made a rolling gesture. I couldn't decide whether he wanted me to get to the point or keep talking. Finally he gave me his card and said to call him if I thought of anything else.

And now the cops were back, but not to talk to us. As they walked up the sidewalk, McGuire nodded toward us. Estevez waved, twiddling his fingers.

"They want to talk to Amy's family again," Kim said.

"This time with Steve," Ed observed.

"Steve knows more than he's saying," Claudia said.

"Nobody knows what Steve knows," Gator said.

"How do you know?" Ed demanded.

Colonel lifted his big block head up from a joint of beef he'd been gnawing. He looked at Ed.

"Calm down," I told them. Colonel regarded the raw bone between his paws. He set his teeth back into it.

"Wait, I've got it," Claudia said. She jumped down off the top of the picnic table, her fingers spread wide, her hands two fluttering fans.

"You've got jazz hands," I told her.

"Nobody knows where Amy is?" Claudia said. "Why?"

Colonel looked at Claudia and barked, then returned to his bone.

"Because somebody stole Amy?" Jordi ventured.

"Kidnapped," Claudia corrected him. "But there's another possibility. Maybe nobody can find her because she doesn't want to be found."

"But she's not with her sister," Marcy said.

"That's because," Claudia said, "Amy ran off with another man."

Asta and Bill had been chasing around the far end of the park. They stopped, sniffed the air, and came running back to the picnic table. They sat smartly, thumping their tails against the turf.

"A pregnant woman with a secret lover?" Marcy said. "Possible. But not likely."

"Totally fucking likely," Claudia said impatiently. "If she's pregnant with that other man's baby."

Asta barked. I looked around the group to see if they were buying it. Ed was nodding. Gator looked away. Jordi blinked convulsively like a set of hazard lights.

"They wanted to get away before the baby was born," Kim said brightly.

I didn't comment. Theirs was such a slender strand of hope. I didn't want to come blundering in with the obvious: Amy wouldn't have left her husband without even packing a toothbrush. Moreover, she didn't take her dog.

"Amy must have wanted it to look like she was abducted so she could get away clean," Claudia added. She looked at me hard, willing me to keep my mouth shut.

"I bet they ran down to Old Mexico," Ed said. He pronounced it Mex-eee-ko.

"Someplace swank," Claudia added.

"Swank?" I repeated. "Isn't that a men's magazine?"

Claudia shot me a withering look. She had dropped the word *swank* like it was a stitch, a missed stitch in her carefully embroidered public persona. Only I knew that underneath all those Prada threads and exfoliated skin and carefully enunciated speech there still lurked a dago chick from upstate New York who glued zircon onto her fingernails and teased her hair with a rat-tail comb.

"I mean that Amy and her boyfriend are probably someplace exclusive," Claudia said. "My mother and Charles always went to Cancún because it was exclusive. Too expensive for the hoi polloi, so you can relax there."

"Who's Charles?" Ed asked.

"My father. He was the CEO of North Arctic Oil."

"Stepfather," I added. "Your mother married Charles when? What year?"

"She married him on the twelfth of what-fucking-ever," Claudia said.

The drapes at Amy and Steve's house swished open. McGuire stood in the window, his hand gripping the curtain pull. He stared at us.

Claudia talked, broadening her tale. Her dreamy narration pressed on like a steady wind filling a sail. We were awash in rainbows over Mayan temples and drink umbrellas in the shade of cabanas and secret lovers on white sparkling beaches.

"I wonder who this guy is," Kim said. "Amy's guy. Probably some high roller. Amy could get any guy she wanted."

I saw Gator clench his jaw. Pairs of little crescents formed at the edges of his lips as if to contain his mouth in quotation marks. Jordi reached into the pocket of his jogging pants and pulled out his cigarettes.

"He's probably filled her room with flowers," Kim said.

"Who?" Gator asked suddenly.

"Amy's secret lover," Kim said. "Her hospital room. Amy's boyfriend has probably filled her hospital room with great big bouquets. The baby is due any day now."

I let myself float into the fantasy. I pictured Amy in a pristine room in a private clinic, surrounded by jungle flowers, verdant and bristling and belligerently pungent.

Estevez and McGuire came out of the house and got back into their car. This time, they didn't wave at us.

"I'm out of here," Ed said. He swung himself off the picnic table.

"Can I catch a ride to BART?" I asked, falling in step with him.

We went through the gates of the park and walked halfway down the street to Ed's van. Colonel loped ahead of us, his platter-sized paws pelting out a samba on the sidewalk.

"You don't think Amy's in Cancún," I said to Ed.

"No."

"You don't think she's run off with a man at all, do you, Ed?"

"No."

21

Wolfgang had arrived a couple of days after Christmas. He had brought me a cashmere scarf and chocolates, and he made the house seem full of people, even though it was just the two of us.

I wasn't as enamored with him as I had been in Berlin. He seemed bigger there. I met him at one of his art openings and he had looked so heroic surrounded by his giant, muscular paintings. I introduced myself. We started talking and he was diffident and low-key in a way that only truly confident people can be. He saw through me in an instant with his painter's eyes. He knew that I was all bluster and bravado and I both loved and feared him for it.

And now he was in my home.

I fixed us rummy eggnogs. I reached under the Christmas tree and picked up the only gift there, an elaborately wrapped package. When he tore off its glittery bow and shiny silver paper, he came to three pairs of white tube socks. He paused and looked at the socks. Then he smiled bravely and thanked me graciously.

"Oh, for God's sake," I said.

I got up from the ottoman, drink in hand, and snatched the socks away from him and tossed them into the fireplace. The flames flicked across the white socks until they curled up into black shavings and fell beneath the log's red heaving embers.

Only then did he laugh, visibly relieved.

"Here, open this," I said. I handed him a small box. Inside was a pair of opera glasses. Gold-plated. Bone-handled. I got them more for me than for him. I wanted him to regard me more closely when I was performing. But I didn't tell him that. I was performing then too.

"They are so beautiful, Max," Wolfy said, watching me through the magnifiers from two feet away. "My God, but such workmanship."

"Yes," I said. "I am a piece of work."

I told him how I'd picked up the glasses in Paris. They were made by a Russian émigré. He was the kind of jeweler who believed that all functional objects should have the senseless splendor of a Fabergé egg. What's the point of owning something if it's not beautiful?

Wolf wasn't beautiful. He was tall, a little taller than me, and thin. He was almost too thin—all angles and lines and planes. His Adam's apple buoyed up and down when he was nervous, which was often. And his already protuberant eyes popped when he was excited, which was seldom. And his chin was too small, and his nose was too big and his ears stuck out in a way that made him look more Appalachian than Alsatian. But he was endearing. I liked the way he'd sweep his blond-red hair to the side, out of his eyes, whenever he was absorbed in something—some article in an art magazine or the very twisty scenes in an old film noir movie, the scenes where the detective cracks the case and explains the entire crime and you still don't get it.

I helped him adjust the setting of his new opera glasses. It wasn't as though the man was incapable of shifting the focus. It was just that I was better at it.

22

"You are not going to fucking believe what's happened now," said Claudia Fantini.

She burst through my front door, her stilettos echoing across the hardwood floor. I was still holding the doorknob when she flung herself into the living room, ripped off her black bouclé wrap, and pinched her cigarette in her teeth so she could smooth her satin sheath with both hands.

"Claudia, this is Wolfgang," I said.

"Oh, hello, Wolfy," she said. She grabbed him by the hand and jerked him in close and kissed him on the lips. She turned to me, her chandelier earrings clanking.

"He's cute, Max," she said. "Younger than I thought he'd be too. Younger than you."

"Everybody is," I said. "Drink?"

"Martini. Tanqueray. Two olives."

She flicked her half-smoked cigarette into the fire and threw herself into one of my barrel chairs, reached over to the occasional table, and picked up the cut glass lighter that was as big as a curling rock. She lit another cigarette, took a deep drag, and exhaled a plume of smoke that reached all the way across the room to where I was shaking her martini.

"For God's sake, Max, bring me that drink. I have big news to tell and I can't tell it sans cocktail."

I handed her the martini. She waved at Wolfgang and me to sit.

"Steve is selling the house," she stated, lifting the brimming martini glass as though it were a talking stick and we were all gathered in the longhouse for potlatch.

"Did he tell you that?" I asked.

"No."

I pursed my lips and got up to make myself a martini. I left my festive eggnog on the coffee table, the ice melting fast, watering down what was left of our Christmas atmosphere.

"You're interrupting," I told Claudia. "Wolfy and I are trying to celebrate the birth of our lord and savior."

"That Realtor bitch thingy was over there today," Claudia said.

"I'm putting on a Burl Ives record," I said.

"Who is the Realtor bitch?" asked Wolfy.

"For the love of God, Wolf, don't encourage her," I told him.

I couldn't find Burl Ives, but I did locate my *Alvin and the Chipmunks Christmas Favorites* LP. I waved the album, trying to distract Claudia and Wolfy with its cover art; buck-toothed rodents wearing sweaters and gazing at a sparkling Christmas tree.

"But Claudia has the information for our case," Wolfy protested.

"Number one, 'zee' information," I said, mocking him even though he spoke English with an exacting British accent, "is not information. It is fabrication, fantasy, and wildly irresponsible conjecture. And second, it's not our case. It is McGuire and Estevez's case."

I sat in the straight-backed chair by the window and crossed one leg over the other to signal that I was bored. I lit a cigarette.

"It's not bullshit," Claudia said quietly.

"You are tormenting a victim," I said, rounding on her. "You are feasting on a human tragedy. It's all happy horseshit around the dog park, but can't we just leave off for one night? Must it consume us?"

"Steve is not the victim," Claudia said, stubbing out her cigarette. She'd only smoked half of it. I kept my eyes on her.

"You're a bitch," I said.

"You're a bitch," she said.

"Who is this reality woman?" Wolfy asked.

"Realtor woman," Claudia said. "Real estate has nothing to do with reality. Her name is Stephanie Saint Claire. She's the biggest, greediest real estate agent in the East Bay." Claudia hoisted her chin upward in what was meant to be a triumphant gesture.

"You'll see her," I told Wolfy. "She's on a shitload of billboards."

"And bus benches, and local TV spots, and on every third fucking For Sale sign from El Cerrito to Alameda," Claudia said. She lit another cigarette with a pert snap of the curling rock lighter.

"How do you know it was her?" I asked.

"I saw her myself," Claudia said. "She's unmistakable. You know that, Max. You met her too."

It had been more than three years ago, but I remembered Stephanie Saint Claire from when she sold Claudia and Larry their house. I couldn't forget her orange suntan and her starchy blond hair, and those crazy blue eyes goring you with maniacal enthusiasm.

"All right," I said. "I'm listening."

Claudia said that she was in the dog park that morning, alone with Asta. She claimed she was incognito. She was hungover so she had wrapped up her hair in a Hermès scarf and set a broad-brimmed hat on her head and hidden her eyes behind a pair of cat-eyed sunglasses.

Stephanie Saint Claire arrived at Amy and Steve's house. She went inside for about forty minutes. Then she and Steve emerged out the front door and, together, they walked around the perimeter of the house with a measuring tape. She wrote on a clipboard. She flitted her hand toward the pair of chairs on the front porch—their red canvas had faded to a mottled flesh color and the wooden legs were peeling and cracked. She pointed to the dead ficus tree in a pine box planter by the front door. Amy had kept that tree in the living room. Steve must have allowed it to perish sometime before Christmas and then dragged it outside. Its branches were dry and bony, leafless. We had all noticed it, and found it strange that the tree died around the time of Amy's disappearance. Ed even suggested that Steve had watered it with lighter fluid, or some other corrosive. I remembered his ill-chosen words; Steve "murdered" the tree.

Claudia told us how Stephanie Saint Claire started down the front walk and swept her fountain pen in the direction of the tired, ragged beds of nasturtiums that fell across the cement. They looked like tangled hair washed up on the beach.

The Saint Claire commented on the honeysuckle that had grown wild and frenzied over the picket fence. I had been noticing that bush myself lately. In the evenings, just as the sun was setting, its sweet odor had become noticeably more pungent, almost sickly.

Stephanie Saint Claire stopped at the end of the walkway. She turned and shook Steve's hand. She nudged the gate open with her knee. It was such a short little gate, like the gate to a child's playhouse. Before she got into her silver Mercedes SUV, Stephanie Saint Claire twirled on her taupe slingbacks, held her fist to the side of her head, the pinky finger in front of her glossy mouth and the thumb by her ear. She mouthed the words "Call me."

23

"The Nazi wants my skin," a woman whispered.

I was standing on a chair adjusting the skeleton that I'd perched at the top of the Christmas tree. The voice startled me so violently that I almost fell off.

"Damn it," I scolded, jumping down, "Baba, must you always sneak up on me?"

"The Nazi. I don't trust him."

"What Nazi?"

She pointed at Wolfgang. He was asleep on the couch. His shoes were neatly placed together under the coffee table. His head and chest were draped over the large, curving arm of the sofa, his cravat was tied around his head like a bandanna, and his long skinny legs were stretched out along the cushions. His sock feet were crossed. Claudia's bare legs were stacked on top of Wolfy's and she lay with her back arched over the sofa's other arm. Her head was propped on a throw cushion. It tilted back a little, which caused her mouth to gape open, and she was snoring loudly through that big Italian beak of hers. But her elaborate chignon, complete with cloisonné chopsticks stabbed into an X at the back of her head, remained perfectly intact.

"That's Wolfy, Baba. He's not a Nazi."

"He's German," she said.

"It's not the same thing."

"Do not trust him," she said. "He knows what you are."

"Thanks for the tip. Anything else?"

"Yes," she said. "There is a man outside in the bushes."

"What? What man?"

"I don't know what man. A *gadje*. He was in the azalea bush. Now he is creeping up the steps. Maybe he means to torch the house. To carbonize us because he knows we are Romany."

"Did he see you?" I asked.

"No one sees me. No one but you," she said. She bobbed her head up and down indicating no while huffing in exasperation as if she were forever burdened with caring for the only idiot in the tribe.

I was just drunk enough to think I could handle an intruder myself. I marched into the foyer to retrieve the baseball bat that I kept in the umbrella stand. I didn't even think to stop and look through the peephole on the door. I flung the door open and held the bat in front of me at arm's length.

Larry was crouched down in front of me. He was setting a pair of gift boxes on the porch. They had been professionally wrapped—at the Burberry store. Larry hovered, suspended in mid-crouch. He looked up at me. I had never seen him startled, and I almost wouldn't have recognized him. His face was blank, as if he hadn't had time to program an expression onto it. But he collected himself quickly.

"Larry! Is this your new routine? Always creeping around with gifts. Some people just ring the doorbell, Larry. It is an option."

"Sorry. Sorry, Max," Larry said. He had recovered. He was standing up straight and his eyes beamed good cheer. He looked tan and handsome and he had lost some weight.

"Are those Burberry gifts for me?" I asked.

"You, yes. One is for you and one is for Claudia," he said. Then he added, "She is here, right?"

"Yes. But she's not receiving visitors at the moment," I said.

A loud, boozy snore rumbled through the foyer. We both knew who it was; since there wasn't a rhinoceros in the house it had to be Claudia.

"Well, that's fine, Max. I'll just drop these off and be on my way."

I could have offered him a drink. We could have sat on the steps, with the front door pulled shut so as not to wake the others. We could have talked. But he disappeared. He hopped down the steps and skittered across the yard like a jack-rabbit. In the late-night quiet I could hear the engine of the Ford Taurus turn over just down the street, and the wheels cranking back and forth, back and forth. Larry must have been making a thirteen-point U-turn, just so he wouldn't have to drive by my house.

I picked up the gifts and went back inside to the kitchen. I opened mine. Prosaically, it was a sweater—a sweater for Christmas. I scratched around the bottom of the box and found the gift receipt so I could take it back to the store and exchange it for something I really wanted—maybe a couple of acceptable shirts or a sport coat in the post-season sale, something that wasn't emblazoned with that tacky tan and black tartan that is only worn by middle-aged women with more brand recognition than taste.

I put the gift receipt in my wallet and folded the sweater back into the box and stashed it and Claudia's gift in the top of my armoire. She'd have a blistering hangover in the morning and I didn't want to have a "Larry" scene with her. Not then. I'd give it to her the next day.

I rousted the two sleepers and shepherded them both into bed and tucked them in—Claudia in the guest room, Wolfy in mine. I poured myself one more brandy, a very short one, so I could sit in the living room alone in front of the glittering, skull-covered tree.

"Do you think Amy is all right?" I asked out loud.

But Baba didn't answer. She wasn't there. Maybe she had gone to sleep. I wondered if they could do that—if the dead could sleep.

24

It had been several weeks, and the news crews still swarmed Amy's house. Never mind that there was genocide in Africa, or an autocratic regime stripping the guts out of our democracy in Washington, or a dozen people gunned down every week in the Bay Area alone—there was one pretty, middle-class, white woman missing in Berkeley. Americans would have to hear about it round the clock.

Whenever Amy's story started to get stale, the infotainment people cast about for fresh angles, for a spark of intrigue, a new wrinkle that their "panels of experts" could volley back and forth ad nauseum.

They corralled Kim and Marcy and Jordi and trained the cameras on them. Marcy couldn't, or wouldn't, comment on Amy's character. Kim couldn't, or wouldn't, stop crying.

Jordi rambled in aphasic monologues: "Is a sinister epicenter to have happen in a cheerful community."

The interviewers liked to film Gator, but they couldn't get him to elaborate on any of his statements, which consisted entirely of "It's a bad deal" and "Can't tell."

Finally, they hit pay dirt when they got Ed in front of the camera.

Ed was wearing a pair of purple mirrored granny glasses; a hand-crocheted yellow, green, and red Jamaican cap over his rasta braids that made it look like he had a Jiffy Pop package on his head; and a T-shirt that asserted IT ISN'T PRETTY BEING EASY.

"Amy is good people," Ed said. "She's not a flake like a lot of people around here."

Ed looked into the camera, took off his glasses. He warned that if it was discovered someone had, in fact, abducted Amy, "it's gonna all come down," and that "what goes around comes around," and he trusted that the perpetrator would know exactly what he meant.

The expert panel gorged themselves senseless on Ed's comments; digesting and regurgitating, and reheating, every statement. They were certain that every utterance was tinged with subterranean meaning.

"What goes around comes around," said the panel's legal expert, a pointy-chinned woman with a blond haystack hairdo. "Those were Candy Bates's parting words that fateful day of the dog attack."

Haystack Head turned her back on the other experts on the panel. She stared right into the camera. The stage's fourth wall—the one that separates performer from audience— came tumbling down. It was very postmodernist. And it was very dismissive of her fellow experts. Wolfy and I loved it.

There was a dynamic among the experts. Haystack Head hated the retired cop. He made faces whenever she forwarded one of her bold speculations. And he wore a mahogany toupee that clashed with his auburn sideburns. The other expert was a forensics guy. She treated him like he was some kind of a drip—probably because he never said anything. Of course, what could he say? There was no corpse.

"What goes around comes around," she said directly to us, the viewing audience. She bobbed her head for emphasis. The haystack shook. "Now that Amy Carter is missing, has Candy Bates's revenge come to pass?"

The former cop did some quick checking. The next day he ceremoniously deflated the Candy Bates theory. Candy was doing thirty days in county when Amy went missing. He adjusted his tinted glasses in a professorial manner.

Haystack Head wasn't going down so easy. Obviously, she countered, he had not considered the possibility that Candy Bates engaged some surrogate to kill Amy.

Mahogany Toupee delivered his coup de grâce, effectively euthanizing the Candy Bates theory. He pointed out, in subdued triumph, that every biker and greaseball and jailbird in the western hemisphere says "what goes around comes around" whenever the occasion calls for profundity.

Haystack Head, unfazed, quickly adjusted her suspicion onto Steve. It's the husband, she said, it's almost always the husband. The forensics guy finally spoke. There was still no body, he said in a voice that was croaky from disuse. He added, now with authority, they had no solid evidence that a crime had been committed. But nobody listened to that guy.

The crews on site liked to interview Steve in his living room, Amy's empty rocking chair beside him. Regardless of what some people in the press were starting to say, the police didn't suspect Steve. Or, they hadn't acted on it. He was the aggrieved husband. Nothing more.

"All we want is for Amy to come home safely," Steve told the television interviewer.

"He is lying," Wolfy said to me. We were watching at home. Wolf was stretched out on my Persian carpet in front of the television like a kid watching Saturday morning cartoons.

"Lying?" I asked. "How can you tell?"

We had just finished smoking a bowl of marijuana and I was feeling rather languid, lying on the Victorian fainting couch in my silk kimono.

"Watch his eyes," Wolf said.

"Our only concern is for Amy and the baby," Steve was saying. "If anyone has seen her, please call the police right away. And, Amy, if you can hear me . . ."

"Now, look," Wolf said, sitting up. He lifted his hand to his hair, brushed it to the side.

"Please, please get word to us, or come home right away," Steve said.

I watched Steve's eyes. They moved up and to the left as he spoke, as if he were searching for the words up there, as if they were stenciled on the port side of his frontal lobe.

"He's doing something funny with his tongue too," I said.

"That's another sign," Wolf confirmed. "See how he probes the corners of his mouth with his tongue? He is a liar."

The phone rang. It was Claudia.

"I don't believe a fucking word of this," she said. "He killed her."

"Does Claudia think Steve killed her?" Wolfy asked, swinging around to look back over his shoulder at me.

"Claudia is a certifiable paranoid psychotic," I said, loud enough for both of them to hear.

"Jordi and Ed think so too," she told me.

"That you're a psychotic?" I said. "They're right."

"They agree that Steve killed Amy," she said.

"I'm hanging up now," I said.

25

There were the obligatory "Missing" posters and news stories and, I suppose, a police dragnet. Amy's family rented a billboard. They put a colossal picture of Amy on it—smiling, pregnant—and a hotline number. The billboard was in kind of a crappy neighborhood in Oakland, over the top of a Vietnamese pho restaurant that used to be a Der Wienerschnitzel. Amy's image loomed in the sky, towering, so much larger than life.

Ed glued Amy's flyers all over his van and drove around. When he wasn't driving, he stood on the corner of Telegraph and Dwight, handing out hundreds more flyers, buttonholing people, recruiting them in the search effort. Jordi and Gator joined nearly a hundred volunteers who walked side by side in a long scambling line across Tilden Park looking for clues, or—and this was the grisly possibility that no one pronounced—Amy's body.

Claudia and I walked the neighborhoods with Sharon, Amy's sister, putting up flyers for nearly a week. We were moving in a spiral, starting at the dog park and radiating out in concentric circles.

Sharon wasn't much like Amy. She was older and bigger, hulking where her pretty younger sister was statuesque. Sharon had wide hips and a flat butt and she wore high-waisted, acid-wash jeans that tapered at the ankles. She styled her brown hair in a kind of square block and used a curling iron to coax her bangs into puffing out so it looked like she had a big conch shell on her forehead. She wore a gold-plate necklace with a flying seagull pendant.

Sharon was good company on our long walks. Even though she was poleaxed with anxiety and grief over her sister, she was pleasant and easy to be around. As if to offset her large physical stature, she was reserved and spoke softly.

We'd managed to cover most of the campus area; the main corridors of University Avenue and Shattuck Avenue; the shopping hubs, Walnut Square and Fourth Street; and worked our way into the adjoining townships of Albany and Kensington and El Cerrito. One afternoon, Claudia and Sharon and I were walking along a street in West Berkeley. That part of town is much as it had been when the shipyard workers lived there during the Second World War. The streets are broad and empty and laid out in perfect grids. The lots are large and flat and, for the most part, planted only with grass and low-lying flower beds. The houses are small and slouching. There is a sense of spaciousness and exposure.

We were walking along the sidewalk when I noticed, ahead of us on the next block, a scarecrow of a figure pedaling a crooked ten-speed bicycle. The cyclist was coming toward us, pant legs flapping around sticklike shins and an old, gunmetal gray parka, unzipped, billowing all around a piercing thin abdomen. The figure creaked along, jerking the curved handlebars in a constant battle to remain upright. I saw the hollowed-out cheeks beneath the dark sunglasses.

"Holy mackerel!" I said to Claudia. "That's Candy Bates."

"Fucking tweaker," she said.

I looked around the bleak landscape. There was no tree to duck behind, no hedge to dive under.

"You fuckers!" Candy Bates screamed. She spasmed her bony digits and locked the brakes. The bicycle lurched up on its front wheel. She struggled to dislodge her dirty white Reebok sneakers from the pedal cages.

"Who is that?" Sharon asked.

"You fuckers," Candy Bates said.

Her mouth was puckered and she was making rising, ballooning gestures with her arms, her feet planted on the pavement and the bicycle pinned between her spindly legs.

"Hey," Claudia said, in a flat tone that I'd never heard her use before. "Don't start no trouble. There won't be no trouble."

"Keep walking," I told Sharon. I didn't need to tell Claudia.

We hustled along but Candy Bates stood her ground in the street. She wrestled the bicycle around and continued to yell at our backs.

"You fuckers got my dog put down!" she screamed. "You fuckers killed my Troy. Serves that bitch right to get herself missing after what you done to my Troy. That bitch is dead. Dead as my Troy!"

I stopped and slowly turned. I've never hit a woman. Actually, I've never hit anyone. But an animal surge of rage came over me and I observed myself walking swiftly toward

Candy Bates. I knew what I meant to do. I was going to knock her down and stomp her into the asphalt—her and her stolen tweaker bicycle.

I did the cowardly thing. I slapped her. My palm striking her cheek sounded like a single hand clap in an opera theater—ill-placed and embarrassing, a spatter of inappropriate applause begun before the aria is over. Candy Bates didn't flinch. She invited me to fuck myself.

"Max. Let's get Sharon out of here." It was Claudia's voice, and it sounded far away.

I looked over at Sharon. She had been so strong this whole time. But now her face was in her hands. The black mascara-stained tears streaked through her big fingers. And I realized that she was a gentle woman inside that mannish physique, and that made the sight of her crying all the more tragic.

26

Amy's story had been titillating when it broke—almost pornographic, as these stories often are. It had a repulsive allure. I think because it married the grotesque with the familiar.

A beautiful young wife takes the dog out for a walk. She is nine months pregnant, with a boy. The couple has already named him Henry.

The husband returns from a day of fishing. He finds the house empty. Later that night, the woman's little dog appears at the front gate. But the woman herself never comes home. She has seemingly evaporated, leaving behind not even a footprint, or a broken twig or a tatter of clothing. She was in the normal world. And then an unseen portal opened up. It pulled her in, and snapped shut behind her.

The husband, handsome and hurt, makes appearances on local news programs, pleading for the safe return of his wife and unborn son. The young woman's family, her mother and her father and her sister, all appear in front of the cameras too. They read their statements, halting but determined. It is a spectacle: macabre and wrenching.

There are sightings. Once Amy is seen in a 7-Eleven convenience store in northern Oregon. She is heavily pregnant. She is buying apple juice. She is with a lean, dusty man in blue jeans and a green John Deere cap. Another time she is spotted in Albuquerque, eating a number four breakfast at the Frontier Restaurant on Central Avenue. Two eggs over easy with a side of whole wheat toast. Someone else claims Amy was holding a newborn baby boy and boarding an airplane, destination Paris. The police follow up. Every sighting is false. Every lead goes nowhere.

The beautiful young woman and her unborn child have vanished. And no one knows what has become of them. No one knows but the dog. And Dixie is not talking.

After a couple of more weeks, Amy's family went back to Stockton. The news coverage died down. Actually, it died suddenly. Amy's television coverage was abruptly displaced when a schizophrenic housewife living in a trailer on the Texas panhandle methodically drowned her four children.

27

"Why do we have to meet at Jordi's house?" I asked Claudia.

She and Wolfy and I were walking up Jordi's front steps. Claudia had insisted we all wear black sunglasses, something about discretion. We looked like we'd just had group cataract surgery.

"We voted to meet here," she told me. "We can't talk about this in the dog park, right in front of Steve's window."

"Yes," I said. "He could hide behind the drapes and read our lips through a pair of binoculars. Steve is superhuman, is he not?"

"It's no joke, Max," she said.

"I think we should be wearing deer-stalker hats," I said. "And smoking meerschaum pipes. We could puff on them while we're ruminating and then hold them aloft, like so, when we're announcing our startling deductions."

The door opened. Jordi was wearing a Hawaiian shirt— a ghastly tossed salad of fuchsia orchids and Day-Glo green palm leaves and muscle-bound surfers.

"What do you call that outfit?" I said. "You look like a Kraut on a sex tour."

"It is Hawaiian," he told me. "I like the tropical life."

"And I suppose this décor is tropical too," I said, stepping into the living room. "Like dengue fever."

The walls were papered in grass cloth. Color-coded tiki glasses lined the shelves. Tinkling strings of seashells hung from the swag lamps. A round papasan chair that was as big as a satellite dish filled an entire corner. Another wicker chair, this one smaller and hung from the ceiling, pirouetted indolently by its chain as though it were an empty butterfly cocoon.

The accent wall was covered with a photographic mural depicting a tropical beach at sunset. The sun was red and fierce through a foreground of dark underbrush and dangling palm leaves.

"Is that Martin Denny you're playing?" I asked, knowing full well that it was.

An LP spun on the turntable, hit a scratch, and a tropical bird shrieked bloody murder over the top of the smooth vibraphone riffs. It screamed again, and again, and again. And it was as though no one heard.

"Yes. It is Martin Denny," Jordi said.

"I knew it."

"Well, of course you know everything, Max," Jordi said. "About music."

Claudia marched straight into the kitchen as though she lived there. I followed her, trying to decide if Jordi had just taken a swipe at me.

I watched Claudia help herself to a glass of wine. She

opened a cupboard and extracted several tins of smoked octopus and pickled mackerel. I poured myself a glass of wine. Claudia pulled a length of botifarra sausage out of the fridge, and a long, sharp knife out of a drawer.

"You really know your way around the kitchen, don't you, Claudia," I said. She ignored me. "Or, should I just say, this kitchen?"

"Yes," she said, and she slammed the knife drawer shut. "I know my way around Jordi's kitchen."

"How about Esquivel music?" Jordi called from the other room. "Crazy enough for you?"

"Go for it," Claudia called back to him, but she was staring at me. She had a knife in her hand.

"You go for it," I said to her in a low tone.

She tossed the knife in the air, grabbed it blade down—the classic B-movie slasher grip—and stabbed it into the cutting board. The knife stuck, wobbled by its tip.

"Stay out of my business, Max," she said.

"What's been going on with you and Jordi? I have a right to know."

"You don't want me to go back to Larry. Right? So I need something else to do. I can't be alone, Max."

Jordi walked in. He stopped and looked at the knife stabbed into the cutting board. He extracted it, telling us to go relax in the living room. He'd take care of the food.

The dog park regulars started arriving in quick succession. Marcy and Kim came. They brought wine. Ed came next. He had a case of beer. Gator arrived last and he brought a bottle of Wild Turkey. We got our drinks and Jordi set up the snack plate on the teak coffee table in the living room.

The women and Wolfy commandeered the big throw cushions. They collapsed on the carpet, draped over their cushions like entropic concubines on a slow day in the harem.

Ed got in the papasan chair and claimed he couldn't get out of it so we had to take turns bringing him fresh beers. Gator sat on one of Jordi's antediluvian stereo speakers—it was as tall as a bar stool. Jordi pulled in a kitchen chair. And I hung suspended from the ceiling in the cocoon chair, twirling and viewing the scene in splice-cuts through the chair's narrow front opening.

There were the usual pointless observations, pet theories, backtracking, and grandstanding that is the hallmark of most Comintern meetings. Kim and Marcy and Claudia didn't like Steve. Actually, they hated him. Ed didn't like Steve either, but with Ed it wasn't personal. Jordi refused to weigh in on Steve's likability as a human. Gator said that whether or not Steve was likable wasn't the point.

"Right," Ed agreed with Gator. "We could like him. We could not like him. It doesn't matter. Hell, people liked Charlie Manson. In fact, they loved that son of a bitch. But the point is not whether Steve is likable, it's whether he's guilty."

"Now we're making progress," I said. "We've actually arrived at the fourteenth century. You people should be on the Supreme Court."

I twirled in my suspended cocoon so as to shut them all out behind its lattice of wicker. I stared at the Hawaiian wall mural. The waves, no doubt teeming with sharks and stinging jellyfish, caressed the beach. It was evening and the sands had grown cool and the palm tree's shadow had grown long. The village girls—girls with skin tawny as aged port, and shining brown eyes, girls like Amy—were nowhere in sight. Perhaps they were just gathering gardenias to put in their hair before coming down to the beach to slip into the warm waters of the Pacific. Surely, I thought, Amy would come out too—perhaps walking out of the surf onto the beach, smiling in the moonlight.

"We've got theories," Ed pushed on. "And we've got facts. We know that Steve's story is fishy—literally."

"Yeah," said Marcy, "he didn't even bring any fish home that day."

"There is a possibility that a third party . . ." Ed was saying.

"Some drifter," Marcy piped up.

"Sure," Ed said. "It's often a drifter. Some drifter could have kidnapped Amy."

They all nodded. I twirled in my cocoon to look at the women. They were watching Ed as he spoke. They were so different, those three: Kim in her childish costume—a neon green minidress and orange tights and her black hair pinioned into two stubby little ponytails at the crown of her head—and Claudia with her hair in a chignon and her black jersey turtleneck dress and heels, and Marcy in that butch mullet haircut of hers and those stevedore blue jeans the size of a side-by-side refrigerator and yet another of her plaid shirts. But, at that moment, they all looked so alike. They all three wore the same grim expression—their mouths were turned down and their faces resolved into the same immobile mask, a tragedy mask. They were a watchful Greek chorus reciting horrors from behind faces that had been scraped out of clay and fired in a kiln. And I realized then that women have a way of knowing brutality, of recognizing when it visits, and of enduring it. Because women—even brawny hod carriers like Marcy—remain physically weaker and so they are perpetual prey. And they know it. They live with it.

I twirled the cocoon chair on its suspended chain. I looked at Jordi. He fidgeted in his seat, crossing his legs first one way, and then another. Gator didn't say anything. He just sat on the speaker and stared at the Wild Turkey in his green tiki glass.

"And we know," said Ed, "that most murders are committed by someone the victim knows."

"You are saying Amy is murdered," Wolfy cried out, his hand smoothing down his hair. "You are giving up?"

"Son, it's hard," Ed told him. "But I think we all have to accept at this point that Amy has met with foul play. Maybe somebody took her, and they are holding her against her will. She could still be alive. And little Henry too. But the truth is—even if she did run out on Steve—she wouldn't go this long without calling her parents, or her sister."

"You said someone she knows," Wolfy said to Ed. "Why don't the police suspect Steve?"

"Amy knows a lot of people," I said, and for the first time I ventured to look directly at Gator. "It doesn't have to be Steve."

"Of course it has to be that son of a bitch," Marcy said. "But the police already interviewed Steve and moved on. He's in the clear."

"We don't know that for sure," Gator said. "McGuire and Estevez are probably watching him right now. They have to gather evidence."

"Oh, really?" Claudia said. She rose to her feet and swung her glass as she spoke.

She was teetering slightly and I noticed that she wasn't drinking wine anymore. She had, sometime in the course of this little powwow, switched to Wild Turkey. I silently cursed Gator, for I knew what a few fingers of cheap corn liquor would do to Claudia Fantini. We were going to be subjected to one of her biker-chick flashbacks—back to the black leather, two-lane asphalt days of her New Mexico teen years. She often slipped into this, her former persona, when she was drunk and angry. That's when her accent changed to the staccato secco of the high desert. And in sentences that fell like jabs she'd talk about predawn motorcycle runs across state lines with ounces of freshly cooked, hydrochloride-based amphetamines stowed under the crank case, and gun-play (usually involving someone named Dirty Dan or Tate quarreling with a woman named Mouse), and police heli-copters over the mesa, and the meth lab blowing up and the dog—a stout brute named Hog—sniffing through the rubble and bringing her a man's severed hand, which he dropped in the dust at her boots.

Claudia stabbed at the air with her cigarette and said, "We are out there every day watching Steve from the dog park. We can see everything that's going down on that whole block. We're not stupid. We'd know if there was heat."

And when she used the word "heat" I couldn't help but squirm. I had to light a cigarette to distract myself from laughing.

"We've all been under surveillance," Claudia continued. She was swaying on her chic high-heeled boots and waving the bottle of Wild Turkey that she had snatched off the coffee table, edging it closer to her tiki glass. She stuck her cigarette in the side of her mouth and added, "We've all had narcs up our ass."

Ed and Gator nodded, taking in the weight of the memories, overcome by outlaw nostalgia. The rest of the group just regarded Claudia blankly and I could only conclude that their asses had always been narc-free.

"Don't you think we'd see if they had Steve staked out?" Claudia filibustered.

"Hell, I can smell pork a mile away," Ed said. "They ain't there."

"But we are," Wolfy said. "We are there."

Everyone in the room became still at these three words. We are there. The crystalline truth of it resonated in a pure, clear pitch. Everyone turned to slowly look at Wolf. They regarded the slender, soft-spoken man—the foreign man—with his spare and careful words.

"We are here, Wolfman," Ed said. "And whoever took Amy didn't figure on us."

28

Claudia volunteered Wolf and me to stay behind with her to help clean up. Wolf stood in the kitchen scraping plates piled high with gnawed chicken bones and shish kebab skewers and cigarette butts. Claudia and I filled the recycling bin with bottles. It took both of us to drag it to the curb. When we came back into the house she noticed something peculiar in the sunroom just off the vestibule. She motioned for me to follow and we slipped into the glass-enclosed room and found a primitive shrine.

"Is he practicing Santeria now?" I asked. She shook her head.

"Well, who's this woman?" I said. "Some cult figure? Some martyred saint?"

"I don't know. This is new."

Jordi had set a three-legged table into one corner. Its sole purpose was to display a framed photograph of a woman. A pair of vases stood beside her portrait, in attendance. Each held a large, crimson rose. The woman in the photograph gazed heavenward in the manner of a religious ecstatic—or a complete nut.

"She's clearly Catalan," I told Claudia, noting the hatchet face.

"Maybe a relative," she murmured.

The woman was young, youngish. I'd say in her early thirties. She was plain—her face was a Cubist study in sharp angles—but she was formally groomed. She wore an ice blue gown with slender straps. Her hair was black and straight and brushed to a luster. The photographer had rendered her in a soft haze, a head and bare shoulders floating on an ethereal white backdrop. She looked like she was about to go to the 1967 senior prom—with her cousin.

"Is this your mother?" I asked Jordi as soon as I realized he had come into the sunroom.

"Does she look like me?" he asked.

"Yes," said Claudia.

"She is my fiancée."

Claudia was standing beside me and I could feel her tense. She touched her fingertips to the table.

"You never mentioned you had a fiancée," Claudia said. I was impressed with her composure. She even managed a smile. And it would have looked genuine, if it hadn't stayed in place so long, and if there weren't so many teeth involved.

"No. I don't talk about Cecilia much," Jordi said. He picked up the portrait and held it in both hands and spoke to it. "But we e-mail every day. And talk on the phone every week."

Jordi looked up at us. His eyes were full of tears.

"Buddy," I said. I'd never called anyone "buddy" in my life.

But it seemed appropriate. I reached my hand to his shoulder, bracing him in a way that I supposed "buddies" do when they console each other after losing arm-wrestling contests or totaling their doolie trucks.

"Don't worry," I told him. "You'll see Cecilia again soon. She looks like a lovely woman. Of course you miss her."

"Oh, yes, she is lovely," he said, jerking his head up. He said fiercely, "She is . . . perfect. But it's not that I miss her."

Then he began to openly weep. Claudia went to the bathroom and returned with a handful of tissues. He accepted them without looking at her and honked his nose into the wad. It gave me a moment to collect my thoughts, which were fairly trivial. The first thing that occurred to me was that Jordi had not named his dog after Cecil Rhodes after all. Not much of an epiphany really. Do people really go around naming their dogs after the lesser figures of world history? That's like naming your dog Bakunin, or General Omar Bradley, or Monsieur Curie.

"It's just that I don't deserve Cecilia," he said, forcing out the words.

"None of us deserves anybody," I said. I turned to Claudia for help but she just stared at me acidly.

"I haven't met Cecilia," I said, "but from what I can see of her here, it looks like you're made for each other."

I looked at the photo again. Cecilia looked like Jordi in a wig. It was the hungry lupine face, the lipless dash of a mouth, and the nose that was so thin and hooked she could have used it to jimmy a lock.

"I betrayed her," Jordi said.

Wolfy stepped into the sunroom. Seeing the drama, he

slowly backed out. I could hear him gathering up empty glasses in the living room.

"But Cecilia ought to be glad that you have a friend like Claudia," I said, just to amuse myself.

Claudia stood motionless, surely calculating some sort of Calabrian retribution involving a rabbit's head and my car antennae.

"Yes. Everybody likes Claudia," Jordi said. "We all love Claudia."

Jordi drew Claudia into his chest, enfolded her in his arms, and started sobbing wetly into her hair. I could see her squirming.

"Here, take this," I said to Jordi, handing him my monogrammed hankie so he'd let go of Claudia. She pulled away and rolled her neck. Her face was red.

"I'm just going to pour myself a little glass of wine," Claudia said. She disappeared.

We were alone in the glass room. The sunlight rained down on us. A stick of incense burned from somewhere. Tendrils of scented smoke floated through the shafts of light, slowly uncoiling into accusing fingers. The light impaled us. It seemed to illuminate us from the inside. We looked ghostly, pale, and we spoke in whispers.

"I cheated on her," Jordi said.

There were a pair of tea lights burning in front of Cecilia's picture. Jordi passed his palm over the flames. Then he closed his fist and shoved it into the pocket of his jogging pants. The candles reflected in the picture frame, the flames became infinite in the picture frame of broken mirrors that surrounded Cecilia's face.

"I had an affair," Jordi said.

"No worries, Jordi. You're not married," I explained, as if I were a legal expert. "You're not married yet. Just engaged. Affianced. Right? So it's not an affair."

Cecilia continued to look beyond us. She was gazing up and into the distance, toward the heavens.

"But, I had an affair with a married woman," he said. "So, you see, Max, even though I am not married, it is still wrong. It is adultery."

I felt Cecilia's eyes on me. They compelled me to glance at her again. Somehow, her mood had changed. She was no longer the tranquil saint. Now she looked angry, homicidal.

"Whatever happened with you and Claudia," I was saying.

"Amy," Jordi blurted out, and I thought the name would crack the glass walls.

"Amy? But what about Claudia?" I asked. "Aren't you two involved?"

"Claudia?" he asked, bewildered.

"Now look, Jordi, we're not in Berlitz School now. This is important. When I ask you a question, do not repeat. Just respond. *Sí?*"

He nodded. I said to him, "Have you been sleeping with Claudia? Yes or no."

"No."

"Fine. Did you sleep with Amy?"

"Yes."

Jordi dropped his forehead into his hand. He released himself over to his sobbing.

"I had an affair with Amy. It was many months ago. I don't know how. It was only a few times."

"Okay," I said. "It's okay, Jordi. It was a long time ago. Now it's done."

It was done. I couldn't imagine it happening in the first place. I couldn't picture that glowing buttery-brown woman—that all-American woman with the perfect skin and the straight white teeth and the long slender legs—I couldn't picture that woman with this gangly, awkward man, with his beaky nose and his pointed chin. But I let myself settle into the notion. I regarded him afresh. He did have big strong hands, and intelligent eyes, and when you got close to him he smelled like a man, like gingery old-fashioned shaving cream and peppery Tres Flores hair tonic and Dominican cigars.

"I betrayed Cecilia," Jordi said. "And I took advantage of Amy."

"I'm sure if you and Amy, uh, if you two did . . . if you were intimate, that Amy would have wanted to."

"Oh, she did want to," he said vehemently, shaking his head. "She insisted. I tell her many times, she is married. I myself was engaged for marriage. It was not right. But she says we don't hurt anyone. It was only between us, nobody else owns our business."

"Correct," I said.

"No, Max. Not correct. We did hurt people. I am hurt. And someday I'll have to tell Cecilia. And she will be hurt."

"Tell her? Why?"

"Because to not tell is to lie."

"To not tell is the manly thing to do, Jordi." I was improvising furiously at this point. "Why would you tell her?"

"Because it is the truth," he ventured.

"Wrong," I intoned. "You would only tell her to unburden

yourself. To make yourself feel better. The manly thing would be to carry the burden of guilt yourself. Don't try to shift it onto Cecilia."

"If I am guilty I only hurt others by admitting?" He just wanted to make sure he was following the logic.

"Yes," I exclaimed. "Yes. You can't burden Cecilia with this. Some things are better left alone, better left unknown."

"There is too much now that we don't know," he said. And he looked toward the wall of glass, its panes streaked with dirt. "And now that Amy is missing, everything is too late," he said. "Now there will never be forgiveness."

"It's never too late for forgiveness," I told him. I wasn't sure where I'd gotten that line. But after I said it, I liked the way it sounded.

Wolf and I walked Claudia and Asta back up the hill to Neuschwanstein. She had a load of crap that we had to sherpa for her: some drink coasters and a large empty Tupperware that had contained yet another one of her runny, pink marsh-mallow salads, and a Twister game that nobody had been in the mood to play. I wedged the entire burden into one gro-cery bag so I could get Wolf to carry all of it. I hadn't needed to ask him. He just picked up the bag and started walking.

"So you didn't actually sleep with Jordi," I said to Claudia.

"Sleep with Jordi?" she said. "Good God, no!"

She unleashed a derisive, maniacal peal of laughter.

"You look like a streetwalker when you smoke on the sidewalk like that."

"Don't try to cheer me up, Max."

We left the stubby little streets of the flatlands and ascended into the Berkeley Hills. The traffic dissipated to almost nothing. The quietness that only the rich can afford enveloped us. The sidewalks wound alongside empty streets, tunneling through green archways of towering oak, and redwood, and eucalyptus trees. The sun dropped quickly in the west. It got bigger as it melted into the horizon, lighting into a great orange flame, grazing the treetops and casting a fire glow around the undulating outline of the leaves.

"I'm happy you didn't sleep with Jordi," I said. "You were being ridiculous. You were acting like a fool."

"I'm lonely," she said.

"I know, darling." I reached over and held her hand.

It was warm for February. In gardens all along the route, crocuses were starting to lift their pert little purple heads from between the cold rocks. It was a chancy move on their part, those stolid little tubers with their defiantly green blades and their short but exuberant lives. Surely there would be another cold snap before spring officially arrived, and all these blossoms would be dealt with severely for venturing out too soon.

"I made a couple of plays for Jordi," Claudia said after a while. "Nothing demonstrative. Just being available. But he didn't pick up. It didn't make any sense—he should have been jumping at the opportunity."

"But now we know it was nothing wrong about you," said Wolfy.

"I never suspected there was anything wrong with me," she said.

"I'm sure. Not for a moment," I said.

"I am shocked," Wolfy said. "I am shocked about Amy and Jordi."

"Well, it's a shocker, isn't it?" I said. "Look at me, I have shock face."

I demonstrated my shock face: eyes bulging and darting with terror, eyebrows arching and knitting madly, teeth biting into the white knuckles of my clenched fist. It was a gesture I'd picked up from Baba. She had first demonstrated it when I told her that I thought I could love a man as much as I could love a woman—which wasn't that much. After she recovered from the initial stunning, she told me that I was affecting bisexuality—just to show off. Those were her words. I was showing off.

Now I liked to bait Baba into making the shock face. I'd think up shocking revelations to sucker punch her with. But she was on to me. She wouldn't make the face. I wondered if, when I told her about Amy and Jordi, she would make the shock face.

Claudia said, "You know, actually this Amy-Jordi thing is a big relief for me. If Amy slept with him, that means he must be reasonably attractive. So, I'm not so crazy."

"This is now reminding me of the girls I knew at the university," Wolfy said. "If one girl thinks you are okay for sex, then the others think you are okay for sex too. And you can have sex for life."

He laughed merrily.

"You slept with women?" Claudia asked him.

"So this is all pretty good for you?" I said to her. "All that matters is you saving face. But what about Amy?"

"What about her?" Claudia said, stopping to light another cigarette. She spoke into her hands cupped around the lighter flame. "This doesn't change Amy's situation."

"And just what is her 'situation,' as you so sensitively put it?"

"Now it is much more complicated," Wolfy said.

"Complicated? What is the matter with you people?" I cried. "Amy is missing. Probably dead. That's pretty fucking complicated, you cavalier bastardos."

Claudia stopped and turned to look at me. Wolfy continued up the street with Asta.

"What do you want me to do, Max?" she said. "Tear my blouse, scratch my face? Cover my head with ashes?"

"I need you to be a human being."

"Don't fall apart now, Max," she said. "Everybody is trying to keep their shit together. Steve's an asshole. Amy could have just left him. People run out on their marriages every day."

"You're the expert," I said, my bitterness turning to cruelty. She looked like I had slapped her in the face. She turned away from me and started walking at a steady, measured pace.

A hush blanketed the stately homes that reclined behind their green lawns like pampered princesses tucked into ornate palanquins. I smelled steaks grilling when we passed a Tudor mansion. Farther along, the folks in the Moorish palace were roasting a chicken.

I caught up with Claudia and marched alongside her, matching my strides with hers. We didn't talk for a while. Claudia smoked pensively and Wolfy stayed ahead of us. Wolf unhooked Asta's leash so he could play fetch with his tennis ball as we traversed the switchbacks leading up to Claudia's house.

"It does force us to think about Amy in a different way," she finally said quietly, just to me.

"This affair business?"

"Yes. I've always thought of her as this pure creature. This untainted person. Now that Amy is missing, all the rocks are getting turned over and all the ugliness . . ."

"That's what I hate about it," I told her.

29

In early March, I took the role of Tonio in the San Francisco Opera's production of *I Pagliacci*. He is a clown. Of course, in *I Pagliacci*, all the characters are clowns. I was one of the jealous ones.

I'd played the role several times. Tonio is in a troupe of itinerant performers. We crisscross Italy's boot in rickety wagons, burlesquing for pennies. A married couple leads the troupe. The husband, Canio, is a charismatic showman. But he is always jealous. His wife, Nedda, is an irresistible gamine. Everyone loves her. All men want her, including me. But she spurns me. So I inform her husband that she has a lover, knowing that this will cause Canio to kill his wife.

Having played the part so many times, I found it increasingly difficult to summon the rage that Tonio requires. And I don't—as myself, as Max Bravo—have the attention span required for revenge. So I had to resort to mechanical acting methods.

When I played Tonio in Paris, I visited the National Military Museum and there, at the new Holocaust exhibit, I found my fury. I had always known that the Nazis exterminated Gypsies in the death camps. In fact, I knew that they had murdered my grandfather. But I hadn't realized how many Gypsies they slaughtered: a quarter of a million.

The catalog of inhumanities became a lurid attraction that I returned to day after day. I started reading more and more about the fate of the Gitanes in the camps. I ordered books online. I bought stacks of books in *bibliothèques*. I pursued the genocidal bastards in reading rooms and museums. I stalked them amid the hushed stacks of stiff books in forgotten wings of libraries. I rode out after them with monomaniacal determination, as if they were still living, breathing men. As if they still trod the earth on their cloven hooves stuffed into jackboots.

The most touching account I found was actually written by a German commandant at one of the camps. He was struck by how trusting and childlike the Gypsies were. They would follow their captors' instructions cheerfully. They huddled in their separate enclosures—they were not mixed with the other prisoners—and played their instruments and sang and danced. It was only near the end, when they realized that the guards were taking the children away to kill them, that the Rom women went wild. They attacked the armed men with their fingernails and their teeth, flailing at them until their starved skeletal arms broke.

I was having coffee at the kitchen table one morning. I was alone. It was a bright, sunny day and Wolfy wanted to get out of the house, so he went over to Berkeley to take Asta to the dog park. I was looking over the *I Pagliacci* libretto and wondering how I could once more summon the necessary hellhounds to play the deceitful, murder-by-proxy Tonio. My reservoir of bile was pretty much dried up. My mind returned to the camps. I thought about a recent article I'd just come across. The Red Cross had just unsealed an entire warehouse full of eyewitness accounts that they had collected at the end of the war. At the time the testimonies were gathered, they were considered far too incendiary to be made public. In the Balkans, my family's homeland, the Nazis had grown tired of bayoneting women and children—they didn't want to waste bullets—and they started tossing live babies into the bonfires.

What does it take? How does a normal man, going about his normal life, suddenly veer onto an avenue of horror? One day you're mowing the lawn. The next day you're vivisecting your wife in the bathtub.

It's the simple questions that have no answers.

In the camps, the children burned alive. Across the street, Amy disappeared. A secret hatch opened and she slipped through it. Was it the same strain of madness that had caused both these events?

"Stop thinking about it," Baba said.

I hadn't seen her come in. She was standing at the kitchen counter. She had opened a package of mixed baklava that I'd just bought at the halal grocery. She was working her way through the assorted delicacies, taking one bite out of each square and setting the nibbled sweets back in the package.

"How do you know what I'm thinking?" I said.

"Just sing," she said. Flakes of gossamer pastry clung to her chin.

"I have to sing to pay for all that baklava you're eating," I told her.

"Sing, Maximilian," she said. "The past does not exist. Only now exists. Live now."

The front door opened and Baba left the kitchen. I set the libretto aside and picked up the *Chronicle* and made a point of reading the society column—just to maintain my insouciant public persona, I suppose. I stared at the photo taken at last night's Pacific Heights soiree, a line of Botoxed and sequined wealthy matrons stared back at me with eyes that were permanently surprised after too many face-lifts.

Wolfy walked in. He was wearing soft canvas shoes and a tangerine polo shirt. It was his outdoor costume. He lifted his sunglasses from his eyes to the top of his head.

"Well, hello, Sporty Spice," I said.

He poured himself a cup of coffee and sat down across the breakfast table from me. He looked at his watch and he looked at me in my kimono and didn't remark on the time. It was after 2:00 P.M. He picked up the sports section.

"Look at this woman," I said, holding up the newspaper. "Her eyebrows are lifted all the way to her hairline."

"I met Larry," he said, very offhand, without looking up from the soccer scores.

"Oh," I said, shifting my eyes back down to the gossip column in retaliation. "Where did you meet Larry? Was he crouching under the hydrangeas?"

"No. He was at Claudia's house. He slept there."

I put down the newspaper and stared at Wolf. I realized my mouth was open.

"You'll have to repeat that," I said.

"He was sleeping at Claudia's house. When I went there in this morning to get Asta for his walk. Larry was there."

"And you met him?"

"Yes. After he woke up. He came downstairs."

"What was he wearing?"

"His pajamas. Of course."

"He has a pair of pajamas at Claudia's house?" I said.

"He was wearing pajamas. This is all I know, Max. And you don't have to yell at me like you are an asinine."

It was the pajamas that got to me. The pajamas indicated premeditation.

"I don't know why you are so disturbed," Wolfy said. "They are married?"

"They are supposed to be separated," I bellowed.

"Well, maybe they reconcile. *Ja?*"

30

We hadn't started group rehearsals yet for *I Pagliacci*. I was still rehearsing on my own at home, early in the morning until about noon. That left vast tracts of my time unclaimed. I was slogging through a wasteland of ennui.

The vacant hours multiplied when Wolfy left. He went to Los Angeles to visit friends, to do some *"kunst"* as he put it. They were building some behemoth outdoor installation, some eyesore. It involved parachute material and barbed wire and an arroyo in the desert near Needles. Wolf tried to explain it to me. They were going to erect this thing using slave labor—an army of art school students—and wait to film a flash flood washing it away. They had a Web site with a live Web camera capturing every anaesthetizing moment. Wolf showed me the site, but I forgot to bookmark it.

I suppose I let myself go after Wolfy left. Baba noticed. She badgered me about slothfulness. She told me that by wearing my kimono all day I was denying my gonads the proper support afforded by jockey briefs. She claimed that this would trigger a condition she referred to as "lazy balls." She described lazy balls in forensic detail—it was a grossly elongated scrotum that could, in the severest cases, reach the sufferer's knees. Sometimes, the balls became so lazy that the gonads dissolved completely, leaving only a long, empty sack to signal that the sufferer had ever been a man with balls at all.

Baba would usually recite these harrowing caveats on indolence from the depths of my Eames recliner—one of my cigarettes burning in between her yellowed fingers and a glass of my good port at her elbow. I noted that as she'd loll in the recliner, her breasts lay flat across her belly and grazed the waistband at the top of her skirt. If she reached over to pick up her port or cadge another of my cigarettes, the breast pouches would part in the middle and go their separate ways, rolling down the sides of her ribs. Her dugs had been drained by her horde of offspring—which she produced with all the efficiency of a Henry Ford assembly line from the age of fourteen until the happy respite of menopause in her mid-forties. Now they were empty flaps that hung under her blouse, causing her to look like she had taped a pair of socks to her chest. She had never worn a brassiere. I wanted to accuse her of letting her own hanging participles lapse into "lazy boobs" but, naturally, I couldn't find a space in the conversation to insert my barb.

Her speeches would come in rapid-fire salvos because she had to fit them in during the commercial breaks of her favorite daytime drama, *A Reason to Live*. If I challenged her theories about "lazy balls," she would shush me and point to the TV, indicating that Cliff—or Ridge or Shale or whoever that lantern-jawed meat-cake was that she liked—was about to break it off with Tiffany, or Ashley, or Breck or some other starchy broad who Baba insisted was not good enough for him.

I hung around the house and watched Baba's programs with her for a while, but eventually, her hectoring drove me out. She had even filched my kimono and wouldn't tell me where she hid it. I was no longer comfortable in my own home.

I started going to Claudia's house every day. Asta was my excuse. One afternoon, after Wolf had told me about meeting Larry, I let myself in and, with Asta trailing behind, I climbed the stairs to Claudia's bedroom. I quietly stepped across her Berber carpeting. The silence in the room accused me of trespassing and caused my bowels to flutter. I poked my head into Claudia's powder room. Her silk nightgown hung on a wall hook and her satin slippers stood neatly on the floor beside the scale.

Claudia's bathroom was fully femme—the walls were papered in vertical black and pink stripes and spritzed with gilt-framed prints of Barbie dolls in evening wear. The towels were pink. The floor was carpeted in four-inch pink shag. The carpet reinforced that this was Claudia's private sanctum; you could never have carpeting next to a toilet that men used. And in the little alcove across from the tub was a marble-top vanity with a scalloped-edged mirror. I had been in this room before, naturally. But I had never been in it unsupervised.

The vanity beckoned me. I sat down on the little pink tuffet, and twirled around to face the mirror. I gazed at my reflection and smoothed my eyebrows and fluffed my hair. I had been sleeping well and I looked good. I figured I could easily pass for thirty-eight, perhaps even a thirty-eight-year-old woman with the right wig and the right lighting.

A parade ground formation of crystal atomizers were lined up in front of me. I picked them up, one by one, and squeezed the balls, sending puffs of scent clouds into the air. I found one that smelled like peonies and sprayed myself with it. Then I perfumed Asta with it.

I rummaged through Claudia's makeup baskets—through the eyeliner wands and the assortment of matte and frost and sparkle eye-shadow rounds in colors ranging from buff to peacock blue. There were lipsticks in snub-nosed black cartridges that looked like bullets. Most of them were saturated colors, aubergine or ruby. I outlined my lips with a go-to-hell purple liner pencil. Then I filled them in with a heliotrope gloss. All I needed to do next was to tattoo a tear on my cheek and put my hair in a fountain and I'd look like a gang girl from the Mission.

Asta barked. He had his front paws up on the vanity now and was craning his neck forward, trying to sniff the assorted brushes arranged in a pink ceramic vase like a bouquet. I twittered the brushes around and selected one that had a white billowing head of natural horsehair. I brushed it along Asta's nose and dabbed it on his cheeks. He barked again and smiled and wagged his tail furiously.

I opened the vanity drawer. It was lined with bottles of nail polish. They were arranged in ascending order of garishness, starting with puce on the left and ending with jug-wine purple on the right. I pulled a fire-engine red from the middle and tested the color on one of Asta's claws. It looked good on him. But I thought that Claudia might notice and start asking questions. I wiped it off with a tissue.

I remembered that I should do the same for myself. I ran the tissue across my lips and as I did, I noticed that the gray streak in my hair had become whiter. Perhaps it was the strain of Amy's disappearance. But I had to admit it was more than that. I was nearly fifty years old. And I didn't like what came next. That streak of gray was one of death's bony fingers rasping at my eyebrow. It threatened the imminent arrival of everything I deserved: sclerosis, periodontitis, an irrepressible urge to talk about nothing but real estate prices.

There would also be the loss of companionship that too often accompanies the loss of youth. I could already hear the thrumming of empty air in solitary rooms. After that, there was only death. Perhaps I would be sent to some circle of hell devised specially for me, where I would be made to sit in a platter of fire—frowning into my jowls—listening to the litany of my outrages recited by legions of wronged lovers, the bitter and the dead.

"All right, Asta," I told him. He cocked his head. "Let's not wallow. Shall we?"

We left the vanity and marched purposefully back into the bedroom. I asked him where Claudia kept the pajamas. He acted as though he didn't understand the question. I started pawing through the drawers in her bureau.

"What's this then?" I said to Asta, holding up a set of men's pajamas.

Their blue and white stripes were faded and the butt sagged and the cuffs of the pants were frayed. They were the kind of pajamas that married people wear.

Asta sat down smartly. I held the pajamas under his nose. He thumped his tail in a lashing motion. He barked.

"That's right, boy," I said. "They're Larry's pajamas, aren't they?"

Asta barked again. Just once. He seemed to be smiling, wiry hairs curled up around his black lips like a pirate's mustache. I folded the pajamas just as I had found them and tucked them back into the drawer.

I didn't actually see Claudia for a week. We spoke by phone and e-mail. I didn't mention Larry or his pajamas. Neither did she.

31

"You know what we need?" Ed said one bright April afternoon. "We need a stakeout. A professional stakeout."

"To watch Steve?" Jordi asked.

"Yes," Ed said. "Steve. Who else?"

"But we can see his house from here, man," Gator pointed out.

"Sure, we can see Steve," Ed said. "But we can't hear him. We don't know what's going on in that house."

Gator and I were sitting on the picnic table and Jordi and Ed were stationed on a pair of lawn chairs that Ed had pulled out of the back of his van. All four of us had just opened fresh beers and lodged them in yellow rubber beer holders—or beer condoms as we called them.

"Aren't you being a bit dramatic?" I asked Ed.

"And aren't you supposed to be here with a dog?" he fired back at me.

He had me there. I usually remembered to bring Asta, but it was a bit of a walk to Claudia's house and sometimes I put it off until I simply forgot. This one oversight, one small slip, had left me vulnerable to receive lectures from a man who slept in a motor vehicle and crapped in a bush. I decided to keep quiet and let Gator do the talking.

"What do you think we need to hear in there?" Gator asked.

"We got to hear it to find out," Ed said loudly. He let out a long sigh and tossed a stick that he had been stripping of its bark.

The dogs were rioting against the far fence. There was a lot of plaintive yelping, but none of us intervened. The women tended to intervene. We didn't. We always let the dogs work it out for themselves. Cecilia was chasing after Colonel, who was being terrorized by the monkey-faced terriers.

"What should we do?" Jordi asked Ed.

"Leave it to me," Ed told us.

The next afternoon Ed showed up at the park with what he called "the right technology." It was a parabolic microphone he had purchased from someone he referred to as The Professor.

"This is like from the seventies," Gator said. He looked at the machine doubtfully.

"So, is this Professor a former member of the Symbionese Liberation Army?" I asked.

"It still works," Ed told Gator sharply.

Ed set the device on the picnic table and began to assemble it. The microphone was shaped like a miniature satellite dish—only it wasn't that miniature. It was easily three feet in diameter. A knot of cables sprouted from it and at the end of each of these cables was a plug as big as a lawn dart. Ed showed us how the cables plugged into a row of sockets in a lead box covered with dials and meters. It was the size and weight of a cinder block. It was the control box, Ed explained—the brains of the machine. Ed put on a pair of headphones that looked like two bagels mounted on a leatherette headband. A gray curling cord bounced down the front of Ed's T-shirt. I noted that the words on his shirt advised QUESTION AUTHORITY. Ed caught the end of the microphone cord and plugged it into the control box.

"And if we put this headset on a creature cobbled together from stolen cadaver parts . . ." I said.

"And run an electric current . . ." Gator continued.

"Listen up, assholes," Ed said. He pulled the headset off. "I'm only going to go through this once."

Ed explained that the parabolic microphone worked a lot like the satellite dishes it resembled. Cable dishes collect and focus radio waves. The parabolic microphone collects and focuses sound waves. It can only collect sound from one direction, and only at low frequencies. This model, from the late 1970s, had a range of ten meters, which, Ed noted, was sufficient for picking up sounds coming from inside Steve's house.

Ed got out his cordless drill. He climbed onto the top of his van—scrambling up the shiny chrome boat ladder bolted on the back—and he drilled a circle of holes into the metal roof. He then whacked the center of the circle with a ball-peen hammer until it caved in. The hole was wide enough to fit the microphone cables through.

Gator climbed up onto the roof with the microphone dish. Ed fitted the screwdriver attachment onto his drill and, while Gator held the dish steady, Ed screwed its brackets into the roof of the van.

After they got the microphone mounted on top of the van, we all lined up along the sidewalk to inspect their work. The dish easily covered half of the van's roof.

"Now that looks perfectly innocent," Ed said. "Like a satellite TV hookup."

"I guess," said Gator.

"Is it typical to have a television satellite on a van?" Jordi asked.

"Hell, Jordi," Ed said. "Wake up, dude. You're in America."

We drew up a schedule and took shifts sitting in Ed's van, manning the stakeout. We parked the van across the street from Steve's house and provisioned it with a cooler full of beer, a digital camera with a zoom, and the parabolic microphone. We named the eavesdropping device Watergate.

We showed the women the operational guidelines that we'd put in a binder. Marcy and Kim and Claudia just looked at it. They didn't say much. We offered to put them on the stakeout schedule. None of them took us up on it.

Ed's van was a tight fit, even though there were usually only two or three of us on a shift. The back half of the van was taken up by Ed's platform bed. The floor was carpeted in red shag, which also ran up the walls and onto the ceiling. On the starboard side was the galley: a cupboard comprised of a small metal sink and a two-burner propane stove top, and a bar fridge and a pantry below. In the middle of the ceiling was a pop-up sunroof that Ed would raise so he could stand upright. But now, with the microphone dish up top, he could only open the sunroof a crack.

A pair of tan Corinthian leather captain's chairs—complete

with a console that held four enormous drink cups—commanded the helm. When he had guests, Ed liked to seat them on the bed and the floor. He would sit in the captain's chair and swivel it around to face inward to the conversation pit.

What wardrobe Ed owned—a collection of sloganeering T-shirts and a couple pairs of fatigue trousers—were folded into a trundle drawer under the bed.

Decades of pot smoke was ingrained in the van's carpeting, where it comingled with the many vials of patchouli oil that Ed must have spilled over the years. It smelled like old ropes rotting in bilge water. Ed maintained the cabin's stench by lighting up a bong at least three times a day. He kept the bong on permanent display on a shelf by his bed. It was a life-sized skull rendered in ceramic, the color of dog shit, and in its cavernous sockets were two red glass orbs, cut in facets so they glittered. The lighting of the bong was a ritual, always begun with the closing of the drapes: back, sides, and, finally, the partition drapes that separated the captain's chairs from the living quarters. Ed had sewn all his drapes himself out of American flags.

We parked the van directly in front of the dog park, with the two oblong side windows facing Steve's house. The windows were tinted so no one could see in, and they bubbled out to afford a wider view.

We kept a log of Steve's comings and goings. He left the house at 7:30 A.M. on weekdays wearing slacks and a sport coat. On Fridays he wore a golf shirt and a pair of khakis. Dockers. He always carried a gym bag. When he came home in the evening, usually at 7:30 P.M., he'd be wearing a track-suit and a pair of cross-trainers. We assumed his work clothes were in the gym bag. Amy had mentioned that Steve went to the gym every day after work. Apparently his schedule hadn't changed.

In the evenings he'd take Dixie out for a walk, assiduously avoiding the dog park. This disturbed us. Pugs need a lot of attention and it was cruel to leave her alone in the house for so many hours.

After he walked Dixie, Steve ate dinner. We checked his re-cycling bin and found stacks of flattened frozen dinner boxes. He was especially fond of Hungry-Man's Salisbury steak.

Steve watched television while he ate dinner, and on into the evening. He liked police dramas and movies that fea-tured pyrotechnic explosions that required the characters to run—one assumes with their hands karate chopping through the air—and dive at the last minute, just ahead of an advanc-ing fireball.

On Saturday mornings, Steve would leave the house at 9:00 A.M. with his golf clubs. He'd return at 2:00 P.M. He would then mow the lawn. We'd turn off Watergate while he was mowing because the roar from Steve's gas-powered Lawn-Boy was deafening. Then he would drink beer. He drank from aluminum cans. We could hear a popping sound every time he opened one. He'd generally drink between eight and ten beers. We counted. As he drank beer—in his recliner, we could hear the chair folding and unfolding every time he got up to get another can—Steve would watch sports.

"Is he watching the Raiders?" I asked one Saturday after-noon.

"Don't be such a fag, Max," Gator told me. "This is baseball season."

"Does that mean he doesn't have a Commitment to Excellence?" I referred to the Oakland Raiders' tagline. Now I was baiting them.

"Oh, he has that," Ed assured me. "Only now it's for the A's."

"Baseball. Right?"

"You got it, buddy," Ed said. He smiled, encouraged by my progress.

Steve was an active observer of sports. He did not countenance failure or incompetence. He often yelled at his television set. Every game was a roller-coaster ride of emotion. He would frequently shout the word yes, which was surely accompanied by a fist pump. Or, conversely, he would express displeasure, calling players pantywaists, showboats, or dumbasses.

Occasionally, while Steve was watching television, the telephone would ring and he'd let the answering machine take the call. It would be Sharon or Amy's father. They'd ask how he was holding up. Had he heard anything new? Steve would turn up the sound on the TV while they recorded their messages. We never heard him return any of the calls.

Ed and Gator and I were near the end of our third Saturday shift. It was around 7:00 P.M., and Ed was wearing the headphones.

"He just opened the freezer," Ed said.

"Salisbury steak?" Gator asked.

"We can't know that, man," Ed said. "Not until recycling day."

"But even then you can't know which dinner he ate on

which day," I said. They both looked at me like I was being an obstructionist.

"Oven or microwave?" Gator asked.

"The dinger just went off," Ed said.

"Microwave," Gator and Ed said together.

Ed let Gator wear the headphones for a while. Manning the Watergate was considered the most glamorous job on stakeout and we all had to be generous with it.

Having handed over the headphones to Gator, Ed, who was by definition our host, opened up his bar fridge and pulled out a brick of sallow Velveeta cheese. He retrieved a box of saltine crackers from his pantry and set up a cutting board on the Happy-Daze ice chest. He arranged the cheese and crackers and three steak knives on the cutting board and tore three sheets of paper toweling off a roll that he kept under the driver's seat. We used the paper towels for plates.

"Got any condiments, Ed?" Gator asked.

"You bet," Ed said. He went back into the bar fridge and emerged with three jars: Dijon honey mustard, capers, and sweet pickles, presliced.

Gator set down the headphones and we three gathered around the makeshift table. Ed sat on his bed, the two dogs, Colonel and Asta, sleeping behind him on his patchwork quilt. Gator and I sat cross-legged on the red shag carpeting.

"How's your opera going?" Ed asked. It surprised me. We almost never talked about work.

"Yeah," said Gator. "It's about clowns, right?"

"Yes. It's about clowns," I said.

"And the one clown kills his wife," Gator said.

"Didn't Caruso play Canio?" Ed said. He shoved a whole saltine, piled high with a slab of caper-covered Velveeta, into his mouth.

"Yes, and more recently, Pavarotti and Domingo," I said.

"Tenors," Gator said. "Do those guys always get the best roles?"

"They generally play the hero. That's not always the best role," I said. "I play the villain, the baritone, of course. Tonio. He's a big lout. A repulsive individual. He's in love with Nedda."

"But he doesn't stand a chance with her?" asked Gator.

"No. He doesn't stand a chance," I told him. "I didn't know you followed opera."

"I don't," Gator said. "I just saw *Rigoletto* in Prague with this chick I was traveling around Europe with. That was good. And then we saw *Cats* in London. And that was the shits."

"I don't remember," Ed said. "Does the husband get away with the murder?"

We heard a knocking. It was the sound of bone on glass. Someone was tapping at the driver's window.

Colonel and Asta were still sleeping. The knocking filtered through their dreams, causing them to pedal their paws and emit muted yelps.

Gator and Ed and I remained stock-still. We looked at one another. The curtain behind the driver's seat was drawn, so we knew we couldn't be seen. We did not make a sound.

It was like one of those movies about a submarine crew—and this was the obligatory scene where the enemy ship is plying the waters overhead and the crew must remain perfectly silent to avoid being detected by sonar. This is usually a very suspense-filled scene. The faces of the crew glisten with sweat. Their eyes are wide with fear. And then someone, some young swabbie, always drops a wrench and the clanging metal reverberates throughout the sub and, one supposes, across the entire ocean.

The knocking started up again. It was a friendly, familiar kind of knocking—just a light rap against the window with a knuckle. Then it stopped again. We maintained our silence but the dogs both jerked up and started howling.

Gator and Ed each grabbed a dog and tried to muzzle them by cupping their hands over their mouths. The dogs squirmed and flopped around on the bed. The two men tried to pin them down with Turkish wrestling holds.

The knocking stopped. Whoever was out there was now listening. They could hear a lot of thrashing and rustling. They could hear the dogs' truncated yelps. They could hear us. The clowns.

Ed looked at Gator and me. He grimaced and jerked his thumb toward the front of the van. Gator shook his head violently.

"They know we're here," Ed mouthed.

"What?" Gator mouthed back.

"Oh, for Christ's sakes," Ed whispered out loud. He let go of Colonel, got up from the bed, and stepped hunched over to the front of the van.

Ed pulled the curtains apart. Steve was standing by the driver's door.

"Steve," he said breezily. "*Qué pasa?*"

"I figured you guys could use some coffee."

"What?" said Ed.

"Coffee. For you. For you guys."

Steve handed Ed a coffee carafe—the kind with the thermal lining that keeps the coffee hot. It was tall and elegant, European design. I thought to myself that Amy must have bought it. She probably got it at Sur La Table. And I hoped she'd got it on sale—I'd seen those same carafes on sale just after Thanksgiving. And then I felt a little sick, thinking about Amy standing there in Sur La Table, big and pregnant and smiling, and the saleslady helping her. And I pictured Amy bringing the carafe home and washing it by hand in the sink with soapy water and rinsing it off and admiring the cheerful red carafe in the sunlight streaming through her kitchen window. Amy had painted her kitchen yellow and red and it was the kind of kitchen that always smelled like fresh coffee and muffins and pot roast. And I saw that big meathead Steve handing the carafe to Ed and he was leering. The son of a bitch was leering.

Ed took the carafe and set it down on the seat. Then Steve handed him a stack of Styrofoam cups—three of them.

"Just leave the carafe on my porch when you're done," Steve said genially. He touched his forefinger to his eyebrow in a casual salute and stepped away from the window. Ed quickly rolled up the window. Through the windshield, we could see Steve walking in front of the van.

"How did he know there was three of us?" Ed whispered.

Gator and I crawled to the port side of the vehicle. We peered through the gap in the curtains and watched Steve swagger across the street. He looked relaxed and confident.

"It's cool, man," Ed was whispering again. "I got a cover."

Ed rolled down the window. He stuck his head out and called to Steve across the street.

"Hey, thanks for the coffee, man," Ed hollered. "We were just in here smoking a doobie."

32

Johnny Miranda poured me a martini. I was his only cus-
tomer. That's the way I liked it. I liked having the Sans Souci
all to myself.

Johnny had the saloon door standing open. It was quiet
out there on Bush Street. The world held still, not waiting.
Just pausing.

It was 4:00 P.M., the magic hour when the sun pauses between the tall buildings and those last rays of light offer an
oblique surrender. The light streaked through the dirty port-
hole windows, glanced across the red velvet walls, and struck
the ship's barometer. High-pressure front moving in, it read.
The copper sparkled, crisp and piercing like drumsticks striking cymbals.

"Did you ever work surveillance?" I asked Johnny.

He flicked the last few drops of gin out of the shaker into
my martini glass, speared an olive onto a toothpick.

Two empty toothpicks sat on the bar in front of me. The
anchors on the wall wore smiling tails, and the cork floats
bobbed in the fishnets strung across the oak paneling.

"A stakeout," I said. "Ever work a stakeout, Johnny?"

"Max, you've been watching too many TV shows."

Johnny Miranda slid the martini in front me, nudging the base of the glass with two fingertips. His fingernails were buffed and his cuffs were crisp and that knuckle-duster pinkie ring of his dazzled under the lights like a parking lot paved with diamonds.

He went to the back room. He said he needed to get more ice.

The great ocean currents rolled beneath my bar stool. I knew a secret about the Sans Souci: I knew that sullen, nautical pastiche of a bar really was what it affected to be—it was a ship at sea.

Johnny Miranda was on deck. The commander.

"You didn't ever park across the street from a suspect's home, in an unmarked van, and monitor his every movement with high-tech surveillance gear? Say, a parabolic microphone?"

Johnny dumped a bag of ice into the metal tray under the bar.

"Max," he said. He put both hands on the bar and spoke directly to me, slowly, like he was talking to a simpleton. "I don't want to know what those clowns at the dog park are doing. Whatever it is, you need to stop. You'll get yourself arrested."

"The police aren't doing anything," I said.

"That's what people always think. It used to drive me crazy. But I can tell you—and you can believe me because I worked homicide for twenty-three years—I can tell you that

McGuire and Estevez are busting their asses every day, chasing down a thousand nitpicky little leads and details. It's not all stakeouts and car chases, Max."

"I'm just a concerned citizen," I said.

"Be a citizen that stays out of the way," he told me.

He started washing glasses, heavy, sturdy little highball glasses. He very deliberately wiped each highball with his white bar towel until it gleamed beneath the red stained-glass lamps overhead.

I had come to the Sans Souci to see if I could run into Claudia after she got off work. Her office was right across the street and she often stopped off for a glass of wine with Johnny Miranda. He was her confidant. There was a time when I hated Johnny Miranda, when I was afraid he had supplanted me as Claudia's best friend—and perhaps even surpassed me by becoming Claudia's love interest. But I had come to a separate peace with Johnny Miranda. I had come to regard him as an ally.

"Bad business about Larry," I said.

"She's doing fine," he said.

He offered me a cigarette. San Francisco had enacted a ban on smoking in bars. But we considered ourselves outside of municipal jurisdiction, being on the high seas. He gave me a light. Then he lit up himself.

"Just when she pulls herself together, Larry comes barging back into her life," I said.

"She's okay now."

"You have no idea how much triage I had to perform on that woman. And now Larry's getting her twisted up again."

"Larry is out of the picture," he said.

I sat up straight on my bar stool and pulled back from my drink as though it had been misleading me.

"Out of the picture?" I said. "What do you know?"

He looked straight at me. He took a drag on his cigarette and blew the smoke over my head.

"I understand the invidious position that you, as a professional, are now in," I told Johnny Miranda. "You cannot betray a confidence."

"I cannot."

"But perhaps I can put forth a theory. And you can offer your expert opinion as to its plausibility."

"We could try that," he said. He tapped a dowel of ash into the ashtray he had set on the bar for us to share.

"I happen to know that Claudia had been seeing Larry again. This has been going on for some time."

"Your sources seem accurate," he said, and he took a drag on his cigarette.

"But now she has broken off with him?"

He picked a fleck of tobacco off his lower lip and examined it. Some people would ignore the gesture. But I knew better. I was encouraged by the way he looked at that fleck of tobacco before he twisted it off his fingertips.

"And I suppose if I were to go to her house tomorrow, and if I were to look for Asta's leash—in, say, a dresser drawer in Claudia's bedroom—I would fail to find a pair of men's blue and white striped pajamas."

"I doubt very much that those pajamas are in that drawer," Johnny Miranda said.

"I wonder," I said, "just where one would find a pair of such pajamas."

"One might," Johnny Miranda said, "find the charred remains of such a garment in the fireplace."

I paid for my drink and scuttled out of the Sans Souci. I had changed my mind about meeting up with Claudia. I didn't think I could hide my glee.

33

Wolfy came back to San Francisco a couple of days after we suspended our Watergate operation. I told him about it and he insisted that we hold the next meeting at my house. Everyone arrived together. They piled out of Ed's van: Marcy and Kim, and Jordi, and Gator, and Claudia.

Claudia was wearing a pair of Levis rolled up to show off how her sharp ankles flicked as she walked in her stacked Famolares. A pair of turquoise earrings that were as big as wind chimes dangled from her ears. She had cinched in the waist of her jeans with a black leather belt studded with silver conches. I suppose it was a southwestern motif.

"Where did you get that shirt?" I asked.

The whole costume puzzled me. But the shirt actually galled me. It was a man's work shirt. Plaid. It was too big for her. She wore it with the tails tied in a knot around her waist, just above her belt. She was clearly emulating Marilyn Monroe's character in *River of No Return*. She was going for a sort of rough-and-tumble, frontier sex kitten thing. But she didn't have Monroe's curves. So she looked more like a transvestite hillbilly.

"It's just an old shirt of Gator's," she said. "He was going to throw it out."

She twirled on her Famolares with her palms beseeching the sky as if to beg the question, *"Voilà, c'est chic, n'est-ce pas?"* We were alone in the front hallway so I reached out, snatched her up by one of her delicate little wrists, and snapped her to attention.

"Max, that hurts."

"Stand still."

"Let go. Let go or I'll scream."

The others were in the kitchen. I could hear them chattering and opening beers and unpacking snacks. The dogs were chasing one another around the kitchen, their claws scrabbling frantically to find purchase on the slick linoleum.

"Now you're after Gator, aren't you?" I said. "That idiot Jordi rejected you. Then you failed again with Larry. And now you're trying to get even by sleeping with Gator."

"I can do what I want," she lashed back.

"You're acting like a dirty hooker. Worse—you're making a fool of yourself."

"Let go. You're hurting my arm."

"I won't have it, Claudia."

I said it just inches from her eyes. I was still holding her wrist. I pulled her in closer to me.

She wrenched her arm out of my grasp. She took a step back and balled up her bony hands into fists.

"I'm not chasing Gator," she said. "I've already got him."

She raised herself up, her shoulders set back. She craned the left side of her mouth into a sneer so high that it almost shut her eye. She put her hands on her hips and swayed side to side like a snake bouncing on its coils.

"You're just jealous," she said. "You want Gator. Well, I got news for you, Max. He doesn't play on your team. He's all man, one hundred percent man. And I got him now. So back off."

I thought she going to spit on me. Instead, she threw herself out of the room. I could hear her making her big phony entrance into the kitchen. She was all brass and bravado. Wolfy, be a dear and get me some ice. Ed, can you get something to mop that up. That. There, where the champagne exploded. You're standing in it. Marcy, darling, can you get this lid off, it's stuck. My God, Marcy, you have the strength of ten men. And then she'd bray at her own jokes like a circus donkey.

I stood there in the empty hallway where she had left me. I felt someone's presence. I turned to look over my left shoulder. It was me: I was in the full-length mirror. My hair was mussed. My silk shirt was crumpled. I was wearing it with my shirttails hanging out. The shirt was a festive paisley, all swirling aquamarine and nicotine and claret. And I saw the bags under my eyes and the sag under my jaw and the sad attempt to hide the extra twenty pounds with a loud shirt— a loud shirt that was hanging out. And I saw that I was a middle-aged man, all alone, with an untucked shirt.

I proceeded to drink like I was at a wedding in Helsinki. Everyone else was drinking beer and wine. I was saturating myself with vodka discolored by drops of grapefruit juice. A couple of people asked me why I was drinking greyhounds.

I explained that I was on a diet. Ed said it looked more like I was on a bender.

In their usual tedious form, the groupthink dissected the Watergate operation. There were two camps. One camp believed that there was still value in the Watergate strategy. The men—Gator, Wolfy, Jordi, Ed, and myself—remained convinced that monitoring Steve inside his home would render some vital lead. We did allow, however, that we needed to come up with another tactic, as Steve had become sensitive to the van-based surveillance. The other camp was a land of women. Marcy, Kim, and Claudia banded into a burning ring of estrogen. They collectively dismissed the surveillance operation altogether.

"You're not going to learn anything by spying on Steve," Claudia stated.

She was sitting on the floor, her legs crossed in the lotus position with her bare feet resting in the folds of her hips, her naked soles facing up to the ceiling. I wanted to give her a good shove. She'd roll right over, helpless, with her legs locked up like that. She was showing off. For Gator, I thought. Her gender confederates, Marcy and Kim, sat behind her on the sofa like a pair of backup singers.

"We have to leave Steve alone," Marcy said.

"Yeah," said Claudia. "Terrorizing Steve isn't going to help us find Amy."

"Are you people on dope?" Ed asked.

"Because if you aren't, Ed could get you on it," I said.

"Following Steve is the only way to find Amy," Ed continued.

"We don't think so," said Marcy.

"We?" Ed asked.

"Me, and Kim. And Claudia."

"Gurl Power!" I said. I raised my glass to the women. "Right on, sisters!"

"You guys have crossed the line," Marcy said. "That dumbbell eavesdropping operation wasn't just stupid. It was criminal. Steve could press charges."

"And what if you guys are right?" Kim said. "If Steve really did kill Amy, what's to stop him from going after any of us?"

"Oh, I'm sure Marcy could take him," I said. "She could smash Steve right into the turnbuckle."

"We don't want to start a war with Steve," Marcy said. "We have a child to think about."

"Only half the time," I said.

That got their attention. They all stopped talking and looked at me. Kim's eight-year-old son was a sensitive subject. None of us ever dared to bring him up. Kim's divorce had been hell on the kid. The custody arrangement split his life in two; he was constantly being shuttlecocked between the dad in Petaluma and the lesbians in Berkeley.

"Excuse me?" Marcy said.

"Just editing for accuracy," I told her. "Kim's son is with you only half the time. The other half, he's with bio-dad."

I sucked down the rest of my vodka. The unmelted ice cubes bobbed against my lips like derelict barges tied up to a crumbling pier.

Marcy shifted. She inched her bulk forward and sat perched on the edge of the sofa, her elbows on her knees. She brought her hands together in front of her and interweaved her fingers lightly, as if to keep them from flying off and committing some act on their own.

I noticed then how very large her hands were, probably larger than my own. Kim remained slunk back into the couch, but her eyes kept flitting from Marcy to me. She rested one hand on the back of Marcy's meaty shoulder. Marcy turned to her and said, "I know. It's okay."

"It's normal that they'd be concerned about Joshua," Claudia said. "It would be negligent not to be."

"He's only with them half time," I persisted. "Isn't Zachary or Moonbeam or whatever his name is—"

"His name is Joshua," Claudia said.

Marcy started cracking her knuckles, one by one. She began to rhythmically sway forward and back, as if building up momentum to spring to her feet.

"Right. Jeremiah," I said. "And what's the bio-dad's name? You know—the fellow that Marcy outmanned?"

I felt a stiffening run through the crowd. But I surged ahead, my words now seeming to come from somewhere outside of me.

"The husband has some name that's not gender-specific. Something neutered."

"Better drop it, Max," Gator said.

"Kelly? Or is it Tracy? I know! Pat! Something."

Marcy had stopped swaying. Now she was still, and intent. She didn't blink. I swerved my focus down—down to the floor where Claudia sat.

"What you fail to grasp, Elly May," I said to Claudia. "What you fail to comprehend is, in fact, the very elemental concept that Steve is the prime suspect. And, as such, he must be under surveillance at all times."

I felt I had counted coup on her. I sat back in my club chair, and my knees fell comfortably open. I let my drinking arm hang down over the side of my chair, holding my tumbler by the rim. I described circles in the carpet with the bottom of my glass. The ice knocked around the glass like balls on a pool table.

"Is he still the prime suspect?" Claudia said, sitting up a little straighter. "We know more about Amy now. We know that her life was more complicated than we had suspected."

"Oh, that's right, Claudia," I said. "Blame the victim."

Jordi reached for the cigar that had been poking out of his shirt pocket. He peeled off the plastic wrapper. Ed handed him a lighter.

"I think surveillance is still valid," Ed said.

"The van thing was stupid," Marcy said.

"Oh, really?" I said. "And your idea was what? Do you have an alternative? You have one? Yes?"

"Yes," Marcy said. "We could mind our own damn business and let the cops do their job."

"Oh," I said. "Yes. The passive option."

She stood up and shifted her bulk onto one leg. She placed her hands delicately on her hips. She pushed that big heater of a belly out in front of her.

Claudia got up off the floor. She was getting out of Marcy's way.

"Don't you see what we're saying, Max?" Kim said. She looked like she was going to cry. "We need to back off of Steve."

"You're just afraid," I told Kim.

"Yes, we are," Claudia said. Now she was sitting in the window seat next to Wolfy, smashed up tight against him.

"And you are afraid," I bellowed at Claudia. "Afraid and weak."

I paused. No one made a move, or a sound. The stage belonged to me.

"You women," I said, and when I said *women* I held the W for a very long time. "You women are always bleating about how invincible you are. How right you are. When the truth is that you lack the stamina, the determination—you lack The Will—to see this thing through."

"It is okay, Max. We are just talking." It was Jordi's voice. I could hear him, but he was sitting across the room and he was getting a bit blurry.

"Yes, we are," I said. "We are talking. Women are good at talking. Talk. Talk. Talk. While we are out in the world— Getting Things Done—they are always clustered around their little coffee klatches talking."

"That's what you need, Max," Kim said. "I'll get you a cup of coffee." She got up and walked into the kitchen.

"Oh, thank you," I called to Kim's retreating back. "Thanks for the caregiving. You girls just focus in on the caregiving while we take all the risks. We will hunt down Amy's killer. We will take the risks. We will do what must needs to be done. We, being men."

"I think you've been hunting too much of that Grey Goose there, buddy," Ed said. He smiled amiably.

But Gator didn't smile. He was sitting on top of my dining-room table. Could the man never sit in a chair? He put his beer bottle down beside him—without a coaster, surely leaving a ring on my vintage walnut burl—and he rested his hands on his thighs. He looked all fresh-faced and lean and loose.

"You look like a guy who's been getting a lot of care lately," I said to Gator.

As soon as I said it, I realized how very right Claudia had been. I wanted Gator for myself. I was a fool. I whirled around on Claudia.

"It looks like you've been giving Gator a lot of care lately, Claudia," I said archly. "That kind of special treatment you reserve for . . . oh, no, wait, you give that special treatment to just about anybody who . . ."

Gator slid off the table, slow and deliberate, like honey pouring over the lip of a jar. He was on his feet. I didn't quite catch how he got from the dining room to where I was sitting. But I remember having the impression that I was in the hands of a professional.

There was a flush of activity—a sort of whooshing motion. I was surprised by how easily I was lifted out of my chair by the back of my shirt. I was pulled along the hallway, dragged on my knees. The pointed toes of my leather Moroccan slippers scraped across the hardwood floor until they left my feet. I looked back and saw them lying in the middle of the corridor, soles upturned and pigeon-toed. They looked like the shoes of a man who had been shot dead and left facedown in a sand dune.

The bright sun assaulted my eyes. I heard a ripping sound and realized that the seams of my shirt were tearing. My top button popped off and disappeared between the planks of the back deck.

And after that I could smell grass and it was fresh like

new-mown hay, although I'd never actually smelled new-mown hay.

I could hear the birds twittering and an airplane passing high overhead. I felt Gator's knee in my back, between my shoulder blades. My nose was digging into the sod. I tasted the wet, black dirt in my mouth and prayed to all the gods in Olympus and Valhalla that the dogs hadn't relieved themselves on that one spot.

Gator had my right arm bent at the elbow and pinioned backward between my shoulder blades. It hurt, mainly at my wrist from the way he held my hand in a torturous, twisted position. He squeezed and my fingers practically touched the inside of my wrist as if I were crippled up with cerebral palsy.

I spit the dirt out of my mouth and turned my face to the side. Gator pushed on my head, impressing my cheek into the turf.

I asked Gator to release me. He pushed my face further into the soft earth.

Ed's gnarly, Teva sandal–clad feet appeared in my, rather close-bracketed, view. This horror was soon replaced by a vision of Jordi's loafers, the upper overhung with rolls of thick white tube sock.

I closed my eyes and wished with all my heart for Wolfy's desert boots to be there when I reopened them. They weren't. However, I could hear Wolfy's voice. I was struck by how very commanding he sounded. Krautish. I vowed then and there to, in future, take every Wagner part that came my way.

"I can't let him up, Wolf," Gator was saying. "Not if he's going to come up swinging."

Wolfy walked around to the other side of me so I could see

him. He dropped down on all fours. He laid his head down on the grass. We were face-to-face.

"Please," Wolfy said. "Please, Max. Be a pacifist now."

"I am a pacifist, Wolf," I said to him, through squeezed goldfish lips.

"You have to promise, Max," Wolfy said. "Be calm. We are your friends."

And as he said that, Gator gave my wrist an extra little tug—just short of snapping it—to let me know what good friends we were.

"I promise," I said.

Gator lifted his hand off my head and his knee off my back. My arm was still wrenched up onto my back; the forced angle held it there like meat on a hook. I tried to move it, but the nerves were dead. I shifted my weight and let gravity tug my arm off my back. It crashed onto the ground beside me. It felt as though it were detached, as though I was lying next to my own amputated arm. I rolled over onto my back and looked up at the sky. It was gray and black and purple, a bruised El Greco sky.

Colonel came pounding over and licked my face. Asta stood on my chest barking, trying to tell me to pull myself together. The men crouched down, and sat on the grass around me. Jordi and Wolf each took an arm and pulled me up to sit, once more, among them.

"Is there something between you and Claudia?" I asked Gator.

"Yes," Gator said.

"Claudia and I are best friends," I said. "We have been

through seventeen years and three marriages together. I love her."

"I care about her too," Gator said.

"How could you?" I cried. "How long have you known her? Six months?"

"I would never hurt Claudia, Max," Gator said.

He unknotted his kerchief from around his neck, handed it to me. I used it to wipe the dirt off my face.

34

After they left, Wolfy drew me a bath. He was muttering something about how I'd better get myself cleaned up. I kept a bottle of bubble bath on the shelf above the tub. He grabbed it and, with a brisk shake, dumped half the bottle into the water thundering out of the faucet. The bubbles frothed up like blooming algae.

I went downstairs, shambled around the kitchen. The dishwasher was running. The next round of small plates and cutlery and dirty glasses stood waiting, neatly scraped and rinsed and stacked along the counter. I picked through the champagne flutes, arranged in their own quadrant, and poured all the remainders into one big tumbler. I brought it up to the bathroom with me, holding on to it firmly as I lowered myself into the tub.

Wolfy picked up the bud vase from the bath-side table so he could sit there. He put the vase on the floor, and absent-mindedly pulled out the one bloodred rose it had held. He had clipped the rose that morning out of my garden. He had wanted the house to look nice for our guests. Now he sat on the little table with the rose in his hands. He tore the petals off, one by one, and dropped them onto the thick drifts of bubbles. The petals smelled like pepper.

I laid back, my head surrendered onto the lip of the tub. I stretched a wet washcloth over my face.

"I just can't keep up," I said from under the soggy shroud.

"With Claudia?" Wolf said.

"With Claudia's love life," I told him. I pulled the cloth off my face and sat up a little. "It was just the other day that you told me she was sleeping with Larry again. And now this."

"Gator."

"Why is she doing this?" I said. "Why is she disrupting my life like this?"

"How can this make trouble for you?"

"I don't know whose side I'm supposed to be on," I told him. "First she wants me to ally with her against Larry. Fine, I can do that. Then she makes a secret treaty with Larry. And all the while, I'm bashing Larry while she's sleeping with him. And now she brings in Gator as this third column."

"Claudia wants to tell you what has happened. She is waiting for you to be in a better mood."

"Right," I said. "My mood. That's the problem."

"Then I will tell you."

I put the washcloth back over my face and rolled my hand, signaling him to speak. Wolf told me that Claudia broke it off with Larry after he confessed to her: he had sex with Amy.

It happened more than a year earlier—right after Amy had the brief fling with Jordi. Amy came to Larry one afternoon when he was alone in the dog park with Asta. She asked Larry if he'd help her hang some curtains. He did.

They drank some wine. They let things go too far. Larry was stricken with guilt and regret before he even got his socks back on. He liked Amy. And he loved Claudia. He didn't want to hurt either of them. It happened just once.

Foolishly, Larry confessed the whole thing to Claudia. He'd been able to keep it a secret for more than a year. To him, it had been a nonincident. But after Amy disappeared, the indiscretion with her had taken on a new gravitas. He felt guilty about it. He couldn't carry the weight of it anymore. He told Claudia.

It had already been a stretch for Claudia to take him back. So when Larry told her about Amy, Claudia threw him back out of the house. She tossed his pajamas into the fireplace, doused them with lighter fluid, and tossed a match onto the crumpled heap of blue and white stripes. All the while, she was drinking gin. Then she started dialing the phone. Gator was the first person to pick up. The rest was tawdry and predictable.

"I think we need to diagram this," I told Wolfy.

"For Amy, she has affairs that go from Jordi, to Larry, to Gator."

"And Claudia tries to have an affair with Jordi—but that's an incomplete. Then she lands back on Larry. And now Gator."

"Help me with the math," I said. "Which one got Amy pregnant?"

"Not Larry." Wolfy was certain of it. I agreed with him.

"Claudia must hate Larry so much right now," I said, sitting up in the tub. I reached for my champagne. "That would explain her going overboard with Gator. Did you see that costume she was wearing?"

"It was not her typical style," Wolf said.

"No, it was hideous. It was like something you'd expect to see at a bluegrass festival."

"She wears his clothes so we know they sleep together," Wolfy said.

"Yes. Like high school. Next thing, she'll show up with his underwear on her head."

"I think you are more concerned about Claudia than about what is happening between you and me," Wolf said.

"Oh, please, Wolf. You know how fond I am of you."

"Fond of is the kind of thing you have for a cat, or for a meal you like to eat."

"What do you want me to say?"

"You can say to all those guys today that you love Claudia. But you cannot say this word to me."

He plucked off the last of the rose petals. He tossed the bare, thorny stem into the wastebasket and stood up.

"If I have to, Max, I can tolerate you seeing another man. I know we are not married and we live very far apart. But if you are in love with a woman, I don't know what to do."

He got up and left, drawing the door shut behind him.

"I don't know what to do either," I said to the empty room.

35

The next morning Wolf got up early and went to Berkeley. He was meeting Jordi and Ed at the dog park. I was just making coffee when the doorbell rang. It was Claudia. She was alone. She wore black sunglasses, a black turtleneck, slim black slacks, and no earrings. Her hair was up, bound in a cream-colored scarf.

"I want to apologize, Max," she said. We were sitting at the kitchen table. Asta was lying under it, his chin resting on his folded paws. She poured cream into her coffee.

"I've been so angry at Larry," she said. "I'm just so angry."

"I suppose I was drunk," I conceded.

"You're my best friend," she said. She reached across the table and held my hand. "We'll always be best friends."

"Sometimes I wish we could live together. Just us. You and me."

I felt awkward as soon as I'd admitted it.

"Sometimes I do too," she told me. "But that wouldn't work. You can't have two vain hysterics sharing the same house."

"Or the same bed," I ventured.

"You're hurting Wolfy," she said.

"I know. I'm a bastard."

"I get tired of consoling your victims, Max."

"Has he been crying on your shoulder?"

"He loves you."

"I love him. Everything about him. He is . . . ," and I reached for the words. "He is a good man."

"He thinks you're using him for sex."

"I am," I said. "And he's using me for sex."

"Promise me you'll treat him with more consideration."

"Well, I don't know how to do that. I'll try. But only if you'll promise me one thing." She nodded. "Don't dress like that again."

"You mean the plaid shirt?"

"And all the turquoise, and the blue jeans. That's the way it starts. It's a slippery slide. Then, one day, you wake up wearing a peasant skirt and Guatemalan backpack."

"And a fleece jacket?" she said.

"In the more acute cases. Yes," I told her.

I took a serviette and dabbed it under her eyes. She had been tearing, just a little. She settled back into the chair on the sunny side of the table. She looked outside to the morning sun burning the night fog off the roses. I poured her some coffee. I made us an omelet.

She told me all about Larry—his steady, patient campaign to regain her trust. He had gotten back into her bed. That was the beachhead. Then he gradually redug the trench that was the routine of their married life. He'd bring over a movie. Then he'd stay the night. Or he'd drop by to trim the hedges. Then he'd stay the night. Or he'd come looking for his book, or his coffee cup, or his missing brown sock. Then he'd stay the night.

Eventually, if he was diligent, Larry would have made it back inside—back into Neuschwanstein, back into their marriage. But, of course, he blew it. He confessed. I found it inexplicable. And sloppy.

It had been months since that night Larry told Claudia he was leaving. In that time they had reconciled, fought, and split again. Now Larry was just another one of those estranged husbands who live alone in a barren apartment without a picture on the wall, without a bath mat next to the tub. He blew his nose on toilet paper because he'd never think to buy tissues. He used paper towels for table napkins. He didn't have a laundry hamper. He didn't have a toothbrush caddy. He didn't have potted plants, throw cushions, candles, or potpourri. He dwelled in his dark apartment like a bear in a cave. But he didn't mind that. He didn't miss the amenities—he missed his wife.

In the meantime, Claudia had stopped thinking of herself as Larry's wife. At first, when he deserted her, she was enraged. She tried to hurt him with Jordi. After he hurt her a second time, she tried to forget him with Gator.

And always lurking in the foreground of Claudia's kitchen-sink drama was the true horror: Amy's disappearance. We searched for Amy. We turned over rocks looking for clues, for reasons. All we found were unsavory revelations. Amy and Jordi. Amy and Larry.

"Claudia," I told her. "It's understandable that Larry had that . . . that moment, with Amy."

"Because she's so attractive," Claudia said.

"That's not it."

"I know," Claudia said. Her voice sounded tired. "It's because Amy's different. She is so different from me."

I picked up Claudia's pack of cigarettes. I lit one and handed it to her. I thought about having one myself, but stopped. *I Pagliacci* was heading into full rehearsals and I couldn't take chances with my voice. I touched the silk scarf around my neck to make sure my throat was properly covered.

"It's not a comparison with you, Claudia," I told her. "Larry wasn't making a choice. He wasn't even thinking. He just did it because he could."

"You make him sound like a barnyard animal," she said.

"Yes. It's all just instinct. Men are programmed to have sex at every opportunity."

"That's a cliché," she said.

She put her cigarette in the ashtray and started clearing the breakfast dishes. She scraped the dishes and rinsed them before arranging them in the dishwasher. She always managed to get twice as many dishes in there as I ever could.

"Here's what I think," I told her. "I think Jordi rebuffed Amy and she was reeling. She was thinking how could *he* reject *me*?"

"The big mystery was how could she sleep with him in the first place. But go on."

"Sure," I agreed. I decided not to mention that Claudia was ready to sleep with Jordi herself. "So, Amy is angry and hurt."

"And humiliated," Claudia added.

"Right. Jordi has humiliated her. She is spurned."

"Yeah. Burned."

"No. Spurned."

"Same thing."

"Amy is pacing around her living room. Raging. She wants revenge."

I got up and paced, and raged, and worried my hands like I was washing them. It was very Lady Macbeth.

"Amy looks out her window." I stopped and looked out the window, shading my eyes with my hand. "And there, across the street, there is Larry. He is in the dog park with Asta. And he's alone."

"So she goes over there and lures him into the house," Claudia said. She frowned.

"And seduces him," I said, easing back into the chair and crossing my legs.

"Why?"

"Revenge."

"Revenge on whom?" Claudia asked.

"Two men," I said. "Steve." I picked up the saltshaker and placed it near the edge of the table. "And Jordi." I picked up the pepper shaker and set it next to the salt.

"I don't know," she said.

"Why are you unconvinced," I said. "Regard—Steve and Jordi."

I swept my outstretched hand toward the salt and pepper shakers.

"Yes, that is a compelling demonstration," she allowed. "But maybe Amy was just looking for sex."

"Sex is never just sex," I said. "Just look at opera. Look at theater, at literature. The theme occurs all the time. Sex is revenge. It's an old standard on every playlist. It's like, say, mistakenly killing your father and sleeping with your mother. Oedipus."

"Yes," Claudia said. "Or, you go to somebody's house for dinner and they serve you your own kids in the paella. Titus."

"Or, you find out that your wife has been sleeping with other men," I said, and I stopped.

"And you kill her and make it look like she was kidnapped," Claudia finished it. "Steve."

We sat quietly for a while. Her image, the image I had of Amy, came to me—her skin, tan, smooth, the easy way she'd stroke my shoulder, laughing, a flash of her face smiling, a blur, turning three-quarter profile, long fingers resting on my thigh, long eyelashes fluttering shut and opening brown eyes, sunlight, amber liquid, gold flecks, the curve of a collarbone, her voice, my name. The pieces of Amy persisted. She seemed to occupy the room as surely as me, as surely as Claudia.

"Amy wasn't who we thought she was," I said.

"I don't care what she did," Claudia said. "She didn't deserve this."

Claudia sat down and crossed her legs. She looked at the cigarette between her fingers. Her hand was draped over her knee, lifeless. Her crossed leg dangled, absently rocking back and forth like the pendulum of a clock that needed winding. Something swept over her face, some thought, and left a crooked smile in its wake.

"Max, I've got it," she said, words tumbling over one another like a crowd stampeding a fire exit. "What if there was a third man. A boyfriend? And this third man is the one. He's the one she falls in love with."

"You mean a man besides Jordi and Larry?" I said. "You're back on that secret lover kick."

"Amy was on a mission, Max. She was looking for a man. We already know that she tried out two of them."

"Why not try another?" I said.

"Maybe she found the one she wanted. The third man."

We both laughed. I felt something very close to relief.

Claudia and I started piecing it all together. We reasoned that wives run off with their boyfriends every day. But how often does a husband, a cuckold, kill his wife? The odds argued for the bloodless scenario.

"Amy could be off with that man right now," I said. "Maybe she's hiding because she doesn't want to share the baby with Steve."

"It's not that far-fetched," Claudia said. "Steve is a dick. But can you really see him killing Amy?"

I could not. I could not see Steve killing Amy, not when I really tried to picture it. The act, to hammer the life out of a person—it was beyond my imagination.

The morning sun rained through the window, lighting up the swirling motes above our coffee cups. The kitchen smelled like toast. I heard the neighbor's car start up. And I couldn't picture anyone I knew murdering another human being. Not even Steve.

It was settled. I tapped the tops of the salt and pepper shakers like they were good boys. Claudia poured us more coffee, the last drops.

We took our coffee out to the back garden. We arranged the two chaise lounges next to each other so as to align with the sun's trajectory. I brought a stack of old decorating magazines and set it between us and we started working our way through them.

Wolf came home later in the day, around midafternoon.

"Steve is selling her car," he said.

"What?" Claudia asked, sitting up and taking off her sunglasses. "Amy's car?"

"Yes," said Wolf. "Jordi and Ed saw him early this morning. He drove it away and then he came back and it was clean and shiny. He put a sign in the window. For sale, $5,500. What is OBO?"

"Or Best Offer," Claudia answered. "People say that when they want to sell something fast."

She held out her hand to Wolfy. He took it, and sat on the chaise beside her.

"I'm going to see if he listed it," I said, going to fetch my laptop.

"Is it there, Max?" Claudia asked, tapping her fingernails on the arm of the chaise.

She flung herself out of the chaise, came and stood over me.

"Here it is," I said. "2004, VW Beetle. Green. Only 6,000 miles. Perfect condition."

"Look at the photo," Claudia said. She pointed her cigarette at the screen. "In the background. That's the dog park."

"How long has Amy been gone?" I asked.

"Four months," Claudia said.

"He knows she's not coming home," Wolfy said. "He knows for sure."

I felt a hollow deep in my guts. I felt myself falling. The fall was steep, because I'd been so high just an hour before.

"Yeah, that's our asshole," Claudia said. "It says right here, call Steve."

Claudia sat back down on the chaise. She leaned forward, let her head hang down. Her face had gone white as Wonder Bread, and her hands hung limp. Wolfy went to get her a glass of water. He came back with a glass of water, and the telephone.

"Who are you calling?" I demanded.

He didn't answer. He looked over my shoulder at the classified ad on the screen. He dialed the phone.

"Hello," Wolfy said into the phone. "I am calling about zee Volkswagen you have for sale. Yes, I can hold a moment."

He pressed the phone against his chest. "I'm holding," he said to us.

"What are you doing?" I whispered. I started pacing the deck. I made little karate chops with my hands as I whispered, "He knows you!"

"He doesn't know me," Wolf whispered. "Whenever I am in the park, always he is at work."

"What about today?"

Wolfy held his finger up to his lips. He raised the phone back up to his ear.

"Yes. I'm here," he said. "Yes. Tomorrow at five P.M. I take the University Street. Yes. I can find you. See you then."

He hung up.

"Tomorrow I go meet Steve to test-drive the car," Wolfy said.

"Oh, my God," Claudia said. "Why?"

"He saw you today," I said.

"I was in the van getting beers when he pulled up. And, besides, I was wearing a hat and glasses."

"I don't care if you were wearing a fucking burka!" I shrieked. "He will recognize you!"

"I want to ask him why he is selling it. And maybe I see something in his face when he answers. Maybe I find out something."

"You'll find out that he's dangerous," I said.

"You'll find out the hard way," Claudia said.

"What will he do?" Wolfy asked. "Kill me?"

36

I couldn't sleep that night. Wolfy was the one who would actually be in danger. And yet he fell asleep before midnight. I chose to stay up, worrying.

I was sprawled in the Eames recliner, wearing a pair of polka-dot pajamas and an argyle cardigan. I missed my silk kimono mightily.

The table next to my armrest was outfitted with the TV remote and a brandy snifter and a bottle of Calvados—I'd grown tired of getting up to refill my glass.

I was watching *A Place in the Sun* on the classic movie channel. Montgomery Clift was playing George Eastman, an eager social climber who has his eye on his wealthy uncle's business. Monty gets a summer job at the uncle's factory so he can learn the ropes, starting at the bottom rung. But along the way he gets entangled with one of the factory girls, one of the girls working on the line. Alice Tripp, that is, Shelley Winters, trips up old George all right. She gets pregnant, just as he's finally made his big entrée into high society and wins the heart of the socialite Angela Vickers. Angela is all moonbeams and magic millionaire dust. He's bedazzled by her money, and by the violet sparkle in her eyes—she is Elizabeth Taylor. And poor old Alice Tripp, who had looked kind of cute on the assembly line in her smock, now looks like a pudgy-faced proletarian lump. Not only that, Alice has decided to play it inconvenient. She expects young George to do the right thing. She expects him to marry her.

"He kills her," Baba said. She was lying on the divan twirling one of her forelock braids round her middle finger.

"Must you ruin it for me," I said. I'd already seen the movie three times.

She shrugged. I could hear the tinkling of the gold coins that were fastened into Baba's braids. The coins—some of them dated back to the 1870s—clinked against the rows of knuckle-duster rings she wore on all her fingers.

It was twilight in the movie. George had lured Alice Tripp down to the lake. They were on the dock and he was coaxing her into a rowboat and the black-and-white picture had gone mostly gray, pale. Shelley Winters was telling Montgomery Clift that it wouldn't be so bad. They'd have the baby and they'd scrimp and get by. She was wearing a cheap sack coat, buttoned up to conceal her illegitimate pregnancy. It wasn't working. She looked as big as a double-wide trailer.

Clift coaxed her into the boat. She was smiling at him. He just kept rowing. He rowed and rowed. He rowed to the center of the lake, to the deepest point. She looked at him quizzically, still smiling, just a little. She trusted him. She looked like a lamb.

"Stupid," Baba spat. "He is bad man. Anyone can see. She should not have got in boat."

"Well, it wouldn't be much of a story if she didn't get in the boat, Baba."

"Why all these women get in boat? Stupid!"

"What all these women?" I said. I turned to look at her. I waved my hand toward the TV and said, "It's just Shelley Winters. He's not going to row Liz Taylor out there too."

"The pregnant women. Sometimes I think you are *dili*, Maximo," she said, calling me retarded in Rom.

"There's just one pregnant woman in this movie, you senile old crow."

"Not all the story is in that box," she said, pointing an accusing finger at the television set.

37

"Take my telephone," Jordi told Wolf. "Put it in your front pocket, under your jacket, like this."

Jordi and Wolfy were standing in the middle of Jordi's living room. Jordi tucked his cell phone into the left front pocket of Wolfy's shirt. Then he closed Wolfy's Windbreaker over it and zipped it up. The rest of us—Ed and Gator, and me and Claudia, and Kim and Marcy—were scattered around the room, watching.

"We'll be listening on my phone," Gator said to Wolfy. "We'll be with you every minute. We'll hear everything you say, and everything Steve says. And we'll record the whole thing."

Gator picked up a miniature digital recorder. He handed it to Wolfy to inspect.

"But Steve might hear you," Wolf said. "He'll hear you on the telephone."

"This is nuts," Marcy said.

"You guys keep fucking around," Kim said. "Somebody else is going to get killed."

"It's okay," Ed said.

"It's not okay, Ed," Marcy said. "Steve is onto you dopes. You're trying to corner him. What do you think he'll do if he's cornered? He's already killed Amy."

Gator stood up from the coffee table that he was sitting on. He laid his hands out in front of him, palms down, as if he were smoothing out a bolt of silk.

"Marcy," Gator said. "If you and Kim keep beaking off like this, you're going to make Wolf nervous. And if he's nervous, Steve will sense it."

"Everybody has to play it cool," Ed said. "This is like smuggling contraband. If you're cool, they don't suspect you. It's your aura, man. Confidence."

Marcy and Kim folded their arms across their chests. Claudia lit a cigarette and averted her eyes. She pretended to stare out the window. Then she got up and went out to the front porch. The other two women followed her.

"I thought they'd never leave," I said.

"We'll stay quiet on our end," Gator told Wolf. "And just to make sure, I'll press this button on my phone. This is the mute function. No sound will come from the phone in your pocket."

Wolfy didn't speak much after that. And when he did it was in terse answers to direct questions. He went to the bathroom twice. Then he said he was ready.

He got into the car we rented for the operation. It was a nondescript compact: a white Dodge Neon. We all stood on the porch and watched him drive away. Then we gathered back in Jordi's living room. We placed Gator's phone in the center of the room, on the coffee table. It was on mute. The line was open to the telephone in Wolfy's pocket.

Wolfy was humming tunelessly. In between meandering fugues, he tried to clear his throat with stabbing coughs. He announced out loud that he had reached Steve's house. He tried to parallel park. It took him three attempts.

He walked up the steps of Steve's porch.

"He's got to stop that idiot humming," Ed said.

We could hear Steve open the door. Wolfy managed some kind of fumbling introduction. Steve told him to wait on the porch. He said that he would get the keys. Steve's voice came back on. He told Wolfy to come around to the driveway with him.

Wolfy told him the car looked like new. Steve said it was his wife's car and she hardly ever drove it.

"So why are you selling this car?" Wolfy said.

"My wife doesn't drive it anymore," Steve said.

"She doesn't like it?" Wolfy asked.

"Here, you can drive," Steve said.

We heard the sound of jingling keys, then a rustling against the phone like Wolfy was waving his arm in the air. We heard the keys clattering onto the driveway. There was more rustling. I heard Wolfy exhale as he bent over. "Okay," he said.

The two car doors opened and closed, one just after the other. The ambient noise on the phone line changed. It sounded contained.

"Oh, it's automatic transmission," Wolfy said. "I forgot your ad said automatic."

"That's good," Ed said. "That's nice, the business about automatic. Sounds very natural, don't you think?"

Jordi and Gator and I agreed it sounded natural. Claudia and Kim and Marcy all looked at one another and made the

222 · Cynthia Robinson

same face—lips pressed into a crinkle of crinoline, eyes rolling.

"My wife prefers an automatic. It's easier to parallel park on hills," said Steve.

"What will your wife drive when you sell this car?" Wolfy asked.

"Follow this exit ramp. South on I-80," Steve told him.

"No," said Jordi. "He should not get on the freeway."

"Where is Steve taking him?" Kim asked.

"Where are we going?" Wolfy asked Steve.

"Let's take it down to the warehouse district around the Oakland docks. There's less traffic there," Steve said. "Less chance of getting run into."

"Why are you worried of someone running into?" Wolfy said. My heart started to beat hard in my chest. I felt faint.

"Turn right here," Steve said.

"But there's nothing out here," Wolfy said. He tried to make his voice sound light, unconcerned.

"Pull over," Steve said.

"What?" Wolfy asked. "By this empty field?"

"Pull over," Steve said.

I could hear that Steve was smiling as he said it. I'm sure the guards in Bergen-Belsen smiled as they told people to get into the trucks, as they told them they were taking them to the showers.

We all edged in closer to the phone. Claudia lit another cigarette and handed the pack to Gator. He lit one and handed the pack to Jordi. Jordi pulled out two cigarettes, one for him and one for Ed, and lit them both. I thought for a moment of

I Pagliacci, then I grabbed the cigarette pack and lit one for myself. The room was engulfed in smoke.

"Where are you from, Wolfgang?" Steve asked.

"Why are you taking the keys?" Wolfy asked.

"Oh, my God, oh, my God," Kim said.

"I'll just hold on to the keys while we chat," Steve said.

I grabbed Ed by the sleeve of his army jacket.

"Where are they?" I demanded.

Ed said he didn't know. He couldn't know. Gator was saying something about how he should have put a global positioning device on Wolf.

"So where are you from?" Steve asked again.

"Baden," said Wolf. "Originally. My parents are still in Baden. But now I live in Berlin."

"And are you on vacation here?" asked Steve.

"Ja."

"Do you have friends here?"

"Some. A few friends," said Wolfy. "Shall we go—continue the driving?"

"Who are your friends?" said Steve. "Maybe I know them."

Gator had been crouching by the coffee table on one knee. He stood up and pulled his car keys out of the pocket of his jeans. He looked at Jordi. Jordi stood up.

"I know someone who goes to Berlin pretty regularly," Steve continued. "He's an opera singer."

There was a silence on the phone. Wolfy wasn't even moving, we could tell because his shirt wasn't rubbing against the telephone receiver. I thought I could hear his heart beating.

"Maybe you know him," said Steve. "His name is Max Bravo."

Wolfy didn't say a word. And still, he didn't move. We heard a car door open, then close. A moment later another door opened—it sounded closer.

"Get out," Steve said.

"Oh, no, no," Kim cried.

"Get out," Steve repeated. We heard the metallic click of Wolfy's seat belt.

Marcy walked to the front door, pulled it open. A bright beam of sunlight shot through the door frame. Marcy unhooked that fist-sized ring of keys that she kept on her belt. Gator held his hand up to her, signaling her to hold steady. Everyone stood still, straining to hear what was coming over the phone connection.

Steve's voice came back onto the phone. It was clear and close.

"You can tell Max Bravo," Steve said. "And you can tell the rest of the clowns to stay away from me."

We heard the driver seat slide back on its metal runner and land with a thud. The door closed. The engine started up. The tires crunched over some gravel. The sound of the engine got softer until it disappeared.

"He's gone," Wolfy said into the phone. "Please come get me."

38

Ed insisted on driving Wolfy to the airport. We needed the van because we had to take everyone. They wanted to see him off, to make one of those histrionic farewell scenes so typical among tribal peoples—Gypsies and Inuits and Grateful Deadheads. There was a lot of clinging, and open weeping, and proffering of packages filled with smoked meat sandwiches for the plane ride, as if the Lufthansa food wasn't comestible.

I didn't cry. It would have been obvious that I was crying for myself, for my own pathetic, and deserved, loneliness. So I performed. I hugged Wolfy. It was awkward—the kind of a hug where you pat the other man on the back. I pulled away and gave him a hearty handshake and admonished him to take good care. I said I'd be in Europe again in the fall. Until then, we'd e-mail. And telephone.

I didn't mean to look in his eyes, but I did. And it struck me then, very hard, that he really was getting on a plane and that I'd be going home to an empty house. That night I would be sleeping alone in my bed. I'd reach over and there'd be nothing. No one.

His eyes were such a soft green, such a rare color. I pulled him close to me and I put my lips on his. I looked into his eyes.

39

"The Catalan is leaving too," Baba told me.

She was sitting at my dining table, her tarot cards laid out in front of her in a cross formation. One of my cigarettes burned in an ashtray on the table. The ash was curled down, long and unbroken.

"If you're going to cadge my cigarettes you could at least smoke them and not leave them burning up," I said. "They cost money. And what are you talking about?"

"The Catalan," she said. "He goes to his woman. She waits on a beach. The water is warm, very aqua. There are palm trees."

I was looking at the Internet on my laptop. It was 11:00 A.M. and I was still in pajamas, lying on the divan. Since Wolfy left, I'd stopped dressing. I hadn't stepped out of the house in three days.

An e-mail came in. It was from Jordi. The subject line read: Farewell my friends.

"Well, aren't you the clever old girl," I said to Baba.

Jordi wrote that he'd be leaving in a week. He hadn't wanted to talk about it when everyone was so distracted, what with stalking Steve and nearly getting Wolfy vivisected—or whatever it was we thought we were doing.

"He's asked that we join him for drinks," I told Baba. "To say good-bye."

"I know," she said.

She finally took a drag on her cigarette. She turned over another card and upon inspecting it, thrust the corners of her lips downward and waggled her head from side to side. She scooped up the cards and put them away, tying them into a red kerchief.

I watched her and couldn't help but feel some sort of familial affection. They say that Socrates was guided by a spirit whom he called his daimon. The creature revealed itself only to him. I wondered if Socrates' daimon was a meddlesome old harpy who tried to run his life, and guzzle all his booze, and steal all his cigarettes.

"You should think about getting married now too," she said.

"Preposterous," I exclaimed. I closed my computer and got up to shower. I decided I would initiate a new policy of dressing before noon.

When I came back into the living room to practice Tonio's duet with Nedda, I noticed something on my piano bench. I thought Baba had left one of her tarot cards. I picked it up and saw it was a photograph.

It was a young Gypsy girl. She looked Kalderash, the tribe of my father's family.

When I turned thirteen, Baba began mailing my mother photographs just like this at regular intervals. They were always young Kalderash girls—no older than twelve or thirteen. Baba got the photos from her one surviving sister who still lived in Romania. The sister was anxious to broker a marriage for me. She saw me as a superior, if somewhat unorthodox, prospect. My father's family was well respected and while my mother's family was unknown—and *gadje*— they were wealthy. The photos came in envelopes accompanied by letters written by a *gadjo* scribe that the families hired to enumerate the girls' dowries. A typical dowry would consist of two horses, a 1978 Lada, various mufflers and exhaust pipes, an acetylene blowtorch, a collection of ornamental plastic citrus trees (for décor), and a trousseau of frilly quilts, pillow shams, and bed skirts. Sometimes there'd be a big item thrown in, like a camper van with oak veneer kitchen cabinetry and teal and coral upholstery on the breakfast banquette. In these cases, there would be a photo of the girl standing in front of the camper van.

My mother didn't respond to any of these offers. But they kept coming until I grew up and went away to study music and performance at UCLA. Mother didn't throw them away either. She couldn't bear to. I think the applications for marriage touched her. The girls were so young, and they looked straight at the camera with such trusting expressions, such good intentions. The carefully crafted letters were dignified and earnest. And the fact that the tribe wanted me back— even though my father had left us and these people had never even met me—was very moving.

The girl in the picture looked to be at least twenty years old. But I knew she had to be thirteen because she was wearing her hair uncovered, without a scarf, the style of an unmarried woman. She was beautiful. That's the way most of them start out. Then they have eight children by the time they are twenty-five, and that takes a toll.

I tried to remember if I'd seen her photo before. I knew that there was a metal box full of photos like this one upstairs, in the attic. Perhaps Baba had been nosing around up there and found this girl. I knew what Baba was up to, of course. She wanted me to marry this child. Perhaps then I could rejoin the tribe, and the *mahrime*, the pollution, of my deracinated birth would be erased.

I looked at the Kalderash girl in the photo. She had eyes like my father's: sly and promising. I actually felt drawn to her. Then I reminded myself that she was a child—a child no doubt living in some squalid caravan in a forest outside of Sintesti.

I propped the photo up against a vase full of lilies on top of the piano. The noontime sun beat its beams through the south-facing window. It struck the blue glass of the vase and backlit the Kalderash girl, making the photo look pale and ethereal. The radiant light seemed to burn from somewhere inside her.

40

We all met at a saloon in Berkeley to have a final drink with Jordi. All his possessions fit easily into his carry-on bag. He had sold the rest—the bamboo and wicker furniture, the Martin Denny albums, the tiki glasses, and the candles that enshrined the photograph of his fiancée.

His dog, Cecilia, was already drugged and passed out in her crate. He planned to fly just to Paris with her that day. Then continue on to Barcelona by car with a friend.

"I wish I could stay," Jordi said. "Steve must be punished for what he has done."

"The Realtor was there again yesterday," Claudia told the group. "Stephanie Saint Claire."

"Suspicious," I said.

"She wasn't there about business," Claudia said.

"What?" asked Jordi.

"It was like they were close," Claudia answered. "Too close."

"Steve put his arm around her," Gator said.

"Around her waist," Claudia said. "Then he tried to kiss her."

"But she pushed him away," Gator said.

"Only because she was aware that we were across the street," Claudia said.

There was more. Just that morning a handyman arrived at Steve's house and started replacing the three or four rotten boards in the picket fence. A gardener came and cleaned up the yard and filled the flower beds with begonias surrounded by cedar bark chips. Curb appeal, Ed noted. They were preparing to put the house on the market.

Once Steve was out of the house, any opportunity to discover evidence there would be lost. Someone, I think it was Marcy, pointed out that the police had already gone over the house thoroughly. If there were anything there, she reasoned, they would have found it.

"I talked with McGuire this morning," Ed said. "He asked me if Amy ever talked about her work."

"What does that mean?" Jordi asked. "Her work?"

"I don't know," Ed said. "Amy never talked about her work with me, so McGuire just dropped it."

"It's nothing," Jordi said. "Those cops have no more ideas. They just ask desperate questions."

"Why would they, Jordi?" Marcy said testily. "McGuire's not an asshole. If he asked about Amy's work, there's a reason."

"Okay, we're getting off track," Gator said. "The cops can do whatever they want. But we need to keep our focus. On Steve."

Gator reached into his pocket and produced an object the size of a grape. He explained that it was a surveillance camera, and it was integral to an elaborate plan that he had worked out on his own. Gator described how we would install the camera somewhere in Steve's house, in some key location.

"Hold on," said Marcy. "Just how are we supposed to get inside Steve's house to install the camera?"

"Let's not get hung up on tactical details," Gator told her.

He explained that the video from the camera would transmit to a single, dedicated workstation. He called it a "live feed."

"Why does it have to go just to one workstation?" Marcy asked.

"Steve has already busted us twice," Gator said. "This has to be absolutely tight. Secure."

"We have to lock it down," Ed said.

"Just like back on the Mekong Delta, right, Ed?" Marcy said.

"This plan is genius," Jordi said. "The technology is correct."

We took Jordi and Cecilia to the BART station. We watched him descend, standing on the escalator, a suitcase in his hand, the dog whimpering in her crate on the step below him. It was an odd sensation to see him steadily lowered down into the ground, below our view, cutting off at the knees, then the waist, and the neck. Finally his head dropped out of sight. And he was gone.

We'd gotten raging drunk at the saloon and were left in that aimless state that daytime drinking locks you into. I had driven over the bridge that afternoon, and I couldn't possibly drive back. I walked up the hill with Claudia to spend the night at her house.

She and I sat in her living room. It was satisfying to feel

engulfed in the cavernous space, to lie on her twin couches drinking wine, watching the panoramic sweep of Claudia's expensive view; the bay, the bridges, San Francisco reclining on its precious spit of land.

The sun fainted into the west, hovering in the ocean's salty breath. It entered the low-hanging clouds, dropping through layers of mist, and it broke apart into horizontal bands of glowing orange—stacked, like an Aztec pyramid. Then the bands fused again into a single bright orb. It blazed carnelian, and melted into the bay, shimmering silver and seeping red—blood pouring into water.

The city lights blinked on, one by one, until the entire peninsula sparkled in the carmine sunset.

I told Claudia that I understood why she found Gator appealing. But, I warned, he was beneath her.

"That's where you're wrong, Max," she said.

"Oh," I said, waving a speared martini olive. "Is he actually the son of a corporate robber baron?"

"No," she said. "He is a robber baron."

"Do you mean he has money?" I asked.

"He has so much money he doesn't know what to do with it," she said.

"Poppycock," I cried.

"Have you ever heard of the *Wraith of Hellfire*?" she asked.

"Isn't that a game? One of those video games with dragons and explosions and broadswords?"

"Yes," she said. She was draped across her couch in a long white sheath of a nightgown. She looked like the exquisite corpse of a silent movie star, on view for a bereaved public.

"Gator invented *Wraith of Hellfire*," she said.

"So he's a programmer, or coder, or whatever?"

"No, Max. He *invented* the game. He is the president of Wraith Enterprises. He's worth like $50 or $60 million."

I had never seen Gator drive a car. I had never been to his home. I had never known him to wear anything but jeans. And I suddenly realized that I knew nothing about him.

I grilled Claudia. How did she know he had millions? How did she know he was who he said he was? Of course, she had checked it all out. Claudia wasn't the type of woman who could be fed hyperbole.

She'd seen his home. It was a penthouse apartment in a tony building—an old brick factory that had been converted into lofts. The apartment was spartan, nearly empty. Gator, apparently, couldn't think of anything he wanted to buy.

He had a car. It was a compact hybrid. I had evidently seen the extent of his wardrobe. His clothes all fit into one closet. And they were just what he wore to the dog park: jeans, boots, plaid shirts, T-shirts.

He didn't even have his own dog. Those two monkey-faced varmints that he walked actually belonged to his former landladies: a pair of mad, geriatric twins who still dressed alike. The twins, Velma and Vera, fussed away their lives in their long-dead parents' Victorian home just blocks from the dog park. They had rented their two-room attic to Gator back in the 1980s—in his pre-Wraith days. He'd lived in it like a monk. He had one table, one chair, and a mattress on the floor. Working alone in that garret, he invented *Wraith of Hellfire*. And he became very, very wealthy.

After he bought his penthouse and sold his company he stopped thinking about video games. He traveled to Tibet. He meditated in ashrams in Thailand. He read—but he always got his books from the library because he didn't want to stockpile them. And he checked in on Velma and Vera nearly every day. That's why we always saw him at the park; he was taking their dogs out for them.

"I thought he was a professional dog walker," I said.

"He is, I suppose."

"Have you seen his bank account? How do you know he really has all that money?"

"It's invested, in really safe stuff like CDs and blue chips," she told me. "And he set up an endowment. He gives away shitloads to programs for inner-city kids and Buddhists and people like that."

I got up to make another shaker of martinis. The phone rang. I could tell that Claudia was talking to Gator. When she hung up she told me that Gator had gotten word that Steve was digging a hole in his backyard.

Apparently Gator had a friend who lived in a flat directly behind Steve's house. This friend—a yoga teacher by the name of Anahata—reported that Steve had hired a landscaping crew. They were getting ready to pour a patio, and had dug up a patch of grass. It seemed benign enough—until Steve crept out into the yard with a hand trowel in the middle of the night. He didn't turn on the porch light. He worked by moonlight. He dug a hole and placed something in it— Anahata thought it was a tool, maybe a hammer.

"It's got to be the murder weapon," Claudia said.

"But why is he burying it now?" I asked. "And why didn't the cops find it before?"

"Maybe somebody has been hiding it for him," she said. "Somebody like Stephanie Saint Claire."

41

Anahata came to the door dressed as a cumulus cloud. She wore gauzy white jodhpurs. A long, white tunic, split up the sides, hung nearly to her knees. Her hair was, presumably, swaddled up in a turban—a tower of ivory muslin that spiraled a foot above her crown. It was the distinctive costume worn by the kundalini yogis.

I knew enough about kundalini practitioners to know that they were on the spacier end of the yoga spectrum. They didn't care about toning their butts or perfecting their handstands. They worked with tantric energy: the energy inside. It's powerful stuff, the kind of stuff that can blow your mind.

"Someone is chanting," I said to her as she showed us into her bare, wood-paneled foyer.

"It's my Saturday morning satsang," she said, smiling.

She had the clear, lucent eyes of the abstinent. They were gray like oysters. Her mulatto skin was burnished gold. Her face glowed, lit up on enough kundalini energy to power all the neon in Vegas.

"We don't want to interrupt," Gator said.

"They won't notice," she told us. Her head bobbled from side to side as she spoke.

Claudia and Gator and I followed her down the hallway. Her naked feet seemed to hover across the bare wood floors. She opened a door at the back of her flat. The chanting hit us like a sonic wall.

"Hari, hari, hari, hari, hari," a dozen people repeated, not seeming to stop for a breath.

They were men and women, young and ancient and in between. They were sitting on the floor in a circle. Their eyes were closed and they held their arms up at shoulder height, their hands in a mudra—the thumb and forefinger touching. They swayed as they chanted. Anahata was right; they didn't notice us.

She motioned for us to follow her. She ducked her head so her turban would clear the doorjamb. We followed her around the outside of the chanting circle and passed through the room to a door on the other side. It opened up to a small, screened-in porch. Anahata closed the door to the studio behind us and the chanting became muted. We could see Steve's backyard.

"When did they pour the cement?" Gator asked.

"Early this morning," Anahata told him.

The wet cement was dark and glistening and the bent wood forms were still in place.

"Where did he dig the hole?" Gator asked.

"In the very center," Anahata said.

"You said it looked like a tool, right?" Claudia asked Anahata.

"It was dark," she said. "I only know the object was the size of a hammer."

"Murder weapon," Claudia said.

"You don't know that," I said.

Now that we were there, I was getting nervous. Sitting in Ed's van with a pair of earphones on your head was one thing, but breaking and entering and implanting electronic video surveillance was another.

"This has gone far enough, Claudia," I said. "You're not G. Gordon Liddy. Let's just stop now."

"I didn't get suited up for nothing," Claudia said.

Claudia was wearing a T-shirt and jeans and a pair of Japanese sneakers that had a split between the big toe and the rest of the toes. It was the perfect outfit for scaling ginkgo trees, or breaking into the homes of psychopathic killers.

"Claudia, just stop and think," I said. "You're the one who always says we should leave Steve alone."

"Gator's got my back," she said. "And you guys."

"That's it then. You're just showing off—trying to impress Gator."

"Fuck off, Max," she said. "I was scared of Steve before. I'm scared now. But that asshole thinks he's got away with killing Amy and that baby. Well, fuck him."

Claudia pushed open the screen door and stole down the back stairs. Anahata reached out and stopped the door before it banged shut.

We had all seen Steve leave with his golf clubs a half hour earlier. Kim and Marcy and Ed stayed down in the dog park, watching in case Steve should return earlier than usual. I dialed Kim's number.

"She's going in," I told Kim.

Claudia easily pulled herself up and over the back fence.

She walked nonchalantly across Steve's backyard like a seasoned criminal. Drug running, like military service, really does prepare one for the challenges that come later in life.

She got to the house and leaned against it, listened. Then she looked casually around the sides of the house and sprang up onto the wheel of the cement mixer that was stowed against the back wall. She stepped lightly from the wheel to the barrel of the mixer. She tugged at the sliding window. It wouldn't move. She reached around to the back pocket of her jeans and pulled out a slim-jim—a piece of wobbly plastic about the length and width of a schoolboy's ruler. She skimmed the slim-jim in between the window and the frame. She eased the window open.

"That was most impressive," said Anahata.

"Yes," I said. "She has skills. That's why she was the most popular girl in rehab."

Claudia pedaled up the stucco wall on the thick rubber treads of her sneakers, pulled herself through the window with her wiry arms. She alighted on the kitchen counter and lowered the window shut behind her.

"She didn't lock it again, did she?" I asked.

"I don't think so," Gator said.

A moment later she was waving at us from an upstairs window. She wasn't in Steve's bedroom. She was in the baby's room.

"What the hell is she doing?" I demanded.

Claudia stood in the window, aping a silent scream. She made circles around her ear with her finger, the international sign language for something in here is crazy.

Gator raised his forefinger and middle finger together,

making his hand into a gun. He pointed it at her. Then he swept his pointing fingers across to the left.

"Get the fuck out of there," he said.

Claudia held up a cupped hand to her ear and crinkled her brow and shook her head. Then she mimed laughter. Gator repeated the motion directing her to Steve's bedroom.

"Quit fucking around," he said.

She smirked at us and turned sideways, dropped down slowly like she was riding an escalator.

"Now she's a goddamn mime," I said.

Claudia popped up in Steve's bedroom window. She held her thumb up. Gator and I returned the gesture. She left the window.

"Okay," Gator said. "Now she's done with clowning around."

"She takes great pleasure in the moment," Anahata said.

"Like a village idiot," I said, putting a finer point on it.

The chanting continued. It seemed to become more insistent. More urgent. Hari, hari, hari, hari, hari. They chanted like blood pulsing. Gator's telephone rang. I could hear Kim's voice, excited.

"Oh, shit," Gator said. "Steve just pulled up."

Gator handed me his phone and slipped out through the screen door. He went over the back fence and into Steve's yard. By then I could see Steve standing in the driveway at the side of his house. Ed was calling out to him from the dog park. Ed opened the park gate and shambled across the street. Steve stood on the driveway, hands on his hips, waiting for Ed.

"Hello," I said into the phone.

"Is Gator in the backyard?" It was Marcy.

"Yes, what the hell?"

"Ed is talking to Steve, trying to stall him," Marcy said. "But he looks impatient. He's trying to break away. Did Gator get the water turned on?"

"The what? Water?"

"The sprinkler?" Marcy said. "Gator needs to turn on the sprinkler in the backyard."

I told her yes. The sprinkler sputtered and then arched up into a furl of jets reaching as high as the roof of the house. The tall spray swayed languidly from side to side.

Gator pulled a knife out of his pocket. I'd seen the knife many times before. Gator used it to pop the caps off beer bottles. It contained a lot of gadgets: corkscrews, and screwdrivers, and leather punches, and flamethrowers and whatnot. He was kneeling down in front of the water faucet, working at it with the knife.

"Is Gator out of the yard?" Marcy asked. Gator stood up and moved quickly.

"He's just over the fence," I reported. "Now he's coming back up the back steps."

"Okay," Marcy said. "I'll signal Ed."

"Signal what?" I snapped.

Marcy called out to Ed. She held the phone up and shook it. Ed waved at her. As he turned back to Steve, Ed acted surprised to see that the sprinkler was on in the backyard. Tall jets of water raked across the sky. Ed pointed to it. Steve turned and looked surprised himself. Then he broke into a run.

"What the hell is going on?" I whispered to Gator.

"Kim just ran to the truck to get her wrench. She's busting the shutoff valve at the connection."

"The connection? What's that?" I asked.

"The city water connection. The pipes are out front, under the sidewalk. You have to lift that concrete cover to get to them."

"Oh," I said. "Of course." I didn't even know how to change a light fuse at my house.

"Give me your phone," Gator told me.

I pulled it out of my pocket and handed it to him. Gator jammed a set of buttons with his thumb. He was sending Claudia a text message. It said, "go 2 kitchn."

"Why?" I asked him. "Steve is down there."

"Look," Gator said, a satisfied grin on his face.

Steve was trying to turn off the water, but the sprinkler was still going, saturating the lawn—and the freshly poured cement patio. Steve stared at the water faucet, then he kicked the side of the house. He bent over at the waist and furtively scanned the ground. He was looking for something.

The patio grew darker as the water seeped deeper and deeper into the cement. Pocks and blotches began to appear on the carefully leveled and smoothed surface. Steve raged, and swore out loud. His face was red and his hair had fallen out of place.

"He's looking for something," Anahata said.

Gator reached into his pocket and pulled out the handle from the water spigot. I looked over at Anahata and she was smiling broadly. Gator and I fell to punching each other on the shoulder.

Steve ran to the sprinkler. Big drops of water strafed his chest.

"Wet T-shirt contest," I said. Anahata suppressed a laugh.

Steve picked up the sprinkler, holding the water jets down

toward the ground, and jogged to the edge of the yard with it. He tried to unscrew the sprinkler from the hose, but in his agitation, he couldn't get it separated. He left it in the corner of the yard. The spray now reached over the fence and drops splattered against the porch screens that we were hiding behind.

"And there he goes to the garden shed," Gator said.

We watched Steve march into the shed and stalk out again swinging a wrench in one hand and a pry bar in the other. He walked up the side of the house and out of sight.

"Is he getting the water shut off out front?" I spoke into the phone.

"Yes," Marcy said. "And he's mad as hell."

"Ask her if it's safe," Gator told me.

"It's safe," Marcy said, having heard Gator's question. "Tell Claudia to go now!"

Gator punched the text message into the phone. We saw the back door open and Claudia step gingerly out onto the back porch. She looked over to the corner of the house that Steve had just walked around and she jumped off the porch.

She sprinted for the fence, skirting the patio, all but missing it—her right sneaker planted onto the wet cement, leaving a signature split-toe imprint.

She cleared the fence, flew up the stairs, and banged through the screen door. Gator grabbed her wrist and pulled her down below the windowsill. She sprawled on the floor, panting.

The arc of water was standing straight up at its full height. Then the spray collapsed, and plunged to earth.

42

We gathered to reconnoiter at the saloon where we had sent off Jordi. When Gator and Claudia and I got there, Ed and Marcy and Kim had already commandeered the big oak and leather booth in the back. Anahata couldn't join us, and I found myself feeling vaguely disappointed.

It was, nonetheless, a festive atmosphere. Everyone was giggling as though they'd just gotten off a midway ride, one of the more death-defying ones—an old roller coaster that shutters and clangs on wood struts, preferably operated by a toothless carnie with passages from the Book of Revelations tattooed across his forehead.

We were very satisfied with ourselves. We had outfoxed Steve. The camera was planted on top of the armoire in his bedroom.

"I just wonder about the placement," I said.

"Claudia, you were like a cat burglar," Gator said.

"I mean," I continued, unheeded, "what will we see in his bedroom? He just sleeps there."

"My friends, you saved my ass," Claudia said, hoisting her beer pint.

"To Claudia's ass," they all toasted.

All except me. I kept thinking about the camera being in the bedroom. What could we catch Steve doing there? Perhaps he would have an affair. I shivered when I thought of Stephanie Saint Claire in a teddy. But, what would that prove? He'd be guilty of bad taste, not murder. I couldn't remember how we'd arrived at the decision to put the camera there. Someone must have suggested it, must have convinced us. I couldn't remember if it was Gator or Jordi.

They talked about how we'd proceed. Gator explained that the Webcam filmed continuously and we could view it from any Internet connection. But that was only real-time. Since no one could monitor the live feed continuously, Gator had set up a workstation to record and archive all the past footage. And he reminded us that what we were doing was highly illegal.

"Where is this workstation then?" I asked Gator. He didn't answer, just got up to fetch us another pitcher of beer.

Kim asked Claudia what she'd seen in the baby's room.

"You know how Steve makes such a big fucking deal about that nursery," said Claudia. "He's always going in there to pray. And he can sense the baby in there, and Amy. And he keeps it ready for the baby to come home. Blah. Blah. Blah."

"Well, is it a place of miracles?" Marcy asked.

"No," said Claudia. "Steve's using it like a junk room. He tosses his old golf clubs and shit in there. There's all these coats stacked up on the crib. There's a pile of empty boxes— shit like that."

Someone called to the bartender to turn up the television. We all looked to see what was on. It was a local news update.

A group of men in black slacks and Windbreakers were on a stretch of rocky beach. Behind them an industrial building loomed against a hard gray sky. It was a brutalist structure of cement slabs and red towers chugging out billows of white smoke.

"That's Hunter's Point," Ed said. "That's the power plant down there on the bay."

The men were gathered around a pipe, as tall as a man, at the water's edge.

Iron bars closed off the front of the pipe so it looked like a giant moray eel baring its teeth. The teeth held something, some lump of flotsam.

"They've got something in the water intake," Ed said. "Buddy of mine used to work at that plant. That's the fish screen. They get a helluva lot more stuff than fish in it."

Two of the men kneeled in front of the pipe, zipping up a large black bag. They picked it up, gently. When they turned and carried the bag uphill toward the ambulance parked on the road, we could see, printed across their backs in yellow block letters, the word CORONER.

Part Three

43

"Welcome to Señor Frog's," Claudia said.

She was standing on my front porch with a bottle of tequila in her hand and two sombreros stacked on her head. She waggled the tequila bottle in my face.

"I told you I'm not receiving anyone," I said, tightening the sash of my kimono.

She barged over the threshold like a storm trooper. Asta barked at me. Then he followed his mad mistress down the hall toward my kitchen.

I hadn't come out of the house in days. I didn't dress. I didn't shave. I didn't answer the phone. I was besotted. And it wasn't just because the body had been discovered. That grotesquery was just the coup de grâce.

I was lonely. A diaspora had hit the dog park like a concussion strike. It was shocking how quickly our group came apart.

It had started when Wolf left. Then Jordi. The dykes, Kim and Marcy, had been talking about moving to Petaluma for months. Less than a week after the body was discovered, they closed the sale of their house and were gone. Marcy drove into Berkeley three mornings a week to teach. I suppose she could have stopped at the dog park now and then. But we knew she wouldn't. And she didn't.

Gator's departure was the most sudden. The day after we planted the Webcam in Steve's house—which was also the day the body washed up—Gator got on an airplane and headed west into the setting sun. He landed in Thailand. His sporadic e-mails reported that he was in the south, on a tiny palm-studded island set like an emerald in the turquoise blue Gulf of Siam. He lived in a wooden bungalow on the beach and spent his days drinking bang lhassis and hanging out with the local squid fishermen.

Even Ed stopped coming around. He was spending more and more time on Telegraph Avenue. His veteran's group— his men's club, as he put it—took turns manning a card table, handing out literature on unexploded U.S. bombs in Laos. He said that he needed to put in extra hours there, that they were gathering donations to fund a bomb removal mission.

Everyone gave a different story for leaving the dog park. But I think that, ultimately, we all left for the same reason. We had failed. We failed to prove that Steve killed Amy. And so each of us ripped up his moorings and left the park that had been, for us, the center of the world. We were disaffected continents. Drifting apart. Inexorably.

"Where the hell is the blender?" Claudia demanded. She tore through my kitchen, opening drawers, banging cupboards.

"The blender is in margaritaville, which I believe is somewhere between Saturday night fever and another tequila sunrise."

Claudia climbed on a chair and found the dust-covered appliance in the back of a cupboard, behind my secret stash of Aunt Jemima waffle mix. She set up the blender, twisted an ice tray over it. A few cubes popped into it, the rest scattered across the countertops and the floor. I went around picking up ice cubes while she dumped a can of frozen lime juice into the blender. She shook in a couple jiggers of triple sec. Then she upended the tequila bottle over the mix and counted to five. She flipped the switch and the blender screamed.

"I was thinking we should get tattooed," she told me, two blenders later.

We were lying on my living-room floor. I was still wearing my kimono. She wore my striped pajamas. We'd given our ensembles a fusion flair by adding the sombreros.

"Tattoos have been taken over by the squares," I said. "Every sorority girl in America has a tattoo now."

"They don't get tears tattooed on their cheeks," she said, pulling a cigarette out of her hatband.

"I'm not doing anything," I said. "I'm not even going to buy a condolence card until we know for sure that the body is Amy."

The authorities had been curiously silent after they found the body on the shoreline. It had been nearly a month, and still there had been no statement. How long could it take to run DNA tests?

"It's gotta be Amy," Claudia argued. "Torso. Pregnant."

"Torso never sounds good," I allowed.

"Neither does partially clad."

"Was she?" I asked. I hadn't even thought of that.

"I don't know," Claudia said. "But partially clad never sounds good."

I telephoned the Cambodian restaurant up the street and placed a delivery order. The mention of Khmer food reminded Claudia that she'd brought a papaya facial mask. We wrapped towel turbans around our hair, applied the green mud, and lay on the floor cushions, pensively puffing on cigarettes through long black holders, waiting for our masks to harden.

"Darling," she said. "I'm sorry about Wolfy leaving."

"Don't speak," I said. "Your mask will crack."

The doorbell rang. It was the Khmer delivery guy. I answered the door with the pale green mud still drying on my face. He took one look at me and backed down off the stairs.

"Hmmm," I growled at him through a flattened ventriloquist's smile. "Phnom Penh?"

He nodded and stepped back up onto the porch. He handed me a plastic sack at arm's length. I tipped him eight dollars and he smiled but he didn't turn his back to me as he left.

We peeled off our masks. They shed in whole pieces, like snakeskins. We sat on the floor eating from the Styrofoam boxes.

"I'm sorry too," I told her.

"About what?"

"About Gator flying off."

"That fucker," Claudia said, stabbing the air with her chopsticks. "Who the hell just flies off to Siam?"

"We've been abandoned," I remarked.

"By men with critter names."

"That," I told her, "is a fucking brilliant observation. Wolf. Gator. My God, the pattern was there all the time. And we were just too blind to see it."

"From now on," she said, "we only sleep with men who have human names."

"Not even pet names," I said. "Nobody named Scooter. Or Tabby. Or Lucky."

It occurred to me that we'd been discussing all of the dog park people in past tense. They had become historical figures. And the dog park itself was a place that existed in another time—like Mohenjo-Daro, or Atlantis. It was a lost civilization.

We hadn't talked about the fact that I, too, would be leaving soon. *I Pagliacci* was going on tour—just in the United States, but I'd be gone for three months. And then, Claudia would truly be alone.

"Have you thought of contacting Larry?" I asked her.

"Why?"

She stood up and went to the fireplace. She leaned against the bricks. Her feet were bare. When she crossed her ankles I was struck by how sharp the bones were, like arrowheads chipped out of flint. You could still see the sparks flying off them.

"Have you tried talking to Larry lately?" I asked.

"I'd sooner fuck Satan," she said.

A scream pierced the silence. I looked toward the kitchen and saw a volley of steam scorching the air. I'd forgotten I'd put the kettle on.

When I brought the tea in, Claudia was still slouching against the fireplace, entertaining a cigarette. Her face was glowing and smooth and a little inhuman. I told myself that it was from the mask. She didn't notice me, not even when I set down the tray. I poured her a cup.

"Larry still loves you," I started, rather awkwardly. "And I know I've been against him, against a reconciliation. But, let's face it, Claudia, Larry's all that's left."

"Nobody is left," she said.

I was startled by her expression. It was blank, frozen calm between emotions, the face of a mannequin in purgatory's display window. The crying was over. So was the caring. She was done with them. All of them. Larry. Jordi. Even Gator. The tears dried up. And only a hard, cracked riverbed of loathing remained. Claudia walked secretively along its horned fissures, on those strong, naked feet of hers.

44

I got out the water pipe. We smoked bowl after bowl of hash.

The last thing I remember, Claudia and I were lying on our cushions watching *Double Indemnity* with Fred MacMurray and Barbara Stanwyck. MacMurray is an insurance adjuster who gets mixed up with a no-good dame; a deadly chiseler who murders a guy's invalid wife just so she can marry him for his money.

"I think most spouses murder each other over money," Claudia said.

"Not passion?" I asked.

"Don't be droll, Max."

Barbara Stanwyck decides she'd like the guy's money a lot better if she had it all to herself. She lures Fred MacMurray into her scheme. Him being an insurance adjuster, he'd know just how to fix it. They kill the husband.

"I talked to Estevez the other day," Claudia said. "He asked me if I'd ever been to Amy's office. Said he was asking everybody that."

The last scene was playing. Fred MacMurray was talking

into the tape recorder, telling his boss that his suspicions were right. There was something fishy about the insurance payout. The dame did steal the money. And Fred helped her do it.

"Estevez asked me if I knew anything about computers," Claudia said. "Big enterprise systems, financial software."

"You? That's a laugh."

"That's what I said. Then he asked me if I knew anybody who did know about that stuff."

"Doesn't Larry sell enterprise systems?" I asked. Now I was concerned.

"Yeah. But Larry doesn't know anything technical. He's just a sales guy. Bullshit artist."

"Gator knows a lot about coding," I said. "So does Jordi."

Claudia was snoring. She'd passed out. Fred MacMurray was about to croak. After he'd helped the dame steal the money, she killed him. Shot him. I draped a blanket over Claudia and turned the sound down on the television.

The morning sun burst in on us like a pipe and bugle band. Asta was eating Cambodian dumplings from a Styrofoam box on the dining-room table. The television was still on.

It was showing another old movie. It was a Western. Big skies. Towering mesas. A man and a woman on horseback, riding off into the distance. The cinematography was nuanced and complex, a profusion of grays. There is no such thing as black and white, not when you really start to look.

A newsbreak flashed on screen, lurid and harsh in living color. The words BREAKING STORY IN MYSTERY HOMICIDE ran along the bottom of the screen. I reached around under the cushions until I found the remote. Claudia was awake, but didn't lift her head. Her eyes were open. She was watching the television too.

I turned the sound up. The reporter's voice pounded over us like hard waves.

He said the body that they'd found down at Hunter's Point had been identified. It was a thirty-four-year-old El Salvadoran woman. Her name was Marta Esperanza. She was eight months pregnant. She was a maid at the Hyatt downtown. Marta had left work on the afternoon of November sixteenth. She never made it home.

45

I was busy with *I Pagliacci*. Claudia attended opening night in Oakland. She sat in the first row, alone. At the curtain call, she rushed the stage with a brace of two dozen crimson roses. She had clipped all the thorns off them herself. She tossed the bouquet directly into my chest and I crushed it to my heart.

Since the dog park gang dissolved, Claudia cleaved to me. We talked about the *I Pagliacci* tour schedule, and how she could possibly meet me at one of the stops. Dallas was out. I knew she would not deign to step one open-toed Prada in Texas. She considered Chicago vulgar. Atlanta wasn't even worth discussing. But I did think there was a chance she'd join me for the last performance, in New York.

I fretted about her. I didn't like leaving her alone, not after everything that had happened, mainly because I didn't feel like it was over.

"How about Jeff?" I said, referring to her partner at work. "Can't he come over to the house while I'm gone?"

"You don't understand advertising," said Claudia. "You're

all best friends at the office, but nobody has time to see you outside of work."

I suggested she spend more time with Ed. That's how perverse our lives had become. I looked on Ed as some sort of bastion of equanimity.

"Ed's going to Laos," she told me.

I was stunned, but not bewildered. I remembered Ed talking about the Laos mission. But I didn't imagine that he and his coterie of fellow crustaceans would scrape together the funds that quickly. I'd been to their display table on Telegraph Avenue. The war chest was an old pickle jar labeled "Laos UXB Relief Fund." It was full of silver coins and a few greasy bills—Lincolns and Jeffersons.

"Now that's a Cinderella story," I said to Claudia. "The donations drive worked."

"Not at the rate those old farts were going," she said.

"Did they all sell their kidneys? Or did they con some wealthy sponsor?"

"Yes," she said. "Gator."

46

Our tour schedule for *I Pagliacci* was willfully perverse. We played Atlanta throughout the second half of July, and Chicago for the whole month of August. I was wondering that they hadn't booked us into New Orleans in time for the fall hurricanes and then maybe swung us up to Buffalo in January. As it was, we were destined to wilt into our greasepaint for a solid six weeks.

I had phoned Claudia from SFO before taking off. Then I called her again upon landing in Atlanta. After that, I called her four times a day for a week before she finally deigned to answer. She claimed to have been sick with a pernicious migraine. I assumed she was on a pills and booze bender, wallowing in the nadir of one of her mood swings.

I was more interested in my own travails at that point. And I enumerated them to her. Our production handlers had us staying downtown, in a high-rise chain hotel. It was a soaring glass and stucco monstrosity that was built in the 1980s and had aged badly, the architectural equivalent of shoulder pads and harem pants. The carpets were worn and the décor was mauve and teal and there were eighteen yards of flounces on the skirt of my bed and eighteen centimeters of grime in the corners of the bathroom floor. At night gangs of drunken businessmen in pleat-front khakis and Top-Sider boat shoes roamed the hallways.

From my thirty-second story window I could see the world's largest Planet Hollywood just below. It sat on a corner facing its evil twin—the world's largest Hard Rock Cafe. Clearly I had arrived at the intersection of Hell's double helix—the genetic coding for bad taste. It was all I could do to restrain myself from throwing a chair through the window and hurtling myself after it.

"I'm battling ennui," I told Claudia. "It started on the drive in from the airport. Miles and miles of suburbs and strip malls. And every strip mall has an XXX shop in it. That's the local anchor stores—porn."

"Oh, don't worry, Scarlett," she told me. "Atlanta burned once before. It could happen again."

When I asked what she'd been doing she became vague. She actually talked about work. The agency was pitching a new account—some dreary Silicon Valley company that manufactured duo processors. I didn't know what duo processors were. Claudia said it didn't matter. She didn't really know what they were either.

She insisted on telling me all about the ad campaign that she and her copywriting partner, Jeff, had devised for the processors people. Apparently they were exploring the hilarious, slapstick side of duo processors. And the creative director—a notorious wet blanket—was trying to squelch their ideas. He was forever trying to clip her wings, I told her. I supposed that was the right thing to say.

Claudia went on to catalog all the various and sundry outrages that she and Jeff had endured over the duo processors project. Her workplace, like all ad agencies, was a seething cauldron of byzantine palace politics. The creative department was populated by swollen, but damaged egos—all of them were frustrated novelists or painters—and they devoted extravagant effort to sabotaging one another's ideas. It was enormously tiresome to listen to.

After nearly an hour of it, I thought we could move on to other, more germane topics. I thought we could return to a discussion of me, and how I felt about Atlanta. Claudia told me I was boring.

I asked if she'd been to the dog park. She informed me that she didn't feel like being interrogated. She abruptly rang off, saying that she had to hurry to get to her yoga class.

I immediately got on the Internet and looked up the schedule at her yoga studio. The last evening class started at seven thirty. It was already eight thirty on the West Coast.

For the next few days, I concentrated on my brooding. It was easy in that environment. I'd stare out my window at the Hard Rock Cafe and perseverate about Claudia. What wasn't she telling me?

It wasn't long before I lost the plot. The Claudia game wasn't as intriguing from a distance as it had been at home. I focused on *I Pagliacci*. The show was well received. Despite being cooped up in my hotel room breathing recirculated air filled with Freon and fibers and Legionnaires' disease, I was in good voice. And I did enjoy our company—most of them were people I'd worked with on various operas for twenty years. The dog park—and all its contents, human and canine—faded into the fantasy that is the memory of things past.

And then Larry contacted me. I was surprised. I hadn't spoken with Larry for months, not since his abortive reunion with Claudia. I actually thought he'd given up on her.

His e-mail was brief. He told me that he was concerned. He told me that I would be too when I saw the photo he was sending me. I clicked on the attachment file and watched the photo image slowly unfurl like a curtain dropping.

It was two people in the dog park. Claudia and Steve.

The sight of the two of them together caused me to exhale violently. If there'd been a chunk of steak caught in my throat it would have hurtled clear across the room.

Claudia was sitting on top of the picnic table. Steve was standing. He was facing her, his thighs touching her knees.

I snatched my cell phone off the bedside table and pressed on Larry's name. The call went straight into voice mail.

"Larry, for God's sake, call me," I cried. "I just got your e-mail."

I shut the phone but continued to clutch it in my fist.

47

We left Atlanta the next morning. I hadn't slept, but I had taken ten milligrams of Ambien and drank nearly a bottle of Malbec in the effort. I was as stoned as Jim Morrison—the Paris years—when my limo collected me the next morning.

I was relieved to be traveling alone—the rest of the company had taken the earlier flight. The Town Car would come, and I could sink into the warm embrace of its Corinthian leather. Malik, my driver, would handle me. He was a big square-headed Persian who was quick in thinking and slow in speaking. During my fortnight in Atlanta I came to recognize him as a heroic figure. And he recognized me as a high-strung neurotic forever teetering on the verge of hysteria.

When he picked me up in the shadow of the hotel awning that morning, Malik took one look at me and said, "Sunglasses in the dark." He turned and picked up my bags, set them in the trunk. Then he opened the rear door for me to slide into the familiar embrace of his impeccably clean, silent-running luxury sedan.

"I'll get you checked in," Malik said, glancing into the

rearview mirror at me, my homburg pulled down over my forehead and my oversized, square sunglasses blackening my view. He added, "I'll walk up to the concourse with you."

"Great," I said. "Security will see me with you and give me a cavity search."

I remembered that, in the Koran, Malik is the angel who stands at the gates of Hell, ushering in some, turning back others.

"You're gonna like Chicago, Max," he said.

"Yes. And I should think I'll like New York even better."

"I love New York," he said, his voice a bass rumble. "I heart New York. Like the bumper sticker."

I watched Atlanta slipping by through the smoky glass of Malik's windows. We had left the defaced downtown core of that once noble city. We sped past the miles and miles of tract homes, past the big-box stores, past the outlet malls. And we cruised the six-lane interstate, the kudzu vines growing so thick in the ditches it seemed that it would overtake the freeway and bury us.

"I've heard this kudzu grows a foot a day," I said to Malik.

"At first, people loved this plant. It was," and he paused until he found the phrase, "it was an ill-advised affection."

I had sent an e-mail to Claudia that morning. I very deliberately waited. I needed time to recover from the initial shock of seeing the photo of her and Steve. I knew that Claudia would round on me if I condemned her, if I was at all shrill. And that's how I felt, of course, shrill to the point of screaming at such a pitch that the blood would burst from my temples and the clouds would wrench down from the sky. Now I was calmer. I was stoned. I hadn't referred directly to Steve in the e-mail. I just asked Claudia how she was getting on. Had she been to the dog park? Had she seen anyone there?

I didn't expect to get anything back from her, not anything beyond the prevarications that she'd been administering to me. She would continue to hide her sordid truth.

"Now look," Malik said. He fluttered his fingers, thick as cigars, at the kudzu-covered ditches. It was a delicate motion that made me think of butterfly wings. "See, Max, the weed covers up everything."

"Do you think it could cover that Planet Hollywood downtown?" I asked him.

He considered the question. Then said, "Perhaps, Max. *Allah akbar.*"

48

Malik was right. I did like Chicago. It was hot and muggy—oppressively so—but the buildings were tall and proud and invented by visionaries. They stood shoulder to shoulder along the Avenue of the Americas and their doors opened at lunchtime and bevies of beautiful, well-groomed people came stepping smartly out onto the wide sidewalks.

I was staying on Michigan Avenue, in a hotel that had been built in the early 1920s and maintained four stars throughout its lifetime. I spent my days walking the avenue to where it ended—the sandy beach on Lake Michigan. There, all the attractive young people from all the small towns in the Midwest gathered to play volleyball and Rollerblade and exhibit their gym-sculpted physiques. It was easy to see how the hamlets and lesser cities of those middle states had become hospices for the elderly, group homes for the incapable. Those towns lost their brightest—their most promising youth had all come north to Chicago.

I often got up early enough that I could walk along the lakeshore. I liked to lean on the railing overlooking the pier and watch the seriously advantaged loading ice chests and picnic baskets onto their private boats, provisioning for a day out on the lake that was really more of a vast inland sea.

I'd walk east to the formal gardens—paeans to order and light and the great civilizing power of the surveyor's transit. I liked that the lawns were trim and the people were coifed and that women weren't vanishing without a trace—or rutting indiscriminately.

The cell phone in my pocket rang and I knew who it was before I even opened it.

"You've been calling me," Claudia said.

"And you are . . . ?"

"Funny."

"I'm just out walking by the lake," I said. "It's gorgeous. How are the microchips holding up?"

"What's that?" she asked absently.

"Your microchip ad campaign—the one that will alter the course of life on this planet as we know it."

"Oh, the pitch," she said. "Yeah. We got that business. It was duo processor microchips."

"You don't sound very excited."

"It's just business, Max. It's not my life."

"What is your life, Claudia?"

She laughed and told me I was her life. It was all about me. Then she laughed some more. It was very stagy, very Noël Coward.

I sat down on a bench and watched an elegant little yacht tugging at its mooring. It had polished wooden railings the color of toffee and wide-planked decks that glistened and chrome that sparkled in the hot sun. It must have cost a fortune just to hire a crew to shine it. Someone, the owner, was paying for gleam. A frilly script cavorted across the little ship's stern describing the words *Ma Folie*.

"Are you seeing anyone?" I asked Claudia.

"I see people every day."

"Stop fucking with me. What are you doing, Claudia?"

She was silent. I returned the treatment. We sat listening to the line crackle, like two children in a breath-holding contest.

"Are you involved with Steve Carter?" I demanded. I would, naturally, be the first to break down. I always gave in.

"I've been talking with Steve," she said. "He's pretty much the only person in the dog park."

A holiday couple was coming up the walkway. They were holding hands and wearing shorts. Grown adults in short pants. Furthermore—and this is typical—their legs were bloated and as white as beluga whales. I fought to contain my outrage.

"Steve is not the monster we thought he was," Claudia said.

I yelled into the phone. "Are you trying to get yourself killed?"

The whale couple's heads snapped toward me in unison. I glared back at them. They both quickly faced forward and doubled their pace.

"Don't tell me what to do, Max."

"Darling," I said, forcing the softness into my voice. "I love you. I don't want you to get hurt. In any way."

"Steve is innocent, Max. And he's been through hell. And we are partly to blame. Max, we persecuted an innocent, tortured man."

"Yes, dear. But still, there are thousands of men you could be dating. You don't need to pick this man who may, or may not, have murdered his missing wife."

"Hey, Max," she said, her voice suddenly changed. She sounded efficient, and preternaturally perky. "I'm just being called to a meeting. Hold on."

I heard a woman's voice in the background. Claudia said she'd be right there. She came back on the line.

"Max, I have to go. Client meeting. I'll call you, sweetie. I'm glad you're having a good tour. Give my love to Nedda and Canio, darling. Ciao. Kisses."

She hung up. I sat, holding the phone. In front of me, the shiny *Ma Folie* bobbed up and down on the tide.

49

"*Love k-o vast, bori k-o grast,*" Baba said to me when I entered my hotel room.

"Oh, my God," I said. "You just scared the shit out of me."

Baba was sitting on my bed, her tarot cards spread out in front of her. I pulled the handkerchief out of my pocket and dabbed the sweat off my forehead.

"I've had a very upsetting morning," I told her. "Please. I need to rest. I'm performing in five hours."

"Don't you remember your own language?" she said. "I said to you, in Romany, money in hand, bride on horse."

"Fine. Thanks for the update. Now, can you clear off? I need to lie down."

She slid off the bed, scraping her cards together into a pile. She went and stood by the window, absently shuffling the tarot deck as she gazed down at the people below.

"You are making good money on this tour?" she said.

"What are you now? My agent?"

I reached into the bedside drawer and pulled out my

blinders. I slipped them on over my eyes and dropped my head back down onto the pillow.

"You could consider getting married now. Now, before it's too late. It's coming, Maximilian. Soon. Old age. Incontinence. Death."

"The incontinence bit is going too far," I said to the darkness. "Please don't be here when I wake up."

She wasn't. Baba had gone. She left behind another photo. I recognized it as the same Kalderashi that Baba had tried to pawn off on me before. But she looked different. In this photo the girl looked a little older and, frankly, more *gadje*.

She was dressed in fashionable jeans—tight bell-bottoms slung low on her hips. Her legs reminded me of iris stamens—long and slender. She jutted out her chest, hands on her hips, proudly displaying how high and firm her small breasts looked in her stylish, low-cut version of a gypsy blouse. Her hair hung long and loose and her face was broken into a crooked pirate smile. She was cracking wise to whoever held the camera.

I tossed the photo into the garbage can. I took a shower and, afterward, dusted myself with talcum powder. I put on fresh clothes and brushed my hair and reached into the wastebasket and pulled out the girl's photo. I propped it up against the base of the lamp on the desk.

50

Claudia and I didn't speak again until after I'd been in New York nearly three weeks. She called and insisted on reading my *New York Times* review aloud. They singled out my performance as being "forceful, and deep to the core. It's as if Max Bravo were himself hectored by the twin demons of love and jealousy."

She was needling me. And I was vexed. I cut the conversation short. I told her I'd see her when I got home in about a week. I hung up rather abruptly and then felt miserable about it afterward.

I corresponded with Larry. I asked him if he was still stalking Claudia. It took him a while to respond—nearly a week—and when he did he said he was in Asia. He'd been bowing and scraping his way across mainland China trying to sell software. He was on his way to Tokyo when he wrote to me. He said that he'd been traveling for nearly three weeks and was hopelessly out of touch with developments in Berkeley. He wouldn't be home for another week. He was worried about Claudia. So was I. But I wrote him back and said that

I'd spoken with her and she sounded fine. I assured him that she wouldn't become involved with Steve. Not intricately, anyway. She couldn't be that foolish.

We performed *I Pagliacci* for the last time on a hot, muggy night at the end of September. Afterward the entire cast went out to a Greek restaurant that we had come to know and love during our stay in New York. I ate a plate of moussaka as big as my head, drank a carafe of house red, and then got into the ouzo. Of course, things unraveled after that. I remember the owner, Jimmy Stavrionadakus, rolling up the carpet so that we could dance on the parquet floor. He taught us the Pentozalis, a folk dance from his native Crete, with a thimble of grappa perched on his head.

By 2:00 A.M. we had spilled enough grappa and broken enough plates to declare that we'd accomplished all that we'd set out to do. We threw fistfuls of cash down onto the table and hugged and kissed every Stavrionadakus in the place and piled into a stretch limo that bore us, like an upscale handibus, back to our hotel.

When I got to my room there was a voice message from Gator. It was too late to call back. The next morning was murderous. I drank a bromide and struggled to the airport and collapsed into my seat that was, thankfully, in first class. I slept across the continent and awoke in San Francisco with a stream of spittle trickling down the side of my chin.

51

For the first time in months I woke up in my own bed. And it wasn't to the sound of birds chirping. The telephone was ringing.

"Dude," Gator said. "I'm in Siam."

"Sawadeekop," I said.

"Can you do me a righteous?"

"And what would a *righteous* be? Water your pot plants? Get your motorcycle out of impound?"

"Dude, I got a call from the lady twins—the ladies who maintain my workstation. There's some kind of glitch."

"I'm not an IT guy."

"Can you just check it out?" he said. "What else have you got to do?"

He had me there. A couple hours later I was driving over the Bay Bridge.

The lady twins lived near UC Berkeley campus, in a once-stately Victorian, a mad Stickley caprice towering over an untended rhododendron dell. The house was in a shambles. There was more grass on the roof than the lawn, most of the decorative scale shingles had fallen from the walls, and several incarnations of paint showed through—patches of blue, and pink, and puce.

I stepped onto the porch. Bobby and Huey, the two maniacal affenpinschers, jumped out of a basket by the front door. They recognized me and offered me their customary greeting; they growled and bared their sharp little incisors like a pair of bilge rats.

The lady twins answered the door together, standing side by side, eerie as a Diane Arbus photograph. They were old, I knew that they were in their seventies, but they both still had a luxurious, healthy head of hair that they wore in shoulder-wide Afros. Their faces were curiously unlined and their Levis were smartly belted to show off their slender waists.

They said they knew I was coming, and that their names were Vera and Velma. And then they proceeded to talk about me as though I weren't there.

"He don't look like he knows nothin' about that workstation."

"Don't matter what he look like. Gator say let him in."

"I'm lettin' him in."

"Gator say let him in."

"I'll just come in then, shall I?" I said.

They told me to follow them. Their big earrings clinked as they sashayed across the foyer on chunky platform sandals. We ascended a wide staircase that switchbacked up to the third-story attic.

The dogs, Bobby and Huey, led the way. They stopped on every landing, turned to leer at me as I struggled up the stairs; my breath choppy, the back of my shirt dampening.

The workstation occupied the attic like a battleship in dry dock. It sat on a large oak table—a hulking gray Frankenstein of a machine cobbled together from a host of dead computers.

The only other thing in the attic was an ancient, sway-backed sofa—its brown leather scratched and worn. A big dog loafed on it. His yellow coat was covered in a flickering Pierrot of red and yellow diamonds—the sun striking through the stained-glass window above him. He lifted his head but couldn't be bothered to stir his paws.

"Is that Colonel?" I asked.

"That's the Colonel," Vera said. "That old nappy-headed fella left him here."

"He went to Indochina," Velma informed me. "He's fighting the capitalist aggressors."

Huey and Bobby ran straight for the sofa. They nestled into the embrace of the Colonel's front legs, the three of them falling into a narcoleptic sleep.

I sat down at the workstation and pulled out a scrap of note-paper. I studied my pencil notes for a moment, then booted up the computer and followed Gator's instructions step-by-step.

The recorded archives dated back to the day that Claudia installed the Webcam in Steve's bedroom. It seemed like a century ago, but according to the files, it had been six months. The twins and I decided it would take too long to start at the beginning. We took a look at the last recording of Steve's bedroom.

Steve came into the room with a small stepladder. He placed it under the ceiling fan. Then he climbed up the ladder and teetered on the top step. He had a nylon rope coiled around his shoulder. He tied the rope to the fan. At the end of the rope was a noose.

"That cracker is crazy."

"He's getting set to hang his self."

"Holy shit," I said. "When was this recorded?"

Steve tugged at the rope to test its load-bearing capacity. Satisfied, he reached the noose up toward his neck.

"This was yesterday," Vera said. Velma pointed to the date stamp at the bottom of the screen.

The stepladder started to tremble. Steve crouched in a surfer's stance, carefully rode out the tremor. The ladder stood still. Steve raised up. He came to eye level with the camera.

"What the—" he said. He registered what, for Steve, was a full spectrum of emotions: curiosity, confusion, surprise, then, his customary mode, anger. He jerked, convulsed by fury. The ladder lurched. Steve tried to steady it again by swiveling his hips, but that just sent the stepladder into a violent tremor.

It tipped. Steve went down holding the rope with both hands. The fan yanked sideways, following Steve's trajectory. Then it ripped out of the ceiling. We heard it prang onto the floor. Steve yelled out in pain, and I was surprised by how womanish he sounded.

A few wires dangled, like torn ganglia, from the hole in the ceiling.

Steve scrambled to his feet, picked up the ladder. Our next view of him was a close-up. He was at the top of the armoire, looking straight into the Webcam. "You fuckers," Steve said. The feed went black.

52

Claudia's front door was locked. I fumbled with my keys, looking for her spare. I had called, but she didn't answer, so I figured I'd let myself in and raid her wine cabinet while I waited for her to get home. I was still laughing to myself; Steve's face, contorted with rage, was one of the most comedic moments I had ever witnessed.

I opened the bolt lock, got two steps into the foyer, and heard a sharp crack. A heavy curtain fell, dragging me to the bottom of an echoing sea.

I came to in the dark. I was on the floor. My wrists were taped together behind my back. My ankles were bound as well. A piece of tape covered my mouth.

I realized that I wasn't alone. A shape lay across from me in the dark. I smelled a faint whiff of peonies, Claudia's perfume. At first I thought she was dead, then I realized that she was kicking me with her bare feet. That must have been what woke me. We were in a small room, a closet, and a sliver of light sliced under the closed door. She was wearing only a little camisole T-shirt and her panties. Her bare legs were duct-taped together like a mermaid. Once she realized I was awake she started shaking her head excitedly and making urgent noises from behind the tape muzzle.

The vague dark shapes began to take form. We were in the pantry. I could see the familiar tins of anchovies and smoked oysters and jars of big, fat martini olives. And the familiarity of it—the very mundane and lovable nature of these provisions—made me wince with sorrow at our exotically cruel fate.

Claudia inch-wormed across the floor toward me. She lifted her face to mine. I could feel her struggling to open her mouth from behind the tape. She loosened her own tape muzzle enough that she managed to bite the edge of the tape on my face. She pulled her head back and slowly peeled it off. I wouldn't have to shave for a week.

"Oh, Claudia," I said. "Are you all right, darling?"

She urgently mumbled something. I told her I couldn't understand. She mumbled again, angrily, and I could make out the word "fucking." Then it occurred to me what she wanted. I craned my neck around, bit the edge of the tape on her cheek, and pulled back with a violent yank. The strip of tape, as long and wide as a lasagna noodle, came off and hung from my upper lip. I shook my head up and down but couldn't get the tape off my lip.

"Darling, could you help?" I begged her.

She bit the tape off my mouth. It stuck on her lip. She became agitated and raked her face across the floor, rolling the tape off her mouth only to have it stick to her cheek.

"Oh, for God's sake, Max," she said. "Get over here and free my hands."

We both inched along the floor, twirling in opposite directions like a pair of pinwheels, until I got my teeth onto the edge of the duct tape on her wrists. Once I loosened that, she pulled her hands apart and freed us both.

We tried the pantry door, but it wouldn't budge. We realized that Steve had propped it shut with one of the kitchen chairs.

"What a cheap fucking trick!" Claudia raged against the door. "Right out of a B-fucking movie."

"Don't worry," I told her. "The lady twins know we're here."

"Do they know that Steve has us tied up in the pantry?"

"Well, no. I, well, actually maybe they don't know we're here. I was just at their house."

"Did you tell them you were coming here?"

"Technically," I said, "no. You see we watched Steve try to hang himself, and then he found the Webcam—and he was pissed—and so I said I'd had about enough for one day."

"What did they say?"

"They said white people are crazy."

"And you said what?"

"I told them I was going home," I said. "Then I decided to swing by here and see you."

She ran her hands through her hair, clutched two fistfuls, and pulled hard until she looked like she had one of those face-lifts that goes a bit too far.

"Well, then this is awkward," I said, as much to myself as to Claudia.

We heard heavy footsteps in the kitchen. There was a thud—
and the sound of liquid slopping around in a metal container.
Steve pounded on the pantry door.

"How are we doing in here, kids?" he called cheerfully.

Claudia looked at me and touched her finger to her lips.
She was right. We didn't want him to know we'd gotten out
of the duct tape.

"I'm just setting up for the barbecue," he said.

We heard liquid splashing on the linoleum and we
smelled gasoline.

"You know it's a shame about the house," Steve said airily. "Stephanie thinks she could get three million for it. But
I guess it was just not to be."

"Max," Claudia mouthed, her face wreathed in terror. A
trickle of dried blood flaked from her chin. I saw that her
front tooth was chipped, and I realized that Steve must have
cracked her in the mouth before he tied her up.

There was a clicking sound. It repeated. Then it became
manic.

"Hey, kids," he called out again brightly. "I have to just go
out to the car and get another lighter. You two sit tight. I'll be
right back."

"Max, what are we going to do?" Claudia whispered.

"Where's your slim-jim?" It occurred to me to ask her.

"I carry it in my ass. Jesus, Max."

I ran my hands down the side of the door. She asked me
what I was doing. I told her I was looking for the door hinge,
maybe I could pop the pins out and we could pull the door
off the frame.

"Shit," I said.

She asked me what. I told her that the pins had been painted over. We may as well have been walled up.

"Oh God, Max," she cried, a fresh welter of tears flooding her cheeks. "I've made such a mess of everything."

I started feeling along the pantry shelves.

"Don't you have some tools in here?" I asked.

"I wouldn't even be in this mess if fucking Larry hadn't abandoned me."

"Nor would I, darling. How about a hammer? Or a chisel?"

"And those other assholes," she said. "Jordi and Gator."

"Maybe just a screwdriver?"

"And I didn't even sleep with Steve. Honest, Max. I was just friendly with him. And then he comes over this morning. He was out of his mind. He busted through the door. He accused me of ruining his life."

"Is that smoke?" I asked.

"Oh God, Max," she said. "I hate dating."

"I smell smoke."

We both panicked. We hurled ourselves against the door, screaming and crying and using up all the oxygen in that tiny enclosure. Claudia composed herself first. She pulled me down to the floor, explaining that smoke rises.

"I smell something plastic burning," she said. "Or maybe it's electrical wire."

"God Almighty!" I said. "It's both. The fire is burning right through the walls."

Claudia picked up a restaurant-sized can of fava beans. She held it over her head and said, "I'm not going down this easy, Max."

She turned to the wall and started hammering at it. She

had the strength of the insane. There is something to be said for a daily regimen of wine, cigarettes, and vitriol.

I grabbed an oversized can of garbanzos and followed her lead. We broke through the drywall inside the closet and started on the Sheetrock that would open up to the living room.

The door swung open.

Larry was standing there, bug-eyed and blanched. Claudia jumped up and into his arms.

I expected to see flames everywhere, but there was only smoke. Steve hadn't set the house on fire after all.

He had pulled the barbecue into the kitchen, filled it with briquettes, and soaked them with lighter fluid. Clearly, he'd lit it, fanned the flames, and then let them die away until the briquettes were white ash, radiating heat—perfect for steaks, or, in this case, a Webcam. It lay on top of the briquettes, like an amputated Cyclops eye, blackened and melting.

We followed Larry outside. Detective McGuire came across the lawn, followed by Asta. Estevez had Steve in cuffs, lying facedown on the hood of Claudia's car. Steve was wearing a pair of baggy shorts, no shirt, and high-top basketball shoes with no socks. Laces undone.

A couple of officers escorted Steve to a squad car. He was docile, and they had to hold him steady to keep him upright. As they drove Steve away, he stared straight ahead.

I thanked Larry. I asked him how he knew we were in there.

"I got back to town yesterday," Larry said. "I thought I should take a drive up here. You know, to spy on Claudia."

Larry pointed to his Ford Taurus, parked up the block.

"And this old lady came up, and she sticks her head right in the car, and tells me to call the police and get in here quick."

"What old lady?" I asked him. The back of my neck felt prickly.

"Some old hippie lady. She was wearing like a peasant skirt and a scarf on her head, and lots of beads—you know, Berkeley."

"What did she say to you? What exactly?"

"She talked funny. Kind of, I don't know, foreign. She said, 'The big *gadjo* is going to carbonize your wife and my Max.' Yeah, that's it. That's what she said. And then she hit me up for a cigarette."

Larry looked around for her. But, of course, Baba would be long gone by now.

53

I was flying to Barcelona. First class. The champagne in my flute was cold and bright and I rejoiced in my good luck at having an empty seat beside me.

I calculated what time I should take my sleeping tablet. I'd have to change planes at Heathrow, which was always a bother, and I didn't want to be too stoned. I could end up in the wrong concourse, oblivious to the fact that I was surrounded by Bulgarians on their way to Blagoevgrad. That's the kind of mishap you don't want to repeat.

I caught myself obsessing about the sleeping pill, the conversation between me and myself banging around in my head. My world had become that small. For the first time in more than a year, I was alone.

Claudia had taken Larry back. She reported to me that they had "reinvented" their marriage. It vexed me. I told her that was very modern of her, too modern for me.

They carted Steve off to jail, then a mental health facility. Amy was still missing, and Steve insisted that he'd had nothing to do with it. He was being charged with kidnapping and mayhem in the incident involving Claudia and me. Estevez and McGuire advised me that I'd have to fly back to California to testify when his case came to trial. It could be a while, they said.

I pressed them about Amy. They clammed up. They said her case was still under investigation.

I popped the sleeping pill and spread out some magazines on the seat next to me, lest some interloper should get a wise idea about snagging it. I started reading the *San Francisco Chronicle*.

The top headline of the business section had Evergreen Mortgage in it. That caught my eye, and I pondered it over my champagne refill until it finally came to me: that was where Amy had worked.

It seemed that Evergreen had suffered a bit of a setback. A company spokesperson released a statement divulging that Evergreen's accounts had been broken into and ransacked. The crooks hacked into the financial transactions server. They sat there patiently for over a year, steadily skimming off a percentage of every mortgage fee. There had been tens of thousands of them. So far, it was evident that the criminals had accreted several million dollars. The company was still assessing the extent of the loss. The investigators had no leads.

"The *gadje* are thieves," Baba said. She added, "And cutthroats."

"Jesus!" I cried. "You almost made me spill my drink."

"I'm glad we're coming back to Europe," she told me, flipping through an in-flight magazine. "America is okay for a visit, but this is our home."

"Yes," I agreed. "You just can't get the good old-fashioned pogroms in America like you get back home in the Balkans."

She produced a photograph. She pulled it out from under her bra strap. I was impressed; Baba only wore her foundation undergarment for special occasions.

"I have her address in Granada," Baba said. "Cell phone too."

She set the photo down on the tray table in front of me. It was the Kalderashi girl again. But she wasn't a girl anymore.

She was a grown woman, tall and regal in a black dress. Her hair was pulled back, sleek and shining against her small, round head. She was fierce, with a stern crease between her eyebrows.

She was singing on a postage stamp of a stage. It must have been a supper club, a very Andalusian affair; bullfight posters on the walls, flowery mantillas, great steaming pans of paella. The place was packed, and every eye was on her.

"She sings," Baba said. "Like you."

"Why does she look older every time you show me her picture?" I asked.

"Ah." Baba sighed. "Because she is old."

"How old?"

"She is thirty-eight, Max. She is an old maid, with no children." Baba shook her head at the enormity of this human tragedy.

"Really?" I said, and I took the photo from her hand. "That's very unusual for a Romany woman."

"She is *dilo*," Baba said, admitting that the woman was crazy. She pretended to consider the situation, then added hopefully, "But for you, Max, it might be okay."

"I suppose I'm *dilo* too," I told her.

I tucked the photograph into the rubber frame of the airplane window. The pure sunlight—shining above the clouds, above the ocean—shone through the Kalderashi woman's image. The light seemed to animate her and, for a moment, I thought I could hear her sing. Her voice was raw and deep and torn, shredded by the tines of a life lived hard.

The jet surged eastward. We crossed that curiously abrupt line between light and dark that airline travelers sometimes experience. You can see it drawn across the sky. Behind us, in the west, the sky was blue. Then suddenly, in front of us to the east, it changed to charcoal.

I could feel the sleeping tablet coming on. It arrived, like a ferry, and I stepped into it and watched the shore recede. The last rays of the sun glinted off the jet wings, and into space— into the enormity.

I knew who was out there. The dead.

Below me, the sea reached to the horizon. It would wash around the curve of the earth, the waters of the Atlantic would meet the Pacific and commingle—and flow to the San Francisco Bay.

The bay that so many people had gone into, and nobody thought of them again. I remembered her name. Marta Esperanza. I had read that she had called her unborn child Jesus. What were they now? A momentary flicker across a television screen. A gruesome urban myth. A lessonless parable presented to the unteachable.

Marta had been found, and forgotten.

News stories still appeared about Amy—but more rarely.

The beautiful, the privileged, the dead. I could never decide whether she'd been a criminal or a victim. Maybe both.

If she had stolen the money, she surely had an accomplice. Amy wasn't a computer expert. The two of them—Amy and her coconspirator—could be together now, with the baby, enjoying their plunder. Or, she could be dead. The accomplice could have gotten greedy.

Whatever Amy was—criminal, victim, both—the public never tired of her. She was so consumable. I knew that eventually they'd devour her completely, every last morsel. Amy, too, would drift into the realm of the forgotten.

I looked once more at the Romany woman in the photo. She was illuminated. *Santo mujer.* I drew down into the darkness, into the duende from which all art and death and eternity issues. I heard the clacking of castanets.

54

I met Jordi for a beer at one of those wooden shack saloons
that used to dot Barcelona's sandy beachfront. I took a table
outside, facing the Mediterranean.

I didn't recognize him when he first walked up. He wore
expensive sunglasses and an Italian suit the color of ripe can-
taloupe. His black shirt was elegant, and freshly laundered.
He wore it open at the collar. His cuff links were gold. So was
his watch.

When I commented on his suntan, Jordi told me he'd been
vacationing in Cuba. He said he liked it there because it was
beyond American influence. I asked him what he meant by
that. He called to the waiter to bring us another drink.

"So they finally caught Steve," he said to me as he was fin-
ishing his second beer. He drank it out of a glass, his pinky
finger slightly raised.

"That must make everyone feel good," he said. "To have
caught him."

"I don't know that people feel good. Relieved, maybe."

I told him how Steve was arrested for assaulting Claudia

and me. Then the police tore through his house. They dug up the patio. Ironically, the "murder weapon" we had seen Steve bury was actually one of the baby's toys—a rattle.

"How amusing," Jordi said.

"That's not the word I would have used."

"Even if Steve didn't kill Amy, he is a bad man," Jordi stated. "It does not matter for Steve to be punished."

Jordi looked out to sea.

"How's Cecilia?" I asked.

"She is to live with people in the country. Is better for a dog to have room. For the running."

"I meant Cecilia your fiancée. Or is she your wife now?"

"I don't know who you are talking about."

He stood up and pulled out a fat money clip. He drew out a twenty-euro note on a twelve-euro tab, and left.

I finished my beer and picked at the rest of the calamari. We'd been sharing it, but suddenly I didn't feel like eating off the same plate as Jordi.

I walked back to my hotel. On the way, I passed a camera store. I'm not interested in cameras, and didn't give the place a second glance.

But as I passed the shop, I was struck by that very primal sense—no doubt emanating from deep in the lizard brain—that I was being watched. I felt eyes on me.

I took a few more steps. Stopped. Turned. Walked back to the camera store and looked in the window.

I saw, in the middle of the display, a picture frame. I recognized it immediately, the *trencada* of broken mirrors. It was the same picture frame that I'd seen at Jordi's house.

And, inside the frame, was the same photograph. It was Cecilia, Jordi's fiancée.

Her gaze was as I had remembered—cast out toward the horizon. But it wasn't fixed there. Her eyes seemed to follow you like a store detective.

I scanned the rest of the picture frames in the window. There was another Cecilia, in a ruby heart-shaped frame. A third Cecilia stared out from a square frame made of bone. Another Cecilia, tiny but unmistakable, was in an open locket. Then more. I thought I smelled something bad, sulphur, maybe. I dabbed my scarf across my forehead, and took some deep steady breaths like I do when I feel a bout of stage fright coming on.

I took a step back, apprized the entire display. All the picture frames held the same image. Cecilia.

I went into the shop. I asked the clerk about the woman in the photograph. Who was she? Just a model, he said. Not famous. Her picture came with the frames. And, as if to clarify, he told me that the woman was nobody.